Praise for LeMone's *Corner Pride*:

"Corner Pride is sociology, memoir and philosophy spun into a novel to be treasured and shared."
—*The Roanoke Times*

"The descriptions of all the characters LeMone brings into the book become live, real and believable."
—*The Franklin News-Post*

"Like the Hemingway novels, LeMone's work is an in-depth study of human character in uncertain times... utterly fascinating. *Corner Pride* is destined to rank among the *creme de la creme*."
—Dr. Melvin Macklin

"LeMone covers that often-ignored middle ground between shying away from inner-city problems and bleeding all over the page with them."
—Virginia Libraries

"*Corner Pride* persuasively captures the dangers and dilemmas inherent in a gritty, 1950s-era, inner-city neighborhood."
—Dr. Jennifer Braaten,
President of Ferrum College

THE SPRING
OF
UNEXPECTED
CONSEQUENCES

Charles Shea LeMone

The Spring of Unexpected Consequences

ISBN: 978-1-936553-28-0

Warwick House Publishers
720 Court Street
Lynchburg, Virginia 24504

This novel is dedicated to Susan Jaime LeMone
who showed me through her actions
the true meaning of unconditional love.

ACKNOWLEDGMENTS

First, I want to thank God for giving me a burning desire to write that nothing could extinguish.

This novel is in print due to the encouragement and support of Donnie Stevens, a precious friend and fellow author.

The story reads so smoothly thanks to Joyce Maddox's excellent editing and Betty Curl's proofreading skills. Amy Moore added the final touch by formatting the book.

I also want to acknowledge two longstanding friends, Latin jazz bandleader Bobby Matos and Jaibe Sivadel for the fantastic work they both did as fact checkers.

The assistance I received from Chele Welsh and Lori Altimus was invaluable when it came to offering me feedback while the story was in progress.

I would be remiss if I did not also give a shout out to L. D. Dixon for suggesting, ages ago, that I write a mystery/thriller in which a bartender was the central character, an idea that led directly to the birth of Nate Holt.

Early drafts of this novel may have languished forever on a cyber space shelf somewhere had it not been for Barbara Jean Stone reminding often that Nate Holt's tale should be revived.

Lastly, I thank Judy M. Watts for taking a concept I gave her to paint the perfect artwork used for the cover. She can be contacted at judy.rohanna@gmail.com.

CHAPTER 1

An hour into my bartending shift at Wally's Tavern, a dingy little dive on 145th Street in Harlem, Blinky Carlson walked into the joint. It was a cold and windy midday on a Friday in the spring of 1957, and the weather had turned his face a mottled red. When he sidled up to the bar to slide onto a stool, I could see something was troubling him. There were a few whites who stopped by for a drink and to place bets through me on the numbers racket, but Blinky wasn't one of them. Being a consummate jazz aficionado, 52nd Street was his scene. Rarely did he venture north unless it was to catch a show at Small's Paradise or one of the other nearby night spots.

"How's life treating you, Mr. Nate Holt?" He spoke in his usual rapid fashion, unwrapping a herringbone scarf from around his neck and sticking a Lucky Strike in his mouth.

"Everything's copacetic." I struck a match for the cigarette and set a coaster down on the chipped bar top. "Name your poison."

"A double shot of Cutty, straight up." He unbuttoned his charcoal gray overcoat, removed a black jeff from his head, set it on the bar top and then, with an unsteady hand, brushed back his thinning, blonde hair.

When I placed the scotch in front of him, he wasted no time gulping half of it down. Except for his hip jazzman shades, which he no doubt wore to conceal a nervous facial tick, Blinky looked like a thirty-five-year-old accountant, which he was, being audited by the Internal Revenue Service. I took care of my regulars and then positioned myself on a stool across from him.

"What brings you so far uptown, Blink?" I asked, giving the narrow room another once-over to see if my services were needed.

"I came to see you." He took his shades off, folded them and laid them beside his cigarettes. "This morning I happened to read an article you wrote a couple of weeks back for *The Uptown Beat*. It was on a gig Miles did down at Cafe Bohemia."

"And…" I urged him on. Only a few months into writing my music column, I was eager for any and all feedback.

"I thought the praise you lavished on him was more than well deserved. I especially liked the part that read, if I may quote you, brother: *'Now that Bird has departed for that big band in the sky, there's nobody on the set moving with the dynamic force and innovation Miles Davis exhibits with his new quintet'."*

"No exaggeration there."

"I was happy to see you also favorably mentioned Coltrane and Cannonball." His right eyebrow jumped up like an exclamation mark, as he seemed to take stock of his reflection in the mirror that ran the length of the bar behind me.

"Yeah, I never thought I'd hear a group like them. All those geniuses together on the same stage."

"Like I said, it was a good piece of writing."

"Thanks, Blink." I replenished his glass and waved off his attempt to pay. "On the house."

"Ever hear of a young kid named Joe Weathersby?" he asked a moment later.

"Can't say I have."

"Well, I'm not surprised. He's only twenty years old and still studying at Julliard."

"What's he play?"

"He's a tenor man, who coincidentally comes from your hometown, Philly." He smiled briefly. "But he's not just any tenor. I'm not jiving, man, when I say this kid's got the bebop chops down and tons of raw talent to match. Given a little time on the set, and any and everybody who seriously follows the music will have heard of him."

"Is that so?" I said, wondering why I'd never heard the fella play. "How long's he been in town?"

"Since the September before last. He came downtown one night, though, for an open-mike jam with Dizzy and some of the cats a couple of months back. I happened to be in the house at the time. Man, talk about extraordinary. He does things in the upper register I didn't think could be done. I mean he's bad, bad, bad!" He downed more scotch. "He even had Dizzy scratching his head in amazement."

"So, when can I hear him, so I can make up my own mind?"

"Soon," he said, a deeply etched frown carved in his prominent forehead. "That is, if Weathersby lives that long."

"Now you've really got me confused." I poured a dollop of Courvoisier into my lukewarm coffee. "Does he have a health problem or something?"

"You could put it that way. Ever hear the name Freddie Tucker bandied about in your travels?"

"Who in the life hasn't? He's a big, ugly lout. But what's he got to do with this kid Weathersby?"

"I'm recording him, see," Blinky said, as the right side of his face twitched. "I been saving dough for years and investing right. So I decided to start doing something I love, like being more involved in the music."

"And…" I said, impatiently.

"So I talked Joe into letting me manage him. Since last week we've been recording some cuts at a little studio down on the Lower East Side. And just when I think we're close to wrapping things up, Freddie Tucker pops up out of nowhere." He took a deep breath and sighed. "So that's why I'm here."

"Can you be a little more specific?"

"I guess I'll have to be." He cracked another brief smile and went on talking. "We were rehearsing the other night. During a break, Joe goes outside to get some fresh air. The drummer I'd lined up, Pee Wee Merkins, has a problem with getting enough duji to stick in his veins. I knew that, of course. I mean, everybody knows he's got a monkey on his back the size of Hackensack. But the cat plays drums like nobody this side of Art Blakey. That's why I convinced myself his habit wouldn't translate into a problem. After all, I'm talking about making a demo tape, not doing a long babysitting road tour."

He paused and pulled another Lucky Strike from his pack. Again, I lit it. He took a deep hit, and slowly blew smoke from the side of his mouth. I excused myself to fill a couple of orders for the morning regulars on hand.

"Anyway," he continued when he once again had my attention, "Weathersby sees Freddie's hassling the drummer about some dough he owes him. From what I heard, he's got Merkins all jacked up by the collar gorilla style, screaming obscenities they could probably hear all the way over to Staten Island. And there's some red-haired chippy with him, too. My guess is he was trying to impress her. Anyway, after watching this as long as he could take it, Joe finally puts his two cents in, simply asking Freddie to lighten up on Pee Wee. Freddie tells him to butt out and mind his own business. Joe says it is his business because Merkins is his drummer. Then one thing leads to another, and before you know it Joe loses his temper and decks Freddie." He slammed a fist into an open palm. "Knocks him right into the middle of next week."

"I suppose it was Joe who told you this?"

"No! Joe wasn't the only one out there." He shook his head adamantly. "There were a couple of other dudes from the band who saw it. Seems like as quiet and laid-back as skinny little Joe is, he's got a terrible temper when he gets riled and packs a mean wallop, too."

An old gent sitting at one of the seven booths that lined the narrow barroom came up to the well for a refill of Thunderbird. I took care of him and another customer and rejoined Blinky.

"Then what happened?"

"That I can tell you firsthand, Nate. Because I was there for that." He paused and his eyes narrowed. "Try to picture this. Freddie comes to, gets up and charges into the studio. He's screaming that Weathersby's as good as dead. We had to hold both of them back. And believe me, it wasn't easy. Took all seven of us, counting the soundman. All the time Freddie's yelling like some maniac straight out of Bellevue, talking about how slow and painful Joe's going to die, saying how he's going to rip each one of Joe's fingers off first."

While I tried to get the full picture of what he was telling me, Blinky paused and batted his eyes several times as though he were reliving the scene.

"Then it gets to the point where," he went on, speaking a little slower, "we can't hold the two of them back any longer. And God as my witness, Nate, I swear what I'm telling you is true. Joe fires on this huge dude again. One punch that sounded like a twenty-two going off and Tucker's out cold again. Meanwhile, I'm scared as shit. So, I rush all my people out of there as fast as I can before Tucker comes to again."

"When did all this go down?"

"Last night."

After an awkward silence, I asked, "What's any of this got to do with me?"

"In certain circles, the skinny is you do favors for friends when they find themselves in a fix."

"Where'd you hear that?"

"A fine looking woman I met recently put me to the wise. Ginny Langsford, a high-priced madam with a ritzy West End address. Remember her?"

"Uh-huh."

"I was giving her some investment advice, and your name popped up. According to her, you cooled out some lame who was trying to put the muscle on her."

"That was awhile back."

"Well, she's just one of the people I've heard mention you as a savior of sorts."

"As I recall, she paid me well."

"That's just the point I was about to make. I know you don't know me from Adam, but I was wondering if you might see fit to help me out if the price is right."

"What're we talking about me doing?"

"Having a little chat with Freddie. I'm willing to make a fair restitution to cool things out. I figure his pride got hurt because the dame with him saw the whole confrontation." He paused anxiously. "So what do you say?"

Before answering him, I took a thoughtful sip from my laced coffee. Some extra cash would make my life sweeter. There was no getting around that. My girlfriend Lillian and I had been looking for an apartment to share, and I was surprised by the asking prices on the choicer pads. Like most people I know, I have a tendency to live beyond my means. My fondness for dressing to kill, coupled with my need to show up on the town at least two or three times a week, kept me pressed for cash. But much as I would welcome the dough, the thought of confronting Freddie Tucker didn't hold a lot of appeal.

"You're a real hip cat, Blink," I finally said. "And I've known you for a long time, but—"

"You mean, I'm all right to a degree. But since I'm not a *member* then—"

"No," I scoffed. "I'm way beyond skin color. In fact, as far as I'm concerned your love for the music makes you an honorary member of the club."

"So where does the but fit in?" He motioned for me to continue.

"Sounds like a man could get hurt pitching his tent with you."

"Maybe, but I doubt it." He sat up straight and motioned for another refill, looking both agitated and fatigued. "Not from what I hear."

I poured another double that I let him pay for this time without responding to his last statement.

Soon as he'd taken a swallow, he went on, "I've got four club owners and two record producers who have checked out three of the cuts we recorded. They're drooling at the mouth and hot to trot. Like me, they think if young Joe opens for a known artist just a couple of times we're talking beaucoup future bucks."

"Why don't you talk to Tucker yourself?" I asked, just to see his reaction.

"Sure!" He blanched noticeably. "Frightening as that prospect sounds, I was planning to do exactly that. But soon as I mentioned it to Joe, his jaws got tight. From where he stands he doesn't think we owe any kind of apology to Freddie. He even made me swear to leave things be. Said he'd drop me as his manager if I did otherwise. Somehow, Nate, I think the kid's not really hip to what a sticky situation he's created for himself."

I took care of the house, and soon I was back in front of Blinky, scratching the freshly trimmed edges of my goatee while wrestling with both sides of my personality, the pragmatic and the risk taker.

"When I came across your article on Miles this morning," Blinky picked up the conversation, "I decided to come see you. Knowing how much you love the music, too, I thought it couldn't hurt. So what's it going be? Do I go back downtown seeing some light at the end of the tunnel or ready to slit both my wrists?"

He waited breathlessly for my answer.

"When can I hear the kid play?"

CHAPTER 2

As the day wore on, I reflected back to the long series of events that led up to me being behind the bar at Wally's, agreeing to help Blinky.

I'd seen action in France during World War II as a member of the 92nd Infantry Division. We were a unit of colored troops assigned to the Fifth Army. Exactly ten minutes after we arrived at the front, we found ourselves in the thick of combat. Days turned into weeks and weeks into months of unprecedented action. When I joined the service, I was a confirmed atheist. But long before I boarded a plane to return stateside, war had converted me into a true believer in the power of prayer.

Back home in Philadelphia, the small-town feel soon drove me northward, ninety miles away to the city that never sleeps. I shared a house in the Bronx with Chris Wilkins, an Army buddy from my original squad. Unable to become a cop like his father because he'd lost a leg in the war, he suggested I join the police force. It seemed like a natural progression to me.

After passing the civil service tests, and faring well in subsequent interviews, I graduated from the academy and was assigned to a midtown precinct. There I was schooled on the job by a crusty old Irish veteran with a wicked sense of humor that he used as a cover for a tender heart. We patrolled the streets around the docks. With five years under my belt, my commanding officer, Lieutenant Braun, approached me about taking a step up the career ladder. Impressed with my work in blue, especially the quality of my written reports, he thought it was time for me to trade in my uniform for a detective's shield.

There was a substantial raise involved, so I thought long and hard before rejecting the promotion.

I'd been around the station house long enough to notice how stressed and haggard all of the detectives were from the pressure that came with the job, and the ungodly hours they logged regularly. Oftentimes, when covering high-profile, politically-charged cases, they were on duty around-the-clock for days on end. It was also common knowledge that the majority of them were either divorced, separated from their wives and children or in marriages at odds. It was also evident that the job consumed and aged them far too quickly. Most of them were out of shape, chain smoking, alcoholic malcontents, popping antacids like candy, dreaming of the long awaited day they could retire with full pensions and finally have time to enjoy life. That kind of lifestyle held no appeal to me.

So I stayed in uniform, walking away at the end of each shift to enjoy an active and passionate life far removed from the job. Lieutenant Braun was incensed by my decision and called me a fool and a nincompoop.

Ten days later, he transferred me to the 30th Precinct in Harlem where I was assigned to a foot beat. I imagine the transfer was Braun's way of exacting a measure of revenge. But I eventually established a rapport with the people along my beat. Six months after the transfer, I moved from the Bronx to the very neighborhood I patrolled on foot.

Then one hot summer night, two years later, while responding to a family dispute, I came close to dying from the trauma associated with a .38 caliber slug. It passed near the center of my chest, missing my heart by a fraction of an inch. My rookie partner was not so lucky. He died from a bullet to the head. That came a moment before I fired off a shot from the ground and put the drunken husband down. Three weeks later, shortly after I was released from Harlem Hospital, I handed in my resignation. Based on a short stint I did as a bartender before the war, I landed the job at Wally's, thinking of it as a temporary transition.

After a few weeks behind the bar, word spread that I was a former cop. Then a pattern began to evolve as many of my new friends, customers, acquaintances and their associates began to call on me to help them with problems requiring investigative know-how. Moreover, I wasn't shy about applying force if the occasion called for it. Nor was I hesitant to break a law or two when I was able to convince myself the ends justified the means. Due to word-of-mouth through the grapevine, I eventually gained a quiet reputation as a successful, unlicensed, independent peacemaker of sorts. And during my years as a beat officer, and while pouring drinks at Wally's, I became acquainted with many of Harlem's shady characters.

One of them was Freddie Tucker, the man I'd agreed to talk to for Blinky. I vaguely recalled that his arrest jacket consisted of numerous charges, such as burglary, assault and battery and pimping. More recently, word on the street had him dealing drugs and catering to the illicit needs of certain jazzmen when they were in town.

~

When my shift ended at six o'clock, I caught a standing-room-only bus south to make a quick stop at my efficiency basement flat just north of Central Park. I freshened up with a shower, shaved and changed into some flashier duds, a beige sports jacket worn over a green turtle neck sweater and brown slacks. Then I ran a shoe brush across a pair of dark brown Stacey Adams comforts. From my selection of hats, I chose a tan stingy brim Stetson and hit the streets before the claustrophobic effect of my small pad undid me.

I set out at a brisk pace to find a gypsy cab. Although the calendar said it was spring, the night air held onto winter's coattails, and I was glad I'd decided to wear a raincoat. Despite the crisp chill in the air, all of the people I passed along Lennox Avenue seemed to have an extra bounce to their steps. After all, I reminded myself, it was Friday night and early enough for anything to happen, good or bad, depending on the stars, if you believe in the zodiac.

When I strolled into Tandy's Restaurant, located a half block from the beauty parlor where Lillian was having her hair done, I was ten minutes early for my date with her. As I made my way toward an empty table in a corner, I acknowledged a few people I knew by nodding to them.

Lillian Warren, who I had been seeing for more than a year, was a dance instructor and choreographer. She was one caramel shade of skin color light enough to have worked as a chorus girl for six years at the Cotton Club. Three years ago, on her thirty-first birthday, she fulfilled a longtime dream by opening her own dance studio. Working with kids gave her a sense of community spirit, and doing it was, according to her, its own reward.

When she finally entered the crowded restaurant, the whole place seemed to grow a few electric shades lighter, as though a film director had called out: lights, camera, action. She always exuded an air of confidence and could have passed for several years younger. With her shapely figure, shoulder length, dark-brown hair bouncing with every step, she was a beautiful sight to behold. Plenty of times I'd heard people compare her looks to the singer turned Hollywood actress Dorothy Dandridge. Although I could see the resemblance, in my opinion, Lillian was in a class by herself. It had taken me more than a month of concentrated effort to finally win her affections. I still thought of that as the best day of my life.

As usual, she was dressed like a fashion plate, stepping live from the cover of *Ebony* magazine. Her classy outfit—a white leather jacket, pink dress, and an oversized burgundy beret— gave her skin a distinctive glow. The heads of men, as well as a few women, swiveled toward her like lead shavings drawn to a powerful magnet. But I was used to similar reactions wher- ever we went. And as she walked across the crowded restau- rant, straight toward my table, I tried hard to restrain the smug expression I was wearing.

Standing as she neared, I pulled out a chair for her.

"I'm glad to see chivalry isn't dead," she said with a gleaming smile.

"Not yet, sweetheart." I did my best Bogart impersonation, sliding her chair in place before sitting across from her.

"So how'd your day go?" she asked, as she removed her flesh-colored gloves.

"Better now that I'm feasting my eyes on you. You look absolutely stunning tonight, dear."

"Talk that talk, mister. You know how much I love it."

During the meal, she brought me up to date on her search for the new pad we were planning to share. She was excited about an available spot in the same building where her dance studio and personal flat were both located.

"Two top-floor flats were converted into one huge corner apartment with a riverfront and downtown view. It even has a dining room and two bedrooms, the greatest kitchen I ever saw, and plenty of space for entertaining." Her brown eyes glittered and danced. "I can't wait until you see it, Nate."

"Sounds expensive."

"Well," she tittered, "what can I say? If you want to dance you have to pay the piper."

"How much?" I folded my hands on top of the table.

"Wait until you see it first. Okay?"

"How about tomorrow?"

"Are you reading my mind again?" She laughed, as she reached out and touched one of my hands. "Tomorrow's exactly when I promised the landlord we'd stop by. He wants to get someone in there as soon as possible. It's been empty for only a few days but it won't be for long."

Halfway through our meal, I tried to think of a diplomatic way to tell her I was breaking off the movie date we had for later that evening so I could check out Blinky's young horn man.

A few days ago, we had made plans to catch a new film all the critics were raving about. It was called *Man of a Thousand Faces*, with James Cagney playing the role of Lon Chaney, renowned for all the misfits and monsters he'd created on the silver screen, like the *Phantom of the Opera, The Hunchback of Notre Dame and The Wolfman.*

Although I tried reaching her shortly after I remembered our date, I'd been unsuccessful. Once more, aware that I was a sucker when it came to delighting in Lillian's beauty, I realized there was no correct way to do what I had to do.

"About later tonight—" I finally blurted, as she was about to speak.

"What about it?" Her lips smiled but her eyes didn't.

"Something's come up."

"Something? As in, something that's more important than us?" She spoke in a subdued voice, but I felt as though everyone in the restaurant could sense her displeasure.

"There's a misunderstanding that could turn ugly unless I do something to quiet it down."

"As you're so fond of saying," she smiled, insolently, "can you be a little more specific?"

The majority of the people who hire me do so off-the-record and prefer to keep the nature of their problems and my involvement confidential. That was just fine with me because the last thing I needed was Lillian knowing anything about my extracurricular activities. I figured if she had the slightest inkling about some of the risks I take, especially in light of her soft-boiled liberal constitution, she'd worry day and night about my welfare. Or worse yet, her knowing too much might be the beginning of the end to our relationship. Even the thought of such a possibility was totally unacceptable to my way of thinking.

Nevertheless, on that night in Tandy's I felt she deserved an honest explanation. In hushed tones, I told her about my talk with Blinky Carlson, painting a simplistic sketch of what I planned to do.

"This all sounds like it could get downright nasty, Nate." Her concern was evident. "Shouldn't you think this whole thing through a little more?"

"Too late, baby. I already gave Blinky my word."

"Is that so?" She twisted her mouth oddly. "Well, I must say your loyalty overwhelms me considering the risks involved."

"Trust me," I said, with a dismissive hand wave. "It won't get dangerous."

"Oh, no? But what if it does?"

"Believe me, Lil, if there was the slightest chance that my talking to Tucker could create a problem, I wouldn't do it. Nor am I looking to play somebody's hero. I have every intention to play it safe."

"If playing it safe was really what you're concerned with, you'd be telling all of this nonsense to your cop buddies so they could sort things out. Then we could be on our way to the movies as planned."

"The only thing I'd get from my friends on the force is excuses about how busy they are fighting real crime. I mean, dig it, unless Tucker backs up his threats with some real action, they've got nothing to act on. You know how they are." I chuckled. "The only thing they'd want to know is what was stolen or who was killed."

"Right!" Not the least bit amused, she pushed aside her half-eaten baked chicken with sweet potatoes and collard greens.

I saw our waitress talking to the woman at the cash register. It appeared as though they were making odds as to whether Lillian and I would be leaving together or apart.

"I promise to make this up to you," I said in my most convincing voice.

"Suit yourself, Nathaniel Andrew Holt," she said, with a long sigh, as though enunciating my full name had exhausted her. "After all, you are a full-grown man edging up on forty and no longer anyone's child."

I ignored the dig, but before I could curb my feelings or clamp my lips, I misspoke, "There's always tomorrow as far as the movie goes."

"Whatever!" She rolled her eyes contemptuously. "There's nothing I like better than being all dressed up with nowhere to go."

I accompanied a sullen Lillian to the front door of her flat, which was directly above her dance studio on Amsterdam Avenue near 137th Street. Along the way, while avoiding eye contact with other pedestrians, who all seemed to be in a better mood than me, I tried to establish an honorable truce.

"I did call you, as I explained, more than once. But I couldn't reach you. My timing must have been off."

"Oh, goody, goody. Hearing that makes everything so much better."

"We're both strong-willed and passionate people, so it only stands to reason that now and then we're going to disagree," I said at her front door, going on before she could interrupt me. "And as you know, I am usually always where I say I will be when I say I'm going to be there. So please let me slide this one time."

"Call me tomorrow," she said, petulantly. "We'll have to see how I'm feeling then."

I almost reminded her about the apartment we were scheduled to see, but decided I'd wait until the morning to do that.

~

Forty minutes later, I paid and generously tipped a gypsy cabby for the lift he gave me to the Lower East Side studio where I'd promised to meet Blinky, Joe Weathersby and the band. The engineer was still doing a sound check when I found Blinky in one of the smoky rehearsal rooms at the rear of the shabby little building. He gave me a furtive nod and then acted as though I wasn't there.

Joe Weathersby was a tall and frail, fair-skinned guy. He appeared much younger than I expected and had peach fuzz for a mustache. Although he was a Julliard student, he looked more like a high school sophomore. He and the piano player were going over what sounded like some intricate chord changes as I found a seat in a corner of the room. If he or any of the members of the band were worried about Freddie Tucker showing up again, it wasn't apparent.

Now and then, Joe seemed to be testing a few licks for their texture and harmony. But even before the band began to kick out a spirited arrangement of Bird's "Ornithology I," I sensed a rare confidence that Weathersby possessed.

My esteem for him grew even more when all six members of the group finally settled down with their instruments and began to play. Blinky hadn't exaggerated with the accolades he'd used to describe the kid from Philly. The other players were good, but they would never draw the raves I was already heaping on the young tenor man. He fingered the Selmer Mark IV to hit each of the notes of the incredibly fast paced tune, going up and down the scales with a casual dexterity and delivering unmistakable tonal clarity.

Young Weathersby exuded even more confidence as he stepped closer to the microphone for his solo. It was as though he were in a trance that allowed him to transcend, contain and blend every sound around him while taking the original score to another level of excellence. From the gut-wrenching bellowing of the lower register to the soul-searing urgency of the higher notes, he played around the tune, adding, subtracting, multiplying and dividing the riff.

Although the composition was definitely Charlie (Bird) Parker's, the young man made it his own in a way I believe would have genuinely impressed Bird himself. I closed my eyes and vividly imagined the deceased legend tapping his foot from the grave while wearing that sage-like smile which so often graced his chubby face.

When the song ended, I opened my eyes to find Blinky smiling like the proud new father of a healthy man-child. I was still being impressed more than an hour later when Blinky announced that it was time to call it a night.

"That's all the time I could book us," he told the band members.

I wanted to approach the budding genius to say something to him, but Blinky pulled me aside the moment I was about to make my move.

"Was I right or what?" he asked, while wearing a full-size smile. "You've got to admit it, Nate; the kid radiates something cosmic."

"He's something special all right," I readily agreed.

"Ain't he though?" As the band packed up their instruments, Blinky nodded his head toward the back door. "Let's step outside where we can talk."

He lit a cigarette as we moved out into a brick-floored, tiny back yard.

"I want your support, Nate. But I have to make one thing clear. I want Joe concentrating on nothing but the music night and day around-the-clock. And I don't need no ripples or beefs coming between us and what we're trying to get done. So let's not involve him anymore than he already is concerning Freddie Tucker." He flicked his thinning hair back as the right side of his face contorted. "Can you dig what I'm saying?"

"If that's the way you want to work it, sure."

"Like I said, the kid's stubborn as a mule. He'd be mad as all get out if he knew I was trying to buy Tucker off."

"You're calling the shots."

In terms of cash, he laid out his offer to me: two hundred dollars for me to deliver his message, along with two hundred dollars to appease Tucker for his embarrassment and to compensate for whatever the drummer Merkins might still owe him.

"Just tell Freddie to leave the kid be."

Blinky's voice was a pitiful plea as he shelled out the cash, looking up at me as though I were the full embodiment of the Supreme Court evaluating his case. "If he agrees, give him the dough and there's another two hundred in it for you later."

"Consider it done," I said and then asked, "Was the drummer you used tonight the infamous Pee Wee Merkins?"

"No!" Blinky spat on the scarred walk as we moved to reenter the studio. "I fired him last night. The way I figure it, he was to blame for bringing Tucker into the picture to begin with."

"Can you give me a description of this Pee Wee joker?"

"He's somewhere around forty-five years old, a real dark-skinned dude from Chattanooga. He's about five-foot-six or seven, completely bald on top, and he's got a laugh that sounds like a hyena's mating call."

"A hyena's mating call?"

"Once you hear it, you'll know exactly what I'm talking about."

CHAPTER 3

I set out to track down Tucker, making Birdland my first downtown stop, and 52nd Street was alive and jumping. When I spied Miles leaving the club with Philly Joe Jones, I hurriedly paid my cabby and jumped out, excited by the opportunity to pay my respects to the man I believed to be a living legend. Miles was wearing the current bebopper's attire—a tight-fitting black suit, a starched white shirt and a thin black tie.

"Miles," I cried out, as I rushed up to him on the busy sidewalk. "How's it going?"

"Hey," he rasped, recognizing me through squinted eyes and slightly tinted eyeglasses. "Everything's cool, my man. How's it going with you?"

"I'm doing just fine, Miles. You going to sit in here tonight?"

"No, man. I just stopped by to see a friend before I head out of town on a West Coast run." He spoke hoarsely, just above a whisper. "But I ought to let you know I really dug the way you wrote on me, man. A lot of so-called critics don't understand the direction I'm taking the music. All they do is second-guess me and expect me to keep playing the same old sounds."

Philly Joe glanced impatiently at his wristwatch and then toward Miles.

"I'm glad to hear you liked my review. I've been thinking we should get together. I'd like to do a biography on you."

"On me?" He laughed that scratchy laugh of his. "Nobody wants to hear nothing I have to say. Besides, everything I have to say comes through my sound, man. You should know that. It's all about the sound."

"That might be halfway true, but I think you're wrong about one thing."

"And what's that, my man?"

"All the hip folks I know would love to hear anything you have to say."

"I don't know about that." He laughed again. "Maybe one day, though. Yeah, maybe one day."

"Just keep me in mind," I said, as he and Philly Joe strolled off toward a double-parked, showroom-new, pink Thunderbird.

For the next hour and a half, I popped in and out of several downtown nightspots before heading north to do likewise in Harlem. Everyone I approached knew Tucker by sight, but no one had seen him that night. Then when I was about to exit The Blue Parrot, I heard a high-pitched, piercing laugh that turned my head. From across the crowded floor, my eyes fell on a bald guy who fit Blinky's description of the drummer, Pee Wee Merkins. I wasted no time sidling up near him at the crowded bar.

"Hey, Pee Wee, what's shaking?"

He appeared to be half in the bag, but the fact that he couldn't place my face didn't seem to disturb him.

"Ain't nothing shaking but the bacon, and the pot's not even hot," he said.

A trio took the stage to set up, so I decided to grill Merkins while the place was relatively quiet. People were ringing the bar so I wedged my way as close to him as I could.

"I heard about your run-in with Freddie Tucker," I said to the side of his bald head. "I hope you guys have squared things up since then."

He turned, eying me suspiciously, and asked, "You tight with him or something?"

"No way! What I'm trying to do is run him to ground on a private matter."

"I didn't really think you were tight with him." He cackled and then let out a high-pitched insidious laugh. "I was just making a joke to myself. Dig?"

"So, what's so funny?"

"Oh…just a thought."

"Tell me about it. I could use a good laugh."

"Just the crazy notion of anyone actually being tight with Freddie." He chuckled and his shoulders shook.

"I see."

"Solid, man. What kind of business you in?"

Although he tried to mask it, I could see a tremendous amount of curiosity light up his red-rimmed eyes. Without mincing words I explained my mission. He looked at me incredulously.

"I'm not sure what kind of drugs you're on, my man," he said, speaking loud for the first time. "But you ought to talk to your doctor about putting you on a new prescription. Because if you think Freddie Tucker's capable of listening to reason, whatever you're takin' ain't working."

The crowd nearby had lost interest in Pee Wee's loud voice shortly after his first few lines. Again I had him to myself. I leaned in closer to whisper, "Why is it you don't seem too worried?"

"I paid off one of his boys just like I promised I would when I got paid last night after the rehearsal." He shrugged indifferently. "If he's still mad, what can I do about that? It's like the song goes: 'Que, Sera Sera.'"

"I think you're forgetting something, though. "

"Like?"

"Since it was you who brought Freddie into Weathersby's life from jump street, I'd say you owe the young brother something in return."

"You do, huh?" He grunted defensively, paused, fondled the wine glass in his hands and then asked, "Like what?"

"What I'd like from you is a simple favor." I reached into a hip pocket, peeled a sawbuck from a wad of cash and folded it neatly to wave it under Pee Wee's nose. "Maybe this'll help."

"Help? How?"

"Where does Freddie live?"

Pee Wee screwed his prune shaped face into an intense parody of moral debate and scratched the side of his face the way I'd seen many a junkie do. Then he announced his decision.

"Why not?" He took the bill. "As long as you don't tell him how you found out his address, I guess I got nothing to lose."

He mumbled off Tucker's address and added one more thought.

"Look, mister-whatever-your-name-is, let me pull your coat to the real deal. No matter what you do short of takin' him totally out of commission, Tucker's not about to forget what happened with Weathersby. Like, read me clear, Jack. Not until all hell freezes over will he ever forget how Joe embarrassed him."

As I walked away, he let out another stream of hyena-like laughter that seemed to cover a lot of ground until it was shut out by the trio's opening notes.

~

It was close to two in the morning when I located Tucker's building near the corner of 118th and Lennox Avenue. It was a rundown tenement. A cavalcade of rancid odors hit me the moment I stepped into the vestibule. The sickening parade of smells grew even more stifling as I climbed the groaning stairway to the fifth floor and rapped my knuckles on the door of Tucker's flat. I knocked twice, and then put my ear to the door. All was quiet. Slowly, I twisted the doorknob. There was some give as I pushed my weight against the door, indicating that all four locks were not secured.

Turning the collar of my raincoat up, I hustled over to my apartment about seven blocks away and grabbed a locksmith's kit and my Colt .38 Detective Special. Then I backtracked to Tucker's crib. The lock gave after a minute of toying with it, and I slipped into the dark flat. With the door closed behind me, I stood stone still. To my relief, the only sound I heard was the non-threatening drone of the traffic from the streets below.

Considering what I'd seen of the rest of the building, Tucker's pad was plush. A long leather couch sat at the center of the room. Two large hi-fi speakers stood like sentries at both ends of the couch. Velveteen artwork hung on the walls along with lots of Polaroid shots of Freddie and a host of different women. Most of them were taken inside various nightclubs.

Soon I became aware of an odor that identified itself as the stench of decaying flesh. Using the faint light that filtered in from a street lamp, I inched my way to the bedroom. On a rumpled king-size bed, Freddie lay naked and face up with his eyes frozen wide in shock.

Blood stained the sheets black. Right smack in the center of his forehead, an ugly gaping wound stared back at me. It was obvious that he had been shot while lying there, most likely while he was sound asleep.

As I neared the front door to make a hasty exit, I heard footsteps in the hall approach the apartment door and stop. Whoever was on the other side of the door knocked several times, using a signal of seven sharp, punctuated raps.

I took a deep breath and anticipated seeing the doorknob turn.

"Shit!" said the voice from the hall. "Where the hell's that nigger this time of night?"

Soon the footsteps retreated. I waited a few moments. Then I followed a slender, shadowy figure down to the exit. When I stepped into the front doorway, I saw Pudding, a neighborhood addict, ambling away and cursing to himself. I stayed in the darkened doorway until he disappeared down a nearby alleyway.

～

After leaving Tucker's bloody remains, I rushed straight to my flat. My adrenaline was still pumping at such an accelerated rate that sleep was totally out of the question. Instead, I worked through a written account of the day starting with notations from my conversation with Blinky and onward. I tried capturing first and last impressions, and anything that might later prove significant.

I wrote longhand in a loose-leaf notebook. As sloppy as my handwriting was, I figured it wasn't about penmanship. By the time I finished the last scribbled word the sun was peeking over the basement windowsill. After I reread what I'd written, I burned the pages and flushed them down the toilet bowl.

From the moment I woke up a few hours later, Weathersby's rendition of "Ornithology I" ran through my mind like a background score. Coupled with the music was the stench of death from Tucker's apartment which seemed indelibly embedded in my olfactory glands. Although I should have felt nothing but relief knowing that he was no longer a threat to anyone, I also felt a nagging sense of unexplainable regret. Seeing the huge man lying there so helpless was a reminder of my own mortality.

The slug the doctors had to remove from near my spine, the one that had almost killed me when I was still in blue, often felt as though it was still embedded in me. At those times, it grew hot and then cold, as it did when I recalled standing over Tucker's corpse.

I had struggled out of bed fifteen minutes after the alarm clock rang. Saturdays and Sundays are usually my days off from Wally's, but I had promised to fill in that day for the weekend man. Before that, though, I had to meet a buddy at the gym where we trained. Weather permitting, I walked on alternate days forgoing a bus, subway or cab. Even though I was running a little late that day, I set out on foot, hoping my first cup of java would finally kick in.

The clock on the wall of the 125th Street gym told me I was eight minutes late. Detective Garret Brown, Brownie as I call him, always arrived earlier than I did. Wearing his red trunks, he stood near the center ring, wrapping tape around his fists, watching two welterweights slug it out. When he spied me, he glanced up at the wall clock and shook his head as a sign of his disapproval.

"You won't have long to wait," I assured him, as I headed toward the locker room to change.

"Good!" his baritone voice stretched the one word out for a full bar.

For the last four years, Brownie and I met at the gym, depending on his schedule on Wednesdays or Saturdays. We'd go through a series of muscle limbering stretches and exercises, skip rope, shadowbox, jab the speed bag and slug away at the heavy bag. Then we'd strap on protective headgear and step into one of the rings to go at each other for a single round, three minutes from start to the final bell. We both held back, pulling the sting off our punches, satisfied that our routine was a way to stay in shape and sharp but not to kill or maim each other. On one occasion, however, things got rough. But more often than not we were both relieved when the round ended, silently convincing ourselves that if need be, we could survive a few more rounds in a regulation prizefight.

At six-foot-two, I had a two-inch height advantage on Brownie. But with his thick weightlifter's body and bulky shoulders, he outweighed me by about twenty pounds. Though I was quicker, he compensated for that by mounting a steady relentless attack.

I changed into my boxing duds, and we began going through our self-prescribed ritual. When it was time for me to hold the heavy bag, his Joe Louis-inspired uppercuts and combination crosses sent gushes of air exploding from the bag, accompanied by clouds of dust mites. He cursed the bag as he slugged it and seemed to be sweating more than usual. After a dozen mighty blows or so, his words became comprehensible.

"This burglary detail is getting to be the pits, brother man." He punctuated his speech with the steady rhythm of his punches. "I don't know if any amount of money could keep a man looking at the same shit I see every day. Each and every day.

Yeah...every...sing...gle...so...li...ta...ry...day! I...may...as
well...be...working...vice!"

"What's so much worse than it was when I saw you last
week?"

"It's those goddamn junkies!" He kept driving steady blows
into the bag, rocking it and me with each delivery. "The way
they live like rats and cockroaches. And there're the kids I see
on that shit! Some of them no more than babies! God, almighty!
Living like animals...they do! And...sometimes...it's more...
than...I can...take!"

He finally stopped punching far past his usual number of
repetitions. Then as though it was an afterthought, he struck
one more blow that sent the bag swinging on its groaning chain.

"I mean...I'm a human being with feelings, too. Ain't I?"

"It's getting that bad, huh?"

"Bad ain't the half of it. A goddamn junky will risk his life
hanging off an eight-story roof to climb in an open window on
the chance that he might find something worth a measly five
bucks to pawn."

"That is desperate."

"No shit, Sherlock." He tightened his already intense sweat-
beaded brows, focused his dark eyes on me with a fierce glint,
and said, "It ain't nothing like when you first left the force,
Nate. Those days are gone. And the really scary part is I'm not
sure if I understand what the new rules are." He shook his head
and blinked his eyes like his own words surprised him. "Worst,
I don't know how the new rules and new order apply to me."

As we walked toward a twelve by twelve foot practice ring,
we strapped on our headgear.

"I may not be a cop anymore, but it's my neighborhood,
too," I said. "Has there really been that much change in the
department?"

"When we're done the round," his eyes darted toward the
ring and to the old gym rat waiting to sound the bell, "I'll fill
you in over breakfast. I'm meeting with Vince and a couple of

other cats at the Chinese joint we ate at last month. You can sit in if you want."

"No can do." I followed him into the ring. "I have to shower and get to work as soon as we're done. So tell me what's cooking."

"Not now I said!" He faced me, gritting his wide teeth and shot a quick jab to my forehead. "When we're done the round."

As soon as the bell sounded, he charged straight at me. After the tense night I'd had with so little sleep, I realized I was ill prepared to face him for three minutes given the foul mood he was in. So right away I started backpedaling.

He stalked me relentlessly, going for my body. A memory of the nagging damage he had once inflicted to my ribcage caused an extra amount of adrenaline to kick in. Defensively, I kept him at bay with a series of jabs and counter punches. He ducked under most of them, using his gloves to ward off others. The punches that did get through were glancing ones.

I started the round circling left, and he followed me, trying to line me up in his sights for an open strike. Then I switched to a southpaw stance, circling in the opposite direction, which also allowed me to stay further away from the knockout power of his right hand. Every time I got him going one way, I'd reverse directions, jabbing with the left hand, then the right.

"You better run!" he growled with a glint in his eyes.

I fought to stay near the center of the ring where I had more room to maneuver and elude him. Against the ropes, I'd be too much at his mercy.

From the corners of my eyes, I could make out a crowd gathering around the ring to watch the sweltering action and cheer us on. About halfway through the round the ring seemed to shrink and my arms began to tire from the blows they'd thrown or warded off and the weight of the sixteen-ounce gloves.

Concentrating even harder as the round wore on, Brownie kept his punches focused on my body. Each time he connected, my guard would lower reflexively. Time and time again, he tried to get a roundhouse bomber over the top, but I was too quick for that to work. Then he'd go back downstairs for my ribs, working on the old pugilistic axiom: work on the body and the hands will drop.

For obvious reasons, I was determined to frustrate him and make sure that he'd have to find redemption for his frustrations elsewhere.

When the round-ending bell finally clanged, I dropped my guard too soon, and he clobbered me upside the head with a roundhouse.

I saw an infusion of red splatter inside my head, and responded with two good blows that landed square to his face. In another instant, all of our decorum was forgotten, replaced by fury. The hail of punches we threw must have made us look like two windmills trying to take flight.

Before too long, three sizable pugs jumped into the ring and pulled us apart. At the insistence of one of the fighters, who reminded us that we were close friends, Brownie and I apologized and touched gloves to symbolize a truce.

I was still trying to keep my temper in check as we showered.

"It's not just the goddamn junkies that have me so uptight," Brownie explained, as we soaped down with steaming hot water showering us full-force. "In the last three weeks, three dealers have all popped up the same kind of dead."

"Can you make out a connection?"

"Each one was done in by a thirty-two slug. Ballistics tells us it was the same weapon all three times."

"Hmm—"

"And there were sightings by more than one witness who described the assailant as male, tall and heavy-set. And dig this. They say the cat's Caucasian." He slurred the last word. "Now tell me what you find odd about that. I mean, way up here right smack dab in the middle of Harlem, and one white cat on his own."

It wasn't hard to follow his reasoning. Nonetheless, I asked, "Are you suggesting a cop is doing it?"

"That's what my instincts are telling me. The eyewitnesses all saw him walking away fast from the sight of the shootings and turning a corner. So there was no make on what he might have been driving."

While I was digesting all I'd heard, he went on.

"I've seen Captain Frye and Lieutenant McKellerhan sweep shit under the rug before, man. But I swear I've never seen them do it with such a wide broom. Something's definitely fishy or my name ain't Garret Jerrell Brown."

Later, as we stepped into the bright sunlight of the street, he began repeating a story I'd heard versions of a few times before.

"When I was a little kid growing up in Mississippi, I saw this county sheriff beat my father to a raw pulp. It happened right in front of our house in broad daylight. All because of some minor traffic violation, and the fact the sheriff never did like my daddy to begin with. You see, he wasn't one of those kiss-ass-niggers. I promised myself right then and there that if any ass was going to get kicked in my life, I was going to be the one doing the kicking."

As we walked the block and a half to where he'd parked his '53 blue and red Chevy Bel Air, he continued speculating about the shootings.

"I wasn't really surprised when the brass ignored the initial rumors about some ofay cat shooting up the night. I figured it was one of those crazy rumors that turn out to be nothing more than another one of those street myths started by some wino or asshole on cloud nine. You know what I mean? But now that it's been three weeks since the first one went down, and two more unsolved cases with similar descriptions from eyewitnesses, I'm not so sure. So I keep asking myself why the brass is still playing this so hush-hush." He shrugged and grunted. "It just don't add up kosher to me, brother."

"When was the last guy gunned down?"

"This morning around two o'clock is when the squeal came. This time it was a big time dealer named Moses Grover. Got his brains blown out in an alley off 118th and Lennox Avenue."

"In an alley?"

"Just like the other two. My guess is the deceased all thought they were meeting *the man* to give him a payoff for protection and got more than they were expecting."

"Hmm…" I said, thinking how close that was to Tucker's flat. "I've heard of Grover."

"I suppose so. He'd been dealing up here for so long the man was practically an institution."

"So, why would a cop on the take kill him rather than keep collecting his rake?"

"Like I told you, too much of what's happening doesn't make sense."

"Well," I said, "now that you've given me the skinny, I'll keep my eyes and ears open, and I'll let you know if I hear anything worth passing on."

"You do that, Nate. Now I'm going to join Vince and a few other cats," he said, as he left me to climb into his car.

My mind was churning faster with each step I took as he drove past me and blew the car horn three times.

CHAPTER 4

Crossing an intersection on Lennox Avenue, halfway to Wally's, I was processing everything Brownie had told me when a tan undercover cruiser cut in front of me. Brakes complaining, it came to a rocking halt inches away. Behind the wheel, Detective Sam Brisco displayed a wry smile as he leaned across to open the passenger side door.

"Get in, Holt!" he commanded.

Brisco was a tall, dark-skinned, stout man, the heavyweight wrestler type, with a shaved head and unnaturally pink lips. A jagged knife scar made a trail from the left corner of his mouth halfway down his fat neck. He was wearing a cheap, brown suit and a frayed, gold necktie twisted into a huge Windsor knot. He sat with the cruiser idling despite the fact that there were horns blaring from cars trying to get by in all four directions of the intersection.

Pedestrians made a detour around the unmarked sedan, looking back at me with frowning faces, as I slid into the front seat.

Ignoring all of that, with a whimsical expression on his face, Brisco studied me disdainfully as a dispatcher's static-filled voice piped over the squawk box.

"So..." he said, eyeing me up and down and licking his thick, discolored lips, "you're walking pretty fast this morning. Why the big rush, Holt?"

"Got to open at eleven."

He turned his critical gaze away and pulled out of the intersection to roll across the corner and brake halfway up the block. Then he twisted his body at what looked to be a painful angle to face me. I waited as though I had nothing better to do, as he pulled out a Kool from a pack on the dashboard and fired it up with a fancy, gold lighter.

"If you're planning to sit here all day," I said, glancing at my wristwatch, "maybe I should walk."

He took his time replying.

"Sometimes I just don't get you, Holt," he said, shaking his head and blowing smoke from the side of his mouth. "You got that front at Wally's, running that numbers operation with Syd Barnes. Then I see you've been hooked up with that pretty dancer girl for a while now. Lillian, I believe her name is. Lives over there on Amsterdam near 137th."

He flicked his tongue like a snake.

"So?"

"To top things off, I hear you're a scribe with a regular column for the local paper, too. Diggit? That kind of greedy mentality worries me to no end. I mean, leave something for somebody else, Jack."

"Trying to make a decent living," I said, sensing that our conversation was going somewhere I was bound to regret.

He chuckled and took the cigarette from his mouth, put the car in gear and pulled into the flow of traffic.

"We all have our jobs to do," I added. "I just do what I can to pick up a few extra ducats."

Though I was a numbers runner, it wasn't as though I was a desperado in the eyes of the local law. The illegal lottery offered people a precious commodity called hope where there should be none. Therefore, the numbers racket was virtually ignored by the police and looked upon as a necessary evil. Furthermore, I made weekly payments to the benevolent order of the local police department via Lieutenant Lyle McKellerhan, which I felt in all practicality legitimized my business. Seventy-year-old Wally Thornton, the owner of the tavern, knew what I was doing. In fact, he was my number one customer. He, and everyone on the street, knew that the police got their share of the action. Consequently, no one would be surprised to see me pull up to work as a passenger in an unmarked police sedan. It was all part of the civilized way business was done in Harlem.

For the next two blocks, in the thick of traffic, Brisco drove silently. I kept anticipating that at any moment he would break the silence. Finally, he did.

"You know," he said, eyeing me rather than the street as he drove, "when I was cruising along back there and spotted you strutting on down the avenue, a profound thought hit me like a flash."

"What was that?" I was expecting him to finally launch into what was really on his mind, knowing his technique of playing cat and mouse as a preliminary tactic to unnerve suspects.

"At any given time, any day or any night, death can strike any one of us down. I mean, any one of us. Know what I'm trying to say, Holt?"

"I...ah—"

"'Cause some folks aren't so lucky. And with me being on the force with a gold shield for so many years and working homicide, too, I know what I'm talking about."

"I don't doubt it."

I was extremely glad when he turned left on 145th. I was anxious to be as far away from him as possible. But he deliberately slowed behind a smoke spewing bus a half block from Wally's. When the bus pulled away, he took his time steering over to the curb. A couple of shaky old-timers were already in front of Wally's waiting for the joint to open.

"So be careful," he went on, "and remember to play it safe when you can, pal."

"What are you trying to say, Sam? Spit it out. Okay? Because I'm tired of whatever game you're playing here like I'm some kind of toy."

"Fine. I can do that." He twisted his body around to face me, like he'd done when I'd first gotten into the cruiser. "Ever hear of Freddie Tucker?"

"Freddie Tucker? Why? Should I've heard of him?" I tried not to reveal concern about the sudden change in the conversation, which did have my mind doing back flips.

"According to my sources, yes, you knew him, Holt. Word is you spent a good deal of time last night looking to run him down."

"Says who?"

"At this point, that doesn't matter. One thing is stone-cold fact, though. Freddie Tucker was found dead this morning." He locked his eyes on mine and held my steady gaze. "I was just wondering if you know anything at all that might help me figure out exactly what went down, and why you were trying to track him down. I was hoping you'd bring the subject up on your own. But, no. That didn't happen. Did it?"

I shifted my eyes toward Wally's and the two stew bums in front. One of them was glancing at his wristwatch.

"I did have a question for Tucker relating to a favor I was doing for a friend." I gazed back at Sam. "But that's neither here nor there, now."

"Look, Nathaniel, that's exactly what I'm talking about," he spoke my name, with his eyes narrowed, as though it was a curse word. "Like I've been trying to remind you. You've got it made in the shade, brother. A good job and a super fine mama to go gallivanting around town, flashing her on your arm. But don't forget you got guys like me who turn our backs on your little numbers running operation. So don't go screwing up a good thing by forgetting who your real friends are."

"Thanks for the—"

"You see, sometimes it's best to play it safe. Other times it's the only way to play it, if you know what I mean?"

"I hear you." I read my wristwatch again and sighed. "All I want to know right now is...are you finished giving me so much friendly advice this morning so I can get to work?"

"Not yet, and you know why?" He didn't wait for me to respond. "In the war I used to have this buck private under me who was something like you. One of those intellectual types who just refused to get with the program, in spite of how many chances he was given. Burns was his last name, and his first name in this story doesn't really matter none. Because the funny thing was that he was trying to desert when he blew himself to pieces stepping on a landmine. While that surprised the hell out of him, it sure as hell didn't surprise me in the least. See, I knew we were covering our tracks. That's why I didn't waste no time shooting him in the back when I saw him fleeing. So, like, when you come right down to it, that chicken-shit Burns ended up killing himself."

He threw his head back and let out a deep-throated laugh. Then, as he reached across me to open the door on my side, he sneered wide enough for his purple gums to show.

"You can bet I'll be talking to you some more, Nathaniel. For your sake, I hope you don't turn out to be as dumb as buck private Burns."

"Thanks for the ride, Detective."

I stepped out of his cruiser and slammed the door hard.

~

As I went about the day behind the bar, my mind spun in overdrive. When I was in Tucker's pad, I estimated he had been dead for at least twenty-four hours. I'd left his apartment door ajar to expedite the discovery of his remains. But no way had I expected Detective Brisco to pop up asking me intimidating questions so early in the day. Even though he knew I'd been tracking Tucker last night, I don't think he suspected me of killing him.

If so, I was certain our conversation would have lasted longer and been held in an interrogation room right around the corner at the 30th Precinct. I was also sure that given Tucker's quarrelsome reputation, Brisco would be looking at a long list of suspects with reasons and the means to see him dead.

Although the cops wouldn't mourn Tucker's passing, a homicide was a homicide, and too many unsolved homicides equaled bad press. Too much negative publicity, and like a lightning bolt from above, the heat seared its way through the ranks from the governor's office on down. Often times, behind the scenes, within a minute's notice, careers were made and broken.

Still, the question of who had killed Freddie Tucker nagged me. Could it have been the vigilante cop that Brownie had hipped me to? Had he doubled his output for the week with two kills in two successive nights? No, I told myself because there was a big bloody hole in that theory. I had seen the wound in the middle of Tucker's forehead, and it wasn't the work of a small caliber .32. But it was the timing of Moses Grover's death that caused me the most concern. About the same time I was gawking at the big hole in Tucker's head, which looked as though it was the work of a .45, not far away Grover was getting his brains blown out by a .32.

At about noon, the private phone behind the bar rang. I wasn't surprised that it was Blinky.

"How'd it go?" he asked right away.

"Your worries are over. Someone took your problem out of the picture permanently before I had a chance to talk with him."

"No joke?"

"You heard me. A brother I know on the force gave me the news this morning. Somebody smoked him."

"Well…" he paused. "I don't know whether to cheer or say a string of Hail Marys."

"I'd cheer if I were you. Then there's still the question of all that cash you laid on me."

"Money's the last thing on my mind. I'm just so relieved that the four bills I gave you don't mean a hill of beans."

"Whatever's fair but—"

"Keep the money, Nate…in recognition for being a real standup guy and for playing it straight with me. You could have told me you talked to him and paid him off, too, and I never would have known the truth."

I thanked Blinky, wished him good luck and told him to let me know where and when the kid's public debut would be.

~

Later that evening, I set out to meet Lillian at her dance studio to see the flat she was so excited about. More than a dozen of her adult students were filing out of the building when I arrived to climb the stairs to the second floor. Her landlord, Harry Swayne, an obese cigar-chomping guy, who had a crush on Lillian, was already inside the studio. Though he was a member of the club, his skin was so pale that next to him, Lillian was dark by contrast. The moment he saw me walking through the door, he fidgeted and pulled a pocket watch from his overalls, glancing at it while frowning. I figured he was irritated that I'd shown up so promptly.

"Right on time," Lillian announced as though she'd just won a bet.

"What are you two up to?" I asked, for laughs.

"Harry was telling me he's in a big hurry. So I'm glad to see you're on time as I predicted you would be."

"Let's get cracking then," I said, smiling in Harry's direction.

Dressed in a pair of leotards, Lillian grabbed a leather jacket from a coat tree near the front door and slipped into it, saying, "I'm as ready as ready gets."

We deferred the elevator because a young couple was in the process of moving an old couch. We followed Harry's slow lead up three flights of stairs. Wheezing with each breath, he informed us that he had a long list of prospective renters coveting the apartment if we passed on it.

"Once I do a little painting, and put some new tiles down in the kitchen and bathroom, we're talking fit for a queen," he smiled Lillian's way, as he fumbled with one key after another until he found the right one to unlock the apartment door. "The only reason I held off renting it was because you've been such a good tenant and you bring so much class to the building, Lil."

The place was everything Lillian had led me to expect and more. It took up the southwest corner of the top floor and commanded a grand view of the downtown skyline. And a peek here and there, between adjacent buildings, revealed slivers of the Hudson River floating by. Lights from a myriad of skyscrapers danced and reflected on the water's sheen.

"I could ask a lot more for this place if I wanted to," Harry said, as he flicked the light on in the master bedroom. "You don't often find so much space on this side of town."

We took the complete tour, and before long Lillian asked me, "Want to take it, Nate?"

"Sure," I nodded, grateful for the extra cash I'd earned from Blinky. "Why not?"

"If you guys are willing to work on fixing the place up yourselves," Harry interjected, "I'll forget about a cleaning fee and half the first month's rent."

"We'd love to do the work ourselves," Lillian said without hesitation. "Wouldn't we, Nate?"

"When can we start?" I asked Harry.

"Well," he said, flexing his slumped shoulders, "I'll turn the keys over to you as soon as I have half of the first month and all of the last month's rent. If you're talking cash, that's one thing. A check is another matter altogether, though. I'd have to wait until—"

"Just a second, Harry," Lillian scoffed. "You've known me and Nate too long to start pulling jive like that on us."

"I know you," he relented.

I was pulling a wad of cash out of a pants pocket when Lillian stopped me with a cutting glance.

"Harry can take a check. Can't you, Harry?"

"Well, I guess a check's okay," he acquiesced with his face turning a bright shade of crimson. "I was just kidding around. I'll leave the keys with you now. You can give me the check first thing in the morning, Lil."

Lillian took the keys and led Harry toward the door by the sleeve of his frayed overalls.

"Just make sure you lock up before you leave," he managed to say before she closed the door on him.

Doing a perfect pirouette, she faced me and asked, "So, honey, what do you think, huh, Nate?"

"You mean about Harry?"

"Get real. Is this place ideal or what?"

"I don't know if I'd call it a deal but I do like it. You really think we can fix it up and move in, though, before the year ends? What is it now, the middle of April?"

"We can do it in no time, and you know it. It'll be fun, too." She playfully poked me in the gut. "Remember what a good time we had redoing the studio last year?"

"I remember some good times, but they had nothing to do with manual labor."

She ignored my statement and said, "I've been running some decorating schemes through my head ever since I got a peek in here. I can't wait to get started."

She rattled off where some of our furniture could go. Before long, I was caught up in her vision. Then she took me by the hand and led me back to the master bedroom.

"This will soon be ours. So start imagining all the fun we'll be having in here." She swept a hand toward the majestic downtown skyline, and then wrapped her arms around me and squeezed tight with a wanton look in her eyes.

"C'mon, Nate. Use that vivid imagination of yours to start seeing what I see. You know that's what I love most about you."

"You're not just saying that because it sounds good, are you?"

She laughed and took a clip from her hair to shake her shoulder-length hair free. Then she pulled me close, stood on tiptoes and smothered my lips with kisses. I was relieved to see her in such a good mood compared to when I'd last seen her the night before.

"Remember telling me how you like me best?" she teased.

"Um… maybe you better remind me."

"Bold and brazen." She nibbled at my bottom lip.

"I see."

Right there on the bare hardwood floor we made love with a passionate urgency. Before too very long, we were lying half naked and exhausted in each other's arms.

"I think I'd better wait a minute or two before I try standing up," she said with her eyes twinkling. "Otherwise, my knees might buckle."

CHAPTER 5

I spent Saturday night and all day Sunday at Lillian's. When I got back to my cramped flat at about one o'clock Monday morning, my phone was ringing. I cut a path around a stack of boxes containing my jazz records and book collection to reach the receiver where I'd left it.

"Nate?" an urgent voice questioned before I could even say hello.

"Who's this?"

"It's me, Blinky," his voice quivered. "I been calling you practically every fifteen minutes for the last seven hours."

"What's wrong?"

"It's about Joe. He called from jail."

"Jail?"

"They arrested him for the murder of Freddie Tucker."

"Come again?"

"Yeah, man. I found out later a detective questioned the soundman at the rehearsal studio. He told them about the fight between Joe and Freddie. But even knowing about that, I'd hardly think they'd arrest and charge him with murder. I mean, can you believe that?"

"There's got to be more to it than that."

"I tried to talk to the cop in charge but he keeps telling me to—"

"Who's the guy in charge?"

"His name's Brisco. And no one's returning my calls. Like I said, I been trying to reach you all night. I didn't know what else to do."

"By now Joe's probably in the Tombs."

"Do you think you can get a lead on what the hell's going down?"

"I'll ask around and see what I can find out. Just try not to get too bent out of shape. I'll call you as soon as I learn anything."

"I'll try to maintain, man. But please, Nate, see what you can find out. This is a bunch of Mickey Mouse shit for sure, and we have to do something for the kid."

"I'll get over to visit him first thing tomorrow."

"They don't allow visitors in the Tombs."

"I have my means, Blink."

At eight o'clock that morning, I began making calls. Despite my best efforts, though, none of my friends on the force, including Brownie, knew the extent of the case they had against Joe. Something told me that Detective Brisco had made it clear to everyone at the precinct that I was to be given the cold shoulder. Brownie being so closed lipped caused me the most concern.

A few hours later, I made my way to the Department of Corrections main detention facility, also known as the Tombs. I carried a briefcase I sometimes use as a ruse and a business card I'd picked up from an attorney who handles some of Wally's affairs. I knew pretending to be a lawyer was the only way I'd be allowed to see Joe.

After going through the courthouse, then down to the basement, and through a long corridor, I entered the jail and took an elevator up to the visiting area. I waited in the renovated building whose very walls seemed to emanate an air of hopelessness and despair from many past ages.

After about an hour, I was informed that Weathersby had been transferred to Riker's Island. Knowing a woman who worked in the filing department there, I dialed her from a pay phone. She informed me Weathersby was being held in solitary confinement. That news complicated matters. I'd once had a run-in with a guard there and knew I could face problems pretending to be a lawyer wanting to talk to a client in solitary.

Later that day, from the phone in Wally's, I reached a friend in the DA's office.

"District Attorney's office. Howard Katz speaking."

"Howie, it's your old buddy, Nate."

"Hey, buddy," his tone lightened. "What's the word, my good man?"

"I've got a friend locked up in Riker's Island. He's in solitary, and I need to talk to him."

"No problem. Give me the unlucky fella's name. I'll look up the case number and call you back in about ten minutes."

"His name's Joseph Weathersby." Quickly, I added, "By the way, knowing how much you dig the hip music scene, I know you'd love to hear the dude play his sax once he's back on the street."

"Oh, now I see why you're so interested in his welfare."

I gave him the number of the phone behind the bar. More than an hour passed before Howie's call finally jingled through. He lit into me as soon as I picked up the receiver.

"Why the hell didn't you tell me the guy you want to visit is an alleged murderer? Huh? Don't you think that information was worth mentioning?"

"Look, Howie, the kid's just twenty years old. I'm a friend of the family. What harm can it do if I get to see him?"

"It's a matter of protocol."

"Protocol? You want to talk to me about protocol?"

"You heard me."

"How about this for protocol, Howard? Who recovered the stolen merchandise that your son got ripped off last year? And don't forget the jam I helped your brother out of about six months before that."

"Well, I—"

"It wasn't the cops or anybody from the DA's office. It was me. Remember?"

"All right. Okay!" he relented. "Give me a little more time on this. Are you going to be at the same number for a while?"

"I'll be here until I hear back from you."

"You could have made things a lot simpler if you had been up front. That's all I'm saying."

"I know, I know. Never again. Okay?"

"Yeah. Right!"

"One more thing. This case against the kid—"

"What about it?"

"I have a gut feeling that his arrest is a case of mistaken identity. Which means the real killer is still running loose."

"You'll hear from me," he said, hastily disconnecting us.

Fifteen minutes later, his secretary informed me that a special visitor's pass would be waiting for me at ten o'clock the next morning.

~

Early the next day, before setting out to visit Joe, I met Blinky at a midtown restaurant on Broadway. It was a dismal foggy morning and the sky was covered with dark storm clouds. Blinky appeared to be struggling with a hangover. Without his sunglasses on, I could see the flesh around his eyes was puffy and he appeared to have gone days without sleep or a shave.

"I don't mind meeting you," he said, with the right side of his face twitching. "But did you have to pick such a god-awful hour?"

"Wally is opening up the bar for me today, so I'd like to relieve him as soon as possible. This makes two mornings in a row he's stood in for me."

"I'm sorry, Nate." He laughed nervously and brushed his thinning hair back with a shaky hand. "Don't pay any serious mind to my squawking. In the mornings I'm always like a bitch on the rag too long, even on the job. But if you want some more dough, I could kick something your way."

"Your savings must be more than I thought."

"What's money if you can't spend it on what turns you on? Right?"

"If I need it, I'll ask for more."

"I insist." He reached into a back pocket and withdrew an old dog-eared wallet and pulled out a fresh fifty-dollar bill and slid it across the table to me.

"Thanks."

An elderly, plump waitress set our coffees down with a jarring abruptness, took our orders in a no nonsense manner, and I got back to the business at hand.

"Tell me all you can about Joe."

"Like what? You don't think he killed Tucker, do you?"

"Can the crap." I dumped one and a half spoons of sugar into my black coffee and stirred. "Whatever you know about him, that's what I want to hear."

"Let's see." Blinky stroked his fuzz-stubbed chin. "Like you already know, he was born in Philly. His father's a doctor who runs his business out of the house in a pretty rough part of town. I guess that's how little Joe got to be so good with his hands."

"That fits. Any man-child raised in Philly learns to use his dukes."

"Anyway," he went on, "when he was about six years old, his mother thought it would be a good idea to have Joe start piano lessons. Not like she wanted him to be a musician or anything as unconventional as that. She just thought it would help with his social refinement, so to speak. Right away, though, he showed a lot of promise. Then when he was about eleven or so, he heard Bird for the first time and fell in love with his sound. That's when he switched to sax."

Our meals came, blueberry pancakes and a side order of bacon, a glass of orange juice and milk for Blinky. T-bone steak, three sunny-side up eggs, hash browns and rye toast for me.

"Although he showed amazing talent on the sax," Blinky continued while buttering his pancakes, "his father was dead set against the idea of his one and only child becoming a professional musician. But Joe already had his mind made up. In the end, with a lot of persistence on his part, he won his old man over, and he let him enroll at Julliard." He paused. "I think you know the rest."

"Have you talked to his family since the shit hit the fan?"

"Yeah," he spoke with his mouth full of jam-laden pancakes. "I had a long distance operator look the number up and gave them a ring. I finally reached his father."

"How'd he take the news?"

"He's taking it hard, of course. It was the whole drug scene fear in the first place that made him so worried about Joe becoming a musician." He grunted and wiped his mouth with a backhand. "You see, he wanted Joe to be a doctor, too."

"Did you find out when the arraignment's going to be?"

"Tomorrow morning."

"Do you have someone lined up to represent him?"

"Yeah, I finally got through to Lucas Haynes. He's going to look into the matter. But because of prior commitments he won't get to speak with Joe until they bring him into court. I hear Haynes is good, though."

"I've heard the same. He used to write political articles for *The Amsterdam News*. I was under the impression he's beaucoup expensive."

"Joe's father said he would pick up the tab. I had to insist on contributing half of whatever the fee comes out to."

"You're a good man, Blinky."

"Thanks a lot." He shook his head wearily and hit the side of his head with an open palm and mimicked a robotic voice. "That's what I keep telling myself; I'm a good man. I'm a good man."

"Don't be too hard on yourself, Blink. There's no way you could have known how convoluted things would turn out."

"I suppose you're right, Nate," he agreed, reluctantly. "It would be nice if you still don't mention anything to Joe about me hiring you to talk to Freddie."

"Don't worry. That's between you and me.

~

In the visitor's reception area at Riker's Island, I could have reread half of Dostoevsky's *Crime and Punishment* while waiting to see young Joe. The longer I waited, the more I could empathize with the anxiety the boy's parents were undoubtedly experiencing. When the time finally came to speak with him, the kid was escorted to the opposite side of a small enclosure where I sat.

He was handcuffed and wore leg irons. A bright shiner had his left eye swollen shut and discolored a purplish red. All in all, he made a pathetic picture when he sat down behind the thick glass partition and picked up the receiver to talk. I introduced myself as a friend of Blinky's, and he acknowledged seeing me at the rehearsal studio Friday night.

"You got to get me out of this place, man," he said. "I can't take this too much longer."

"I know what you're saying. Nobody likes being locked in a cage. But tell me, how'd you end up in solitary confinement?"

"Some cats in the cell block where they put me tried to punk me out."

"Sorry to hear that."

"I'd die before I'd let that happen. They can keep me all boxed up like some animal in the dark, or move me back to the general population. Either way, nobody's punkin' me out as long as I'm alive."

"First things first," I said calmly. "When the cops picked you up, what kind of questions did they ask?"

"They wanted to know everything like what time I left the studio Thursday night and where I went from there."

"Where did you go?"

"Home."

"Straight home?"

"Uh-huh."

"What time did you get there?"

"About midnight or so, I guess."

"And where's home?"

"A little furnished crib up on Edgecombe."

"Step by step, take me through what happened."

"I was all jacked up thinking about some kind of bright future blowing my horn." He closed his good eye momentarily, as though he were trying to recall a long ago, half-forgotten past. "I had damn near put that shit with Tucker out of my mind. And, like I often do, I went up on the roof and did some shedding."

"Was anyone with you?"

"I wish I could say yeah, but I was by myself."

"How long were you up there playing?"

"About an hour. I'm not really sure, but something like that."

"Then someone must've heard you."

"Probably not."

"I don't get it. You just said you were shedding with your horn up on the roof of your building, right? If that's true, someone had to hear you."

"Unfortunately," he shook his head forlornly, "I always stuff a towel in the bell of my sax when I practice at home or on the roof. That way I don't have to deal with any complaints."

"I can see why the cops didn't buy that line. After all, as I recall the hawk was out in full force and it was colder than a witch's tit."

"Long as it's not freezing, the cold doesn't bother me. When I'm playing, no matter how cold the weather, I stay warm." He spoke with credible conviction. "Just ask some of my schoolmates at Julliard. They know shedding up there on the roof is something I do all the time."

To help verify his story, I had him supply me with a few names and phone numbers, which I jotted down.

"So," I said, "go on. What else happened while they were interrogating you?"

"I admitted to the cop questioning me, Detective Brisco, about having a run-in with Tucker. Anyway, he already knew about all that. So I figured no big deal there. But he kept harping on and on about where I was around midnight. On and on all night and through half the morning, he and the other cop there in the room with us took turns. They were asking me all kinds of stuff, like where I'd hid the gun I shot Tucker with. Like I was supposed to know what the hell they were talking about. Going over and over the same stuff."

"Stuff? Like what?"

He collected his thoughts before answering. "According to how I put it together since then, someone on the floor below Tucker's place heard what sounded like a gunshot. They opened their apartment door and saw someone running down the stairs. They also said some ofay chick was with the guy."

"Did they indicate what the white chick might have looked like?"

"Kind of." He lifted his handcuffed hands and scratched the tip of his nose with a forefinger. "They kept asking if I knew a white chick with short red hair."

"Do you?"

"Naw, man. I was dating a white chick for a while. Last year, when I first hit town."

"Did she happen to have red hair?"

"Yeah, but she had long, red hair. Back then anyway. I suppose it's still the same, though."

"What's her name?"

"Do we have to bring her into this? I mean, I only went out with her two times before we decided to call it quits."

"Why'd it end?"

"It was mostly on my say."

"Why? What went wrong?"

"Just the extra headaches, man." He shrugged his slender shoulders and looked down at his restless fingers pounding out silent rhythms on the narrow countertop in front of him. "I mean, as it stands, a guy and a girl run into enough problems without opening the window for a lot of racial bullshit on top of everything else."

"Even so, I may need her name."

"Only if push comes to shove," he said, with a dramatic sigh.

"Just in case you don't get the full picture, we're not talking about a misdemeanor or petty offense stacked against you, Joe.

We're talking cold-blooded, premeditated homicide, which is a capital offense. If a jury convicts you, the judge could sentence you to life in prison. That's if you're lucky. Then you'd have the opportunity to mount appeal after appeal for just about forever. The electric chair's the other option he could take. There are folks right now trying to abolish capital punishment in the state. As of yet, though—"

"You think I don't know how serious this shit is?" he said, in a raised voice.

He stared through the wire-meshed, fortified glass. Then he let out another prolonged sigh and collected himself to speak with more composure.

"Here's all I know. They put me in a lineup with about five other colored cats. But none of them looked a thing like me. All of them were either short, fat, or old as Methuselah. Someone behind the looking glass must have pointed me out because, as you can plainly see, here I am locked up for murder. And I've never in my whole life broke one law worth mentioning."

"Well," I finally said, "here's the situation. Tomorrow you'll appear for an arraignment. There'll be a lawyer there to represent you. Blinky picked him out and he's the best at what he does. His name's Lucas Haynes. If you agree to let him represent you, which I know you'll do, he'll be able to confer with the DA's people and get a better idea of what kind of case they have against you."

"I don't get to talk to this lawyer until then?"

"This is just an arraignment. Think of it as the first step where not much goes down. The only time you'll be asked to say anything is when the judge asks how you plead. Then he'll set a preliminary hearing date."

Dejectedly, Joe nodded his head.

"By the way," I said, "Blinky called and talked with your father."

"That's good to know." He blew out a compressed mouthful of air. "How's he taking all this?"

"Naturally, he's upset. But he's in your corner and together he and Blinky are going to foot the attorney's bill."

"I hope it ain't a waste of their money."

"Just keep this in mind. If you're innocent, as I believe you are, you don't have anything to worry about."

A long silence followed.

"Out of curiosity," he said, as he leaned closer to the glass that separated us, "what's your stake in this?"

"Blinky's a friend."

He puckered his lips, blinked his good eye a few times and seemed satisfied with my answer.

"And..." I added, "you're one hell of a horn man. I especially like what you do with 'Ornithology I.'"

"Thanks, man," he said, smiling faintly. "I dug it right away when I first heard it, especially when I looked up the word and found out it means the study of birds. That was the first one of Charlie Parker's complicated tunes I learned. I still get a big charge out of wailing it. I always see all kinds of birds while I'm playing."

"You'll be playing it again soon."

"I sure hope you're right."

I wanted to offer him more encouragement but felt helpless to do so. I shrugged and promised him I would do everything within my power to get him released as soon as possible. With that done, I stayed long enough to watch Weathersby shuffle away in manacles as he was being escorted back to solitary confinement.

CHAPTER 6

A torrential rain was falling later when I climbed out of a Yellow Cab in front of Wally's Tavern. The joint was relatively deserted when I stepped through the door two hours later than I'd promised. Old man Wally was sitting behind the bar, going through a battered ledger he used to keep track of business. He glanced up briefly and then dropped his eyes back to the book. For his age, he was a spry and wiry fellow who claimed to be seventy years old but looked more like he was going on eighty. The first thing I had noticed about him when we met years ago was his wizened old eyes that seemed to have seen it all, and his impatience was legendary.

"How's it going?" I asked, as I hung my raincoat on a hook behind the bar and rolled up my sleeves. "Slow, huh?"

"You can see that much yourself," he said, eyes still studying the ledger. "I was expecting you earlier."

"I got held up longer than I thought." I poured myself a cup of coffee, black, and added a double-shot of Courvoisier. "Did I get a lot of action on the numbers this morning?"

"Less than usual," he said, almost inaudibly. "Damn rain slows everything up. You'd think some of these old cusses think they're made of sugar."

"I wouldn't want to be the one to tell them differently."

"I'll tell you one thing," he said, dryly, "like I told Syd Barnes when he picked up your betting slips this morning. If I don't get a hit soon, you guys are going to lose your best customer. I been due too long playing seven different numbers every day."

"Hey," I shrugged, "we're all due."

"That's what you always say, six months running now," he said, as he closed the ledger.

"What else can I say, Wal?"

He stood and stretched his scrawny arms above his head, old bones creaking noisily.

"I'm going to get out of here and take care of some chores up at the house. If the old battleax calls before I get over there, tell her I'm on my way."

"Sure you don't want to stick around and keep me company for the fun of it?"

"Full of wit today, eh?" He frowned in my direction and paused as he rounded the bar. "Oh, by the way, that Lieutenant McKellerhan stopped by to pick up his action. He had a drink, and then left about fifteen minutes ago, looking real angry."

"He always looks that way to me. Did you tell him I had some important business to take care of?"

"Ain't my job to go explaining nothing to that man. I just told him to come back later."

"Thanks a bunch," I muttered to myself.

After Wally left, I replenished the few remaining regulars with a drink on the house. Having established the feeling of goodwill, I went to the cigar box where I kept my betting slips.

Deciphering Wally's tiny and cryptic handwriting, I learned who had bet what and for how much. I smiled as I noticed that Wally had doubled the amount of cash on his picks for the day, boxing most of his numbers to give himself a better chance of winning. I could also see that, like me, he was keeping faith in 248, which had come close to hitting a week back. I guess Wally remembered the time he'd missed hitting his favorite 721 by one digit and had backed off only to have the number pop up like a smiling jack-in-the-box the very next day.

～

About four o'clock, the rain let up and only a light drizzle fell. Soon the place began to fill with the usual weekday crowd.

I found myself busy pouring drinks and playing the crowd as the congenial trouble-free man behind the bar. Gertie, a daily fixture at Wally's, was pestering everyone for nickels to drop in the jukebox to play "Topsy Part II" as though she were getting paid a commission for each time it spun.

Just as I was feeling removed from my own concerns with less than two hours left to work, the music stopped as Lt. Lyle McKellerhan's huge frame darkened the doorway. He was wearing a wide-brimmed hat and was draped in an olive-green rain slicker. While I was busy serving a couple of orders, he walked to the far end of the bar and perched on a stool that seemed to be perpetually vacant whenever he showed up. I finished listening to a joke I'd heard more than once and acknowledged his presence.

He was a bear of a man with a beefy-red face and bushy, gray eyebrows, deep-set, steely-blue eyes, a thickly veined bulbous nose and thin lips which were unaccustomed to smiling. Conversely, I gave him a carefree smile, as I leaned on the bar top across from him, playing on the familiarity of knowing him when I was still on the force before he made his present grade.

"Sorry you missed me earlier."

"Mishaps like that can create problems," he said, woodenly.

"Believe me, it wasn't a planned thing."

"Planned or not, I have better things to do than come back and forth to this lousy dump. I mean, that's certainly not what I get paid to do," he said, with a curled lip. "Get me?"

"Certainly," I replied, with just enough insolence in my voice to convince myself I wasn't brown-nosing up to him.

I left him and reached into the pocket of my raincoat to retrieve the envelope containing his weekly payoff and slapped it down in front of him.

"There we go."

Unceremoniously, he ripped the envelope open. Impervious to whoever might be watching, he wet a thumb and counted the bills. Content with his count, he folded the bills neatly, unsnapped his slicker, stuffed his take into the breast pocket of his shirt and pushed the used envelope aside like so much trash.

"You're in a grim mood today," I commented.

"Look, Nate, like I already pointed out, I don't like having my time wasted."

"Got time for the usual?" I gave him a subdued smile.

"Why not?" He snapped his slicker shut. "You know my taste."

I set two coasters down and poured him a double shot of rye and broke the cap on a bottle of his favorite beer, Pabst Blue Ribbon. He chugged the liquor and chased it down with a mouthful of cold brew.

"I'd strongly suggest you do one thing for me, though," he said, in an ominous tone. "If you see fit, that is."

"What's that?"

"Tell that old coot you work for that it would be wise for him to stop copping a 'tude whenever our paths cross."

"Aha," I said, suppressing a grin. "So it's old Wally who's got you so uptight?"

"I'm not used to taking rude lip from nobody."

"Rude?"

"It's just his attitude that might need adjusting."

"Hey, Mac, he's just an old man trying to run a business and struggling to make ends meet. I'm just glad he puts up with me and lets me run my operation out of his joint."

"You see, Nate," he sneered, "that's just the point I'm trying to make."

"What point?"

"Screw the old bastard!" McKellerhan growled. "With one phone call to my brother-in-law, I could have the Board of Health come up with a slew of reasons to close this dump down." He snapped a finger against the broad palm of his hand.

I opened my mouth to challenge him but thought twice and bit my tongue.

"You think this petty cash," he patted the breast pocket where he'd stuffed his take, "means diddlysquat to me? If you do, you're dead wrong."

"I'll talk to him." I sighed. "Tell me, though, Lyle, is there anything else on your mind?"

"Why do you ask?"

"Because I just can't see you letting a stubborn old codger like Wally get your goat."

"As a matter of fact," he said, as his eyes hardened, "since you brought it up, there is another bone I have to pick with you."

I surveyed the bar to find a few of my customers restive and anxious for service.

"Let me fill the trough. I'll be back in a jiffy."

"Good." He glanced at his wristwatch and said, "I've got a little more time to kill."

Soon I was back in front of him.

"So what else is on your mind?"

"I had an interesting chat with Sam Brisco the other day and your name came up."

"How so?"

"Seems as though he suspects you of sticking your nose where it don't belong."

"Yeah. I believe he indicated as much to me when he gave me a lift last Saturday."

"And...you were straight with him?"

"Not entirely." McKellerhan showed no reaction and waited for me to continue. "Something about him ticked me off. At the time, though, I was unaware that Freddie Tucker had bit the dust."

"So exactly what was your involvement with that two-bit punk anyhow?"

"As you probably already know, the kid you guys booked for his murder is from Philadelphia, like me. His father is a friend of a friend. Knowing I live up here, he asked me to quietly keep an eye on Joe to make sure he didn't fall in with the wrong crowd. So when I heard about the altercation he had with Tucker, I decided to have a talk with the thug to see if I could smooth things over."

"Did you manage to have that talk?" McKellerhan asked, as one of his bushy gray eyebrows arched.

"I tried to track him down Friday night but didn't have any luck." I shrugged in the face of his impassive gaze. "Scout's honor."

"I'd like to believe you," he finally said, after weighing my words. "You could have made things a lot simpler if you had been up front with Sam from jump-street."

"Next time I see him, I'll apologize. Because I certainly wasn't looking to break any laws when I went after Freddie. In fact, my only aim was to prevent any more trouble from going down."

"Well," he cackled, "looks like you failed to be the Good Samaritan."

"Maybe so, but I don't think the kid's guilty."

"Far as I'm concerned, the case is closed. From here on it's up to a judge and jury to decide his fate."

"I'm just wondering if you guys didn't wash your hands of the matter too soon."

"To tell you the truth, from the very beginning all I saw was another no-good junkie dead. But it's still a matter of principle. With all those cowboy shoot-um-ups showing on television every night of the week, I think too many people in this precinct have made the mistake of thinking these streets up here are the Wild West revisited." He knitted his brows and squinted his cold, blue eyes. "Part of my job, however, is to destroy that myth anyway I can."

I nodded, unable to think of anything else to say.

"Okay, Nate," he said stiffly, as he rose from the stool. "I'll buy your friend of a friend of the family line for the time being."

"Well, I am being straight with you, Lyle."

He adjusted his wide-brimmed hat in the mirror behind me and gave me a farewell nod, before saying, "See you next week, I hope, at the usual time."

~

It was close to ten o'clock that night when Lillian and I took a break from painting the new flat. Using paint thinner and a bar of Lava soap, we scrubbed our hands clean just as the Chinese food we'd ordered arrived. We sat picnic style on the floor of the empty living room, using paper plates and admiring our work.

"Almost done," Lillian made the assessment, as she served me a generous helping from the take-out cartons. "Damn if this place isn't starting to look even better than I thought it would."

"Yeah," I agreed. "One more night should get it for the rest of the trim. Then I'll get started on the tiles."

We ate silently for a while, and then Lillian cocked her head slightly and stared at me with a troubled expression distorting her face.

"What's bugging you, Nate?"

"Huh?"

"You heard me. You've had your forehead screwed up for half the night. So would you mind telling me what's up?"

I considered evading her question but answered honestly.

"It's the Joe Weathersby thing."

"I had a feeling that's what it was. I can imagine how you feel, but you did the best you could for him, honey."

"I guess it's more than just him." I sat my paper plate down, having lost my appetite. "It's the whole drug scene that's gotten under my skin. I've seen too many people's lives turned upside down behind that shit. Too many of them innocent of nothing more than knowing a junkie or being related to one. Men forsaking their families, kids stealing from their parents and brothers against brothers. It's plain madness and seems like it's getting worse each day."

"No doubt about it," she said, with a sigh. "It's getting so people don't even feel safe in their own homes with all the burglaries and break-ins happening. Everywhere I go, I see people I thought I once knew, nodding and sleeping in the doorways, wearing the same old raggedy clothes day in and day out. And they line up all day long in front of those pawnshops that are taking over the neighborhood. I make sure I hold tight to my purse whenever I'm out by myself. It's a doggoned crying shame how bad things have gotten."

"Ain't that the truth?"

"There's something else that upsets me even more. I see more and more young girls out there, some of them still in their early teens, peddling their asses with no sense of shame. One look at them and you can tell all they have on their minds is getting a few dollars for another fix. For all I know, I've got girls in my classes today who could be out there tomorrow doing the same."

She put her plate down beside mine with her observations producing another long silence.

"A few years ago," I finally said, "when I was still on the force, we were lucky to make ten to twelve drug busts a week. According to what I hear now, the count is ten times that. It's like some kind of modern day epidemic."

"You'd think the city would be able to do something about it. I mean, what do we pay taxes for?"

"That's the real pity of it all. If the powers that be weren't profiting in some way, believe me, Lil, we wouldn't have this problem. For the most part it's only the guys on the bottom rung getting popped. They get put on probation or they do a little time and they're right back on the street like nothing happened. But you have to remember, dear, the small time dealers and the poor souls they sell that shit to are just pawns in the game. The big shipments that come into the country and trickle down to the colored neighborhoods wouldn't get through if big money wasn't changing hands at every turn along the way."

A siren grew out of the distance, wailed by and the sound began to slowly fade.

"Although I hate to admit it, you're probably right," Lillian said, with a sad far-off look in her eyes. "It's still a damn shame that's the way it is."

"I know this sounds crazy," I said in a level, carefully measured voice, "but sometimes I wish there was something I could do about it."

"Now you're absolutely right," she said, brusquely. "You are talking out of your mind."

"I know."

"You stuck your neck out enough just by promising to talk to a creep like that Freddie Tucker character." She shivered. "Jeeze! I'd say you were lucky the way things turned out."

Nodding silent assent, I wondered what she'd think if she knew I'd tracked Freddie down. What if she knew how he looked and smelled when I found him dead in his flat with a .45 slug in his head? But those were memories I was determined to keep to myself.

"Earth to Nate." Lillian shook me by a shoulder gently, wearing another inquisitive expression. "Now where's your mind gone off to this time?"

I took a deep breath as a faraway thought hit me.

"I was just thinking about a down-home saying my grandfather once told me."

"Which was?"

"He said it takes a long time to grow hay from seed. More time for a horse or a cow to digest that hay, but you can spread their manure in no time flat."

CHAPTER 7

About noon, on the last day of April, Horace Yancy came into the joint, looking especially dejected. Horace had been the plumber for Wally's Tavern long before I started working there. He wore his workman's garb: dark-blue coveralls and large, scuffed, black boots. As usual, his shoulders were sloped like a man who carried too much baggage. He had a long, basset hound face that always seemed etched with worry. Even on the occasions I'd seen him and his wife out on the town, dressed to kill, he wore a sour look on his face as though the blues were a lifelong experience impossible for him to shake.

I poured him a draft as soon as he slid onto a stool at the far end of the bar.

"How's tricks?" I sat the beer down on a coaster in front of him.

"I doubt it can get much worse," he mumbled in a voice that held onto a tinge of his North Carolina roots.

"Working hard or hardly working?"

"Work ain't got nothin' to do with it." He clutched the beer glass with a huge, dark hand before taking a healthy slug.

"Want to talk about it?"

"Matter-of-fact," he glued me with his rheumy old eyes, "that's why I'm here."

"Go for it. A lot of people consider me a good listener."

"'Member my son, Rudy?"

"Sure. He used to come in here all the time when he was working with you. How's he doing?"

"He ain't doing nothin' now, Nate. He's dead."

The bluntness of his statement stunned me.

"I'm real sorry to hear that, Horace. He was such a vibrant, fun-loving guy."

"Wouldn't been but twenty-three years old coming up soon."

I took a deep breath, and then asked, "How'd he die?"

"He was killed." Horace lowered his eyes. "That's how."

"Well, I'll be damned. How'd it happen?"

"I only know what some detective told me."

"What detective?"

"He's a member of the club. Got a shaved head and ugly lips."

"Detective Brisco?"

"That would be him." He sipped on his brew again.

"He's a tough cop, but he's a straight shooter. So what did he tell you?"

"It was that dope that killed Rudy."

"Heroin?"

"Uh-huh." He shook his angular head up and down. "I knew Rudy was doing the stuff. That's why I fired him awhile back. Thought that might make him wake up and get himself cleaned up."

"Too bad."

"For a short time, he seemed to be doing okay. But I saw him a few weeks back. One look told me he was back on that junk."

Someone at the other end of the bar signaled for service. I excused myself from Horace, refilled a few more drinks, and gave someone a pickled pig foot. Soon I was urging the bereaved father to continue.

"What makes you think it was murder?"

"According to the cops, there's been a turf war going on around 116th Street, a war that involves some junk that'll kill you."

I knew something about that. Since Freddie Tucker had gotten blown away, a power vacuum had come into existence. Brownie had also told me about the new plague that was killing off junkies, now that the phantom shooter had stopped filling them with hot lead from a .32.

"Anyway," Horace went on, "one of the gangs made sure some bad dope got mixed up in the other dealers' supply. It was pure poison, too, man. Rudy was just one of the poor suckers who got his hands on the stuff."

"Sounds like murder, all right."

"That's why I came to see you, Nate. I'm hoping you can help me out."

"Exactly what do you expect from me, though, Horace?"

"I just want to know the low-life punks responsible. That's all."

"And...then what?"

"Look, Nate, I'm a war vet, like you. I fought the Germans and they'd never done a damn thing to me personally. So I think I'd know exactly what to do to some low-down dope fiends who could pull a dirty trick like the one that killed my boy."

"We're talking real serious business here, partner." I glanced down the bar to make sure our conversation was still a private one. "The kind of business that could get a man killed quick."

"I know that," he said, staring straight into my eyes.

"Besides, if the cops were able to tell you as much as they did, maybe you should let them wrap this up in their own time."

"Who you trying to josh, Nate?" His face turned even sterner. "You can call all of those coppers straight shooters all you want. But you know as well as I do that if they weren't getting kickbacks, none of this crazy shit would be going down in the first place."

I couldn't argue with his logic, especially since it was the same brand I'd suggested to Lillian.

"Pick up a newspaper," he continued, "and you can't find a word about any of this. No, Nate, I think you know the only justice most of us can count on is the justice we make for ourselves."

He was too close to right, again, so I remained silent.

"If I'm asking too much," he spoke clearly, while his eyes pleaded, "just tell me right out. I swear I won't waste no more of your time."

He polished off his beer.

"If I say no, then what will you do?" I asked.

"I'll find the son-of-a-bitches myself. You can count on that."

I got a picture of straight-laced Horace Yancy walking up to street dealers asking incriminating questions. I knew he wouldn't last long doing that. Another customer came and sat up front, looking anxiously toward me for his double shot of gin and tonic.

"Tell you what, Horace," I said, when I was back in front of him, "let me sleep on it. Tomorrow you stop by. Then I'll let you know if I'm your man."

"I'll show up around the same time." He slid off the stool. "All those bastards have got to learn there are consequences for their actions."

~

When my shift ended, I returned a few overdue books to the library that I had been too busy to crack open, let alone read. Then I picked up some dry cleaning, and dropped by to see one of my bedridden numbers customers to pay him a hundred dollars he'd won on a quarter bet. My percentage of the win, and the tip he gave me, reminded me of why I'd gotten into the racket to begin with. It had been awhile since any of my customers or I had seen any luck.

The sun had long since set by the time I got home to the new flat. Thanks to bank loans that both Lillian and I had gotten, modernistic paintings, colorful African prints and two ceremonial masks hung on the walls. Our many shelves in the living room were lined with a large collection of our hardbound books. My record collection of jazz, blues, boogie-woogie, doo-wop, and Latin jazz lined a corner wall. Three sculptures were appropriately placed. And at the hall leading to bedrooms, a black panther of life size proportions stretched itself with its paws reaching up high on the wall.

The aroma of Lillian's cooking greeted me the moment I stepped through the door. I removed my shoes and crossed our honey-colored Berber carpet and headed for the kitchen.

"What smells so doggone good, baby?" I smiled at the striking image she made clad in a black leotard, as she stirred the contents of a saucepan.

"We're having Nate's special marinated lamb chops and Lillian's lasagna with fresh garlic bread and a tossed salad. All made with love." She smiled back at me and wiggled her generous hips. "By the look on your face, I know I don't have to ask if you're hungry."

"You've got that right."

During our candlelit meal in the dining room, Lillian reminded me that she would be busy working every evening for the next few weeks. She had recently replaced another choreographer for an off-Broadway production, which was due to open in less than two weeks. The play was a musical extravaganza depicting the Harlem Renaissance. Much as I wanted to go to one of the rehearsals, she insisted that I wait until opening night so that I could fully appreciate what she, the producers, the director, the actors, musicians and the dancers were trying to convey.

"I'll be back about eleven o'clock," she said, in a promising way. "I may be all keyed up with a lot of energy left to burn. Think you'll still be awake then, Mr. Holt, or taking one of your long walks you say you need for exercise and to clear your head?"

"Want to wager on how I'll be or where I'll be when you get back?" I tore into a chunk of garlic-buttered bread and stuffed it into my mouth.

"No," she laughed, "not since you put it that way."

"Good!"

"Seems you like my lasagna."

"With a name like Lillian's lasagna, I loved it even before I tasted it the first time."

Shortly after Lillian left the pad, I sat down to my portable typewriter to polish off a jazz review I was writing for *The Uptown Beat*. It was already two days past deadline, so I could only hope it would be accepted for the following edition. As I applied my hunt and peck typing technique, it soon became apparent that my concentration was too far off the mark to get any real work done. I found myself constantly thinking back to my conversation with Horace Yancy.

Now that we were living together, it was harder to keep my personal preoccupations from Lillian. The Horace Yancy dilemma was one such problem I didn't want clouding her thoughts. Yet there seemed no escape from thinking about the conversation I had with him earlier that day. Everything about Horace's present problem tied in with Joe Weathersby's predicament. After Lucas Haynes requested a postponement, the young man's trial was due to start in eight weeks.

No matter how I looked at it, though, it was as clear as one plus one adding up to be two. If I backed off and let Horace go it alone, it would be like signing his death warrant. On the other hand, if I discovered the identity of the dealer or dealers responsible for killing his son, he'd no doubt go hunting for them. Either way, before the dust settled I knew someone was going to end up dead no matter what I did. I racked my brain for another solution. I realized that my friends on the force could do little to protect Horace from taking a route that would lead straight to his grave. Only I held the ticket to his survival.

Most of all, one thing he said kept haunting me, "All those bastards have to learn there are consequences for their actions." Still, I realized that consequences cut both ways.

Already Detective Brisco and Lieutenant McKellerhan were questioning my connection to Weathersby. The last thing I needed was more cause for them to hound me. But, the more I reasoned the more I saw there was only one decision I could make. I had to give Horace a reasonable chance of coming out of the whole mess alive.

After listening to Bird's "Ornithology I" for the second time, a restless urge to scout the drug market turf overtook me. To do that, I decided to dress down for the occasion. I put on an old pair of dungarees, a torn sweatshirt and stuck my feet into a pair of rundown sneakers. Then I slipped into a flight jacket with frayed sleeves, which I'd picked up years ago from a Salvation Army outlet for just such occasions. Lastly, I donned a big, wide apple jeff, which had splattered paint stains on it that matched the living room walls.

I pulled the brim of the hat down as low as possible, as I stepped from the vestibule into the street. I passed elderly Mrs. Gilmore carrying a bag of groceries inside. Even though I held the door open for her, she didn't seem to recognize me or she would have said more than, "God bless you, son."

It was a brisk night, yet the wind was still. I walked, taking quick, long strides with my hands thrust deep in the pockets of my dungarees. With my shoulders hunched, and head bent toward the cracks in the pavement along Amsterdam Avenue, I tried to be as anonymous as possible to all the folks I passed along the way.

A skinny hooker approached me as I walked east on 126th Street and was about to turn right on Lennox. One mean glance in her direction, gritting my teeth, was all it took for her to stop in her tracks.

"Go ahead," she said to my back. "I never needed you!"

When I reached a foreboding dark stretch of 116th Street, known as Heroin Alley, I noticed that most of the streetlights were burned or shot out. Immediately, I spied a loose cluster of ghostly figures stationed along the block hawking their wares. As I passed among them they called out to me, advertising their goods.

"Whacha need, brother? I got five spots of the best."

"Want the boss duji? Three to five bucks."

I ignored their advances and kept my pace lively while furtively observing the dealers.

Farther down the block, I saw a tall guy wearing a long, olive-drab leather coat with a fur collar turned up. He stood in the doorway of a burnt-out tenement building with his arms folded across his chest. The second his eyes appeared to focus on me, he stood more erect. Then he spat over the side of the stoop railing in my direction. One of the three cronies who stood at the foot of the steps, a skinny guy wearing a blue car coat with the hood up, approached me.

"I got whatever you need, boss." He rapped two teaspoons together like castanets. "Duji, coke, reefer. You name it, daddy-o."

I slowed to a stop, still aware of the tall guy in the doorway eyeing me.

"How much for the duji?"

"Five dollars a pop," he said, in a high-pitched, irritating voice.

I dug into a pocket for a five while the skinny dude looked proudly toward the guy in the doorway. He handed me a tiny plastic bag and I gave up the five and pocketed my score.

"Suppose I want more?"

"No problem, ace. Like, I'm easy to find. Here all the time."

"I mean more," I whispered, "like weight."

"What you talking? Three, four, five bags, maybe?"

"No," I snickered. "I need more like two hundred dollars worth."

"Wow, daddy-o. Like, that's a lot of action, my man." He clicked his spoons less vigorously.

"Fine," I said, as I turned to walk away. "*Like,* I guess I'm talking to the wrong man, *like.*"

Skinny skipped after me. I could almost feel the eyes of the dude in the burnt-out doorway follow us.

"Hold on, daddy-o," Skinny entreated, as he caught up and fell in stride with me. "Don't be in such a hurry, like. I got major pull to cop whatever you need. But you gotta understand I don't walk the street with all my stash jammed in my pockets, you know? I don't have no license, like, from the city to sell this shit, you know? But trust me, like, cap. You picked the right man to get whatever it is you want and more."

"Who the hell are you trying to bullshit, me or you?" I smirked. "You're obviously not the man I need to see."

"I swear I'm more connected than I might look. I can score large or small quantities. Just let me know what you need."

"I already told you that." I stopped walking and pinned him with a hard glare. "Tomorrow I'll be back with two hundred bucks, cold, hard cash. I've got some dudes coming to town. So if this bag I just copped ain't the real deal, *like*, you just lost some big-time business."

"You'll dig what I gave you for sure," he said enthusiastically. "That I ain't worried about, like. I always got nothing but the best smack around."

"Then I'll see you tomorrow." I grinned. "If that goes well, you and I may get to become lasting friends."

I gave him a firm pat on the shoulder and retraced my steps along 116th. Fast stepping again, I turned the corner on Lennox Avenue and tossed the white poison into the first sewer mouth I passed.

CHAPTER 8

The next morning I was behind the bar for less than an hour when Horace Yancy walked through the door. I served him a tap beer.

"On the house," I said.

"What did you decide?" he asked, ignoring the beer.

"After thinking through everything you told me, I decided to follow my heart." I paused while trying to find the right words. "Not long ago I made a vow to do everything I could to stop the flow of drugs into the neighborhood. Although I'm not sure anything I do will have a lasting effect, still, I've got to side with you."

"God, I'm so glad to hear that. I been praying all night." Horace was visibly relieved, as he took a long swallow of beer. "So tell me what it's going cost me. I'll be glad to pay you whatever you say."

"It's only going to cost whatever my out of pocket expenses are. Not a penny more."

"I can't let you risk—"

"You have no choice, Horace," I said adamantly. "Much as I could use the dough, I'm not helping you for the cash. And that's the end of the discussion."

"If you say so, I guess I can't change your mind." With a sigh he sat erect. "What's your first step going to be?"

"I already took it."

"Say what?" His left eyebrow rose.

I filled him in on the reconnaissance run I'd made the previous night.

"What'd he look like?" Horace inquired. "The guy in the doorway."

"I didn't really get a good look at him because he stayed in the shadows. I think I'd recognize him again, though. He's about my height, six two, maybe, two hundred pounds, full-length leather coat. Holds himself real cocky-like."

"You think he might be one of the cats I'm after?"

"I'll know more tonight. That's where your money comes in. Two hundred dollars is what I'll need to carry on me."

I explained the setup.

"No problem," Horace said. "I'll bring the dough with me tonight and we can go together."

"Whoa! Who said anything about you going along?"

"Since you're doing all this for me at no charge, I've got to back your play." He spoke with devout conviction written all over his long and bony face. "Those are my conditions."

"Okay," I acquiesced. "But you follow my lead and let me do all the talking. We can't be certain we're dealing with the right people yet. Read me?"

"You can count on me, Nate." Horace nodded his head. "Just tell me where and what time."

"Pick me up at nine-thirty on the northeast corner of 136th and Amsterdam."

"I'll be there," he said. "But there's one thing you ought to know."

"What's that?"

"I will be packing hardware."

"So will I," I said. "So will I."

~

My wristwatch read nine-thirty exactly when I slid into Horace's new, dark-green Mercury Montclair. He was dressed as though he pictured himself to be some kind of movie gangster, wearing a camel hair overcoat, a double-breasted brown serge suit, a wide tan and black tie, and a black Chicago cut

Stetson. I wore an outfit similar to the one I'd worn the previous night. We talked over a radio broadcast of a Knickerbockers game. The Celtics rookie center, Bill Russell, was dominating the boards, and Boston was up by six points.

"Where to?" he asked.

"Let's come in from the opposite direction they'd expect."

"Point the way," he said, as he pulled away from a stoplight and switched the radio off with time running out and the Knicks behind by eight.

"What kind of gear you packing?" he asked.

I patted the piece, which was snug in its shoulder holster and replied, "A thirty-eight special."

He reached somewhere within the depths of his overcoat and withdrew a gat that looked like a .45 with an eight-inch barrel.

"Damn," I said, taking a gander at the huge revolver. "Where the hell did you get that dinosaur?"

"It's a Colt I hang on a rawhide strap that I wear over my shoulder. Made a big hole in my pocket so I can get to it fast." He smiled as he fondled the piece. "It's called a Peacemaker."

"I see." I scratched my head dubiously. "Let me remind you again, Yancy—"

"I know. I know. I follow your lead."

We parked a block-and-a-half away from our destination and began footing it. My mouth felt as though I'd swallowed a whole bottle of bleach, and my stomach churned like a washing machine. The sensations were familiar to me, but I hadn't experienced them in a long time. With each step, my heart seemed to beat faster and my temples throbbed loud enough to almost make me believe I could hear the pulsing above our marching footsteps and the steady drone of traffic on the streets.

When we stepped onto the notorious dark block, I immediately spied our quarry congregated around the same burnt-out building. They were all concentrating their attention away from us. We were about twelve feet from them when the tall cat in the doorway, smoking a huge reefer, noticed our approach.

"There he is!" he alerted his boys, pointing at us.

The skinny guy and two others turned, shock written on their faces. They were still dumbfounded as I spoke congenially.

"Hey, Skinny. Got the goods or what?"

Before he could reply, the guy in the leather coat made his way down from the stoop and joined the circle. He was about twenty-five hard years old with sharp West Indian-like features and smooth caramel colored skin.

"Like, you the cat looking to make a big score?" he addressed me with a slight Jamaican accent.

"One and the same."

"Solid. Like, my name is Johnny G. Dig it, slick?" he spoke arrogantly. "What's yours?"

"Just call me Cash."

"And your spordiotee friend?" he asked, pointing the acrid smelling joint toward Horace.

"He doesn't have a name."

"No name, huh?" Johnny G cackled and ran the narrow slits of his eyes across the two of us. "So what's the deal? You want to talk business or what?"

"That's what I'm here for. You got the stuff?"

"I sure do."

"Let's see it then."

"No problem," he said, as he stuck the reefer in a corner of his mouth and reached his left hand beneath his coat. "Now where'd I put that bag?"

In a flash, a silver plated .22 jumped forward clutched in his hand. In an instant, he had it pressed against my right temple. His three flunkies appeared as shocked as I was.

"Do some talking fast, like," Johnny spat the words out. "C'mon, Cash. Whacha got to say for yourself?"

"Not so fast!" Horace said menacingly.

Johnny G kept the gun to my head, as his eyes wandered to the suspicious bulge in Horace's coat. Slowly, Horace exposed the cannon in his hand. It was aimed directly at Johnny G's heart.

"Looks like a stalemate," I said. "But all we came to do was make a purchase and talk about the future, Johnny."

"Like, what kind of future?" he asked, as though talking casually with a gun pointed at him was something he did all the time. "C'mon, Cash, man." He pressed the rod deeper into the side of my head growling around the joint in his mouth. "Cat got your tongue or what?"

I tried to clear a dry lump from my throat and licked my parched lips.

"I'm only looking for the right connect. I want to move the score south. I'm talking Philly, B-More and D.C. If things go well, our plans are to branch westward."

"How come I never seen you around before now, Mr. Cash? Like, suddenly you come from out of nowhere on my turf, Jack!"

"This is a new venture for me."

Johnny thought my story over for a few beats while ignoring whatever play Horace might make. Then, without another word, he took the gat from my head and stuck it away. Together, Johnny G and I turned our attention to the big Colt .45. Its aim remained true to Johnny's heart.

"Mess with us," Horace snarled, "and I'll turn this whole block into the O.K. Corral faster than you can say Jack Johnson."

"That won't be necessary," I said, soothingly. "I think we all have a better understanding now."

"In this business," Johnny directed himself to Horace with a cocky grin and his chin raised, "you can't be too careful. Solid?"

"You ever draw down on us again, Johnny, I'll pump you full of holes sure as shit stinks." Slowly, Horace's cannon disappeared beneath his overcoat.

Johnny nodded toward Skinny.

"Give it up," he said.

Skinny handed me a plastic bag of dope. I opened it, stuck a finger inside and tasted the bitter contents like I knew what I was doing.

"It's even better than what you got the other night, chief," Skinny said with pride.

"Just checking." I resealed the bag and stuck it in my leather jacket.

"I told you I don't be bullshitting. Didn't—"

"Shut up, Brad!" Johnny barked at Skinny. "I'll handle things from here."

He relit the joint with a lighter and offered me a drag.

"No," I said. "I'm in this strictly for the profit."

"So a steady connect is what you're looking for?"

"That's right. In fact, I'll be needing a lot more from you by Friday."

"Ain't nothing to it, Cash. Brad and all these dudes work for me. See? I got the handle on whatever you want. Like, you need a truckload, you talk straight to me from now on."

"Let's talk five hundred bucks worth. What kind of action would that get me?"

"For five yards," Johnny stroked his narrow chin, "I'll make you a real sweet deal, sport. I'll give you three times what you're holding now." He smiled. "And...like you already know, it won't be all stepped on like you might find if you were dealing with anybody but me."

"Yeah," I lied. "I noticed the stuff tonight was better than that shit I got yesterday."

"That's just the way it goes." Johnny shrugged. "Now that you're dealing directly with me your troubles are over."

"Would this Friday be too soon for you?"

"No time's too soon for me."

"Good."

"Next time, though," Johnny added, "we'll meet at midnight. Like, let's say, in Morningside Park. There's less traffic to worry about doing such a big transaction. Dig?"

"Where in the park?"

"Let's make it near the corner of 123rd."

"I guess that wraps things up for now. So...we'll see you then."

"That's cool, Cash. But just the two of ya'll is all we expect to show up or you won't want to be nowhere near there."

"Whatever you say, Johnny. You're the boss."

Horace and I backed away several paces and then hoofed back to his car. Neither one us spoke a word the whole time.

~

I soaped and scrubbed a thick coat of fear off my body with a long shower. That done, I poured a snifter of Courvoisier and stretched out on the living room couch to the sounds of "Charlie Parker with Strings." I drank myself into a semi-stupor and was drifting off to sleep when I heard a key trip one of the front door locks. I tensed, my mind somewhat disoriented, glanced around the room and found the wall clock lit by ambient light. It read ten minutes after twelve.

One of Lillian's legs broke the plane of the doorway, as I feigned sleep. Through squinted eyes, I watched her hang her jacket on the coat tree before she turned to me.

"Nate," she said. "You still awake?"

I lifted my head slightly. "Huh?"

"It's just me, baby." She crossed the room, sat beside me and planted a light kiss on my forehead. "I thought you were going to wait up for me again."

"What time is it?" I asked, drowsily.

"About midnight. I had to stay a little later." She stretched out on the couch beside me and placed one of her dancer's legs across my thighs. "You wouldn't believe how behind schedule we are. Given twice the time we have to get ready, I'm not sure I can whip this group into shape in time for the opening."

"You'll do it," I mumbled.

"Will I?" She reached inside my shirt, stroked my chest and pressed her body closer. "You certainly have a lot of confidence in me."

"That's 'cause you're so deserving."

"Why do you say that?" she cooed into my ear.

"Because we're so much alike."

"How's that?"

"You know how we are." I yawned. "I've told you a hundred times before."

"I know," she said, running her nails down the center of my chest while nibbling at one of my earlobes. "But you know how much I like to hear sweet talk come out of your mouth."

I sighed, and then said, "We're both intelligent, strong-willed, passionate people."

"You've got that right." She took her hand out of my shirt and ran her fingertips across my lips. "So what have you been up to all night?"

"Nothing much. Mostly resting."

"None of your long walks, eh?"

"Not tonight. Just lying up here alone with my thoughts."

"That's kind of what I've been thinking about all the way home." She drew herself closer, pressing her pelvic bone to my hipbone. "You up here all by yourself and me working on the play. Seems like we never have time to spend together since we moved in. Makes me want to take advantage of what little time we do have together. Know what I mean, honey?"

All at once the dynamic nature of our intimacy hit me. Seldom did she want to call it quits until she'd had at least six orgasms. She said that was due to my mastery of lovemaking, and I had reason to believe her. Initially, it had taken three heated sessions to push her over the top. Since then, more than once, I'd begun to wonder if I'd created an insatiable monster.

Suddenly, her clawing at me felt overbearing. Perhaps it was the tension I'd been experiencing since becoming involved with Blinky and Horace, and meeting with the dealers earlier.

"Well, we're here now." I eased her legs aside, as I sat up and stretched my arms above my head. "Why don't you make some coffee? After all, I was sleeping when you walked in."

"I didn't mean...just like that!" she snapped, and sat up beside me. "You don't have to wake up just to please me, you know. If that's what you're thinking, you can go right on back to sleep and never wake up as far as I'm concerned."

"Now I'm confused." I stood up scratching my goatee as I stared at her. "I'll get the coffee myself."

She followed me into the kitchen and leaned against the doorframe.

"I was going to ask if you would mind having an open house party next weekend. But catching you in such a grumpy mood, I'm not sure that's such a good idea. Maybe we should wait for a better time."

"Look, Lillian, you come prancing in here all jazzed up, and that's all fine and dandy. All I'm asking is a little time to get with it." I ran tap water into a small pot for instant coffee. "You want some?"

She hesitated, momentarily, frozen in the doorway.

"Yeah. Fix me a cup, too."

I pulled two cups from the cupboard, set them on the kitchen table and looked at her. She was smiling coyly, running a hand through her hair.

"I'm going to take a quick shower and slip into something less dignified," she said. "So get the water hot."

CHAPTER 9

The next day right after Syd Barnes, the numbers' banker's footman, picked up the betting slips, Brownie and his young plainclothes partner, Vince Parker, stopped by Wally's. They ordered a couple of Piels beers on tap to wash down the corned beef and pastrami sandwiches they'd picked up at their favorite delicatessen. Tempted as I was to direct the conversation toward the neighborhood drug scene, specifically on 116th Street, I restrained myself. I figured if Johnny G popped up dead in the near future they'd both remember our talk too well. Instead, the subject turned to politics and the recent ratification of the Civil Rights Act.

"Hallelujah! Can you believe that?" I said, wearing a big Stepin Fetchit smile. "One of these days comin' up soon, us colored folks can vote down South."

"Front page news, huh?" Brownie smirked with a bitter frown etched into his forehead. "The first civil rights legislation passed since the Reconstruction Era. But I say it's too little and way too late to celebrate."

"You have to figure we'll be better off with it passed, though," said tall and lean Vince. "The ballot could prove to be the biggest weapon for our people, ever."

"Say what?" Brownie exclaimed. "Are you drunk on a half glass of beer or just out of your rabbit-ass mind?"

"Well," Vince said, uncertainly, nodding his long, hatchet-shaped face up and down, "that's the way it appears to me."

"Weapon? You call giving our people in the South the long overdue right to vote a weapon?" Brownie stared at Vince as though he were contemplating having him committed to the mental ward at Bellevue. "You can't really believe that bullshit, do you, Parker?"

Vince sighed, knowing from experience that he wasn't going to get anywhere arguing with Brownie.

"No!" Brownie laughed derisively. "You can't really be dumb enough to buy into that liberal, double-talk bullshit you read in the papers or hear on television. You're just spouting that propaganda they brainwashed you with in those two years of college you took. Luckily you didn't stick around for the full course."

"Here we go again," Vince said.

"That's right. What I want to know is how can you still believe all that crap after working out here in the real world?" A staccato stream of laughter rumbled from his chest. "I mean, take Harlem for instance—"

"Take it where?" Vince tried for a laugh but failed.

"What happens if it snows tomorrow?" Brownie went on. "Tell me. Okay?"

"I have an idea, G. B.," Vince said. "But I suppose I'd be wrong again. So why don't you enlighten me, brother?"

"Before the last snowflake hits the ground, those city snow plows will have downtown open for business as usual. You can bet your black ass on that, too." He grunted. "Up here we'll still be sloshing through muck, hoping the weather will turn warm enough to melt the snow. So don't tell me about the power of the goddamn ballot and insult my intelligence by calling it a weapon. Especially when you know that too many of the men walking the streets we work ain't eligible to vote because they got bad rap sheets. Then there's all those brain-dead folks who're just too countrified and Jim Crowed to know they're entitled to vote. So if the vote don't half-ass work up here, what good do you expect the right to vote will ever do in the South? That's what I want to know."

The three of us, and everyone else in the bar within earshot, held a respectful moment of silence reflecting on Brownie's lengthy diatribe.

"We live in two separate societies." Following the prevailing silence, he went on, "One is where a missing white kid is almost enough to bring out the National Guard. Another is where you know what happens even if twelve colored kids go missing. Not a damn thing. That's what!"

"Guess you've got a point there, Garret." Vince said. "Looks like everybody's given up on Harlem."

"Everybody but the landlords, pawnshop and liquor store owners. I'll tell you where the real Harlem is, though, Vince. It's a state of mind." He wiped a glob of mustard from his graying mustache and tapped a forefinger to the side of his head. "Some of us have it. Most don't!"

"What do you think about all this, Nate?" Vince asked me.

"I have to go along with my buddy," I said, as I poured them two more beers. "As long as we have a president like Ike in office, Congress can pass all the bills they want but it won't mean jack-shit. For example, look at the Brown decision on school integration. That was passed when, three or four years ago? Still, today less than 10 percent of the schools in the South have been integrated and not a single one in the Deep South." I pounded my fist on the bar top. "Not a single one!"

"You're kidding." Vince looked at me in disbelief and turned to his partner. "Tell me he's joking, G. B."

The older detective ignored him and drank from his frothing glass.

"Laws aren't worth the paper they're printed on, if they're not enforced," I added. "The folks in the South still have to be registered. Talk about risky business, how many people will want to take on that responsibility?"

"You said a mouthful there," Brownie said. "Check it out. There's only one word our esteemed President Eisenhower's ever said on the race issue, and that's patience. But I think that Ike, and all his rich golf playing buddies, and the rest of America's going to wake up one dark morning and find out that us so-called Negroes are sick and tired of all the bullshit they've been force-feeding us for the last umpteen years. Most of all they're going to find out that we're sick and tired of being called Negroes and treated as second-class citizens."

He pounded a fist on the bar top twice as loud as I had.

"Teach, Brother Brown," a dapper, elderly man sitting nearby said.

"For goddamn sure," Brownie went on, "one fine day they're going to find out that we're fresh out of patience and dealing with our problems in a nonviolent way."

Brownie paused a beat before continuing in a subdued voice.

"Don't get me wrong. I respect Martin Luther King and all he stands for. But all he's done is wake some folks up to the inequities we face. But everybody can't buy into a turn-the-other-cheek philosophy. That goes against the grain of our day-to-day experiences and everything that America stands for. What was slavery but the worse form of violence against generations of Africans? Then look how they stole land from the Indians and broke one treaty with them after another whenever it suited their Manifest Destiny philosophy."

"Hear! Hear!" I said, pouring myself another shot of cognac before addressing Vince. "We've been turning the other cheek too long. Our people want results, not the same old-fashioned tingly feelings that come from singing gospels in church once a week. That's why you will see more and more thinking people turning to the Black Muslim faith and becoming more and more militant. Mark my words, Vince, that brother Malcolm X knows what he's talking about and who he's talking to, too."

"Times have changed, man," Brownie directed his words to Vince again. "And thank God someone knows that and how to put what's important in the right words that can reach people about subjects they would rather pretend don't exist."

Noticeably, Vince's face toughened into such a fierce mask of disappointment that I had to shift my glance across the room. You would have thought someone had just broken the news to him that there was no Easter Bunny and Santa Claus was dead.

"Don't take it personally, Vince." I gave him a consoling pat on the arm. "I learned a long time ago that reality can be a real bitch sometimes."

"But," Brownie interjected, "it's far better to deal with the ugly truth straight on than live with our heads buried in the sand."

"Amen to that!" the dapper man exclaimed.

~

I was sitting with my back to the pay phone reading *The Amsterdam News* when a junkie named Pudding shuffled through the front door. The last time I'd seen him was the night he'd knocked on Freddie Tucker's door, and I followed him down to the street to see him disappear into an alleyway.

He had been around the neighborhood as long as I could remember. By looks, I estimated him to be between thirty-five to forty years old. Rumor had it that he'd fought off the duji habit countless times but kept finding his way back to the needle. I never knew if he was using, trying to clean up, dealing or what. Nevertheless, I gave him the benefit of the doubt, reasoning that as long as he didn't cause any problems inside Wally's he was all right by me.

Making his way to the far end of the bar, he nodded to me with a respectful smile and went straight for the pay phone. He wore old, faded, assorted ill-fitting clothes that appeared fairly clean. But the scuffed brown shoes he wore were cut open at the front and his bare, crusty toes hung over the front end of the soles.

At first, I paid more attention to the article I was reading than Pudding. But soon I overheard a phrase or two, and the context of what he was saying hit me. From there on, I found myself totally captivated and straining to hear every last word.

"Hear me out, man. I be true blue, like. If Johnny G don't got it, nobody do." Whoever was on the other end of the line must have said something briefly before Pudding took over.

"No, baby. Like I been trying to tell you in plain English, you been off the scene too long to know what's going down. Freddie Tucker's history. So is Moses Grover. Both of them got knocked off sometime back. Today Johnny G's the man, because Wayne Wesley's out of business, too."

He paused and chuckled.

"On the lam, is what I hear. He couldn't take the pressure and packed it in."

Listening with the phone receiver pressed tight to his ear, Pudding paused again before responding in a mocking tone.

"How you think? Johnny G did them dirty. That's how!"

I missed some of what he said when I turned my attention to the racket Gertie and some old fart, wearing a mailman's uniform, were making. Cackling like a flock of geese, they stood up from the front booth and headed out the door, arm in arm.

"That's what I'm telling you, baby. You know the dude I'm talking about. Last name's Garrison. Johnny Garrison. But he calls himself Johnny G. We both know him from way back when, I'm telling you. The tall cat with the 'daylight come and me wanna go home' accent. He used to be one of Freddie Tucker's lieutenants."

Pudding paused again for a few beats. "Now you get the picture. He's the cat I'm talking about. And you want to know how he did it? Simple baby, he had one of his main boys pretend to go over to the other side. But it turned out—"

Just as I was about to fall off the stool, leaning closer to hear Pudding, one of my customers sitting nearby demanded a refill. I flashed him a hand signal for patience, but the old-timer wasn't to be put off so easily.

"That damn newspaper ain't going nowhere, Nate!" he bellowed and pounded his wine glass on the bar top, while looking in Pudding's direction. "Come and hit me up. Can't you see my empty is drying up and getting dusty from the dirty air you let in here?"

By the time I'd sweetened his glass with muscatel, Pudding had finished his conversation and was making a shuffling exit.

~

As I climbed into Horace's car later that night, low dark clouds from off the Atlantic swept fast across the night sky. It had been raining on and off for most of the evening. Occasional lightning pierced the sky and thunder rocked the world around us as we rode in silence. Earlier we had said all that needed to be said during a brief conversation on the phone. When he dropped me off two blocks from our rendezvous point, he gave me a little salute as he pulled back into traffic.

I turned my collar up against the wind and took a circuitous route to Morningside Park. Unlike the previous night, I wasn't feeling fear. That emotion had been replaced by a cold, calculating state of mind, bent on nothing but self-preservation and the sweet measure of the revenge Horace was yearning to get.

All revved up, I made my way to a spot at the northeast corner of the park. As soon as I got there, I spotted Horace approaching from the opposite direction. We were both dressed in black to blend with the shadows and met under a wide-leafed tree. From there we surveyed the lay of the land. Nearby was a streetlight that had burned out or been shot out. At the foot of it was a lopsided bench, and behind that was a line of unruly bushes. A walking path crossed from east to west and separated us from the unlit bench.

The sky grew darker and more ominous, as Horace cupped a cigarette and struck a match. He took a few puffs and passed it to me. Although I'd given up smoking after the war, I took a hit, inhaled deeply, then took another long drag. I could feel a burning sensation in my spine where the almost deadly slug used to be.

"I been thinking about Rudy a lot lately," Horace said, in a low voice, fighting the wind.

"So have I." I passed the cigarette back to him.

"He was a good kid until he started running the streets. But you, if anybody, know how it is up here. By the time he was twelve years old, he was already running with the wrong crowd.

Stealing hubcaps, snatching pocketbooks and who knows what other stuff he was up to that I never got wind of."

I nodded, knowing Horace needed to share his thoughts with someone willing to listen. So I did, close-lipped. After all, what could I say to a father grieving the death of his only son? Besides, no matter what I thought of Rudy, he was dead and there was nothing I could do to change that. I was there to help Horace.

"But why him?" He flicked the cigarette to the ground and crushed it out with a toe. "Most of his friends came from broken homes. Them I could see going out and getting into mischief. Too many of them didn't have no fathers putting bread on the table, clothes on their backs and giving them a good kick in the ass now and then when they needed it. And my wife, she couldn't have loved that boy no more than she did. But God knows why, from the day he turned fourteen, he was spending most of his time locked up in every youth detention house you can name."

"None of us are saints," I said, to fill an awkward silence. "I remember Rudy being a young man who was trying to find the right way. I guess he just slipped one time too many."

"I guess so." Horace shrugged and kicked the earth with the heel of a shoe.

Then our attention turned to a car, with one headlight out, when it slowed and cruised by at a crawl. It was an old, black '49 Ford Tudor with the timing off and a bad cough from a faulty carburetor. Apprehensively, we watched it chug by slowly and disappear from sight and then sound.

"You're right, Nate," Horace picked up the conversation. "He was trying to be responsible. Even started going to night school to get his high school diploma. Trying to get by, and I think he might've made something of himself if all that poison wasn't so easy to come by."

"It's a lousy shame, all right. That shit's my enemy and anyone who deals it."

"But," he spat, "as far as the police go, they don't give a rat's ass one way or another. To them it's just dope fiends killing dope fiends."

Then we heard the same Ford returning.

"Time to split up, Horace."

CHAPTER 10

As a misty rain began to fall, the old Ford, with one head-light and a faulty carburetor, cruised the park twice more, then stopped at the curb. Six figures filed out. Johnny G led the way. A faint glare off dark metal flashed from under his long, leather overcoat, a sawed-off shotgun, I suspected. They sauntered toward the broken bench, which was the general location we hoped they would choose. As soon as they reached the spot, Johnny G looked around suspiciously.

Meanwhile, I could vaguely distinguish Horace's dark form. He was moving closer to their position. The wind suddenly whipped up and tore at my eyes as bits of soot and debris came at me with an earful of their words.

"What now, G?" Skinny asked.

"I'll, like, put the shotgun right over here," he said, walking a few paces closer to me to prop the weapon against a tree on the same side where I was hiding. "Rock, Tee Boy, Terry and Primo, split up. So, like, all they see is me and Brad."

"I'll go this way," one of them pointed east. "C'mon, Tee Boy, you go with me."

"Right on, Rock." Johnny pointed toward the direction that ran by my position. "Terry and Primo, you two go that way. Everybody, keep your eyes open and give the signal the minute you spot 'em. They should be here in about twenty minutes."

"Sure 'nough!" one of them said.

"Yeah, like," Johnny G giggled, and said, "me and Brad'll be here acting real natural, like. Then when Mr. Slick-Ass-Cash and his no-name friend come to deliver our dough, we surprise 'em like they ain't never been surprised when we all do what I told y'all to do."

Walking fast, two of the scouts passed a few feet from where I was crouched behind a bush.

"Right!" Skinny said, as he aimed a small caliber pistol here and there. "Then Blam! Blam! Blam! I'll show that son-of-a-bitch Cash something he don't wanna know about some goddamn skinny."

"Yeah," Johnny said. "Like, I can't wait to see the look on their faces just before we blast 'em away."

One of the young thugs, going toward the hedge where I'd last seen Horace's shadow lurking, slowed his pace and paused. Cautiously, he stepped closer to the dark bushes, pulling something from his pocket. Suddenly, he jumped back a step and popped off two caps from a piece that sounded like a .22.

"G!" he yelled. "I think I got one of 'em."

I stayed in a crouch, creeping closer to them, glancing over my shoulder at the guys who had passed by me. They were a good sixty yards away but heading back fast. Then Horace's .45 erupted. The guy with the .22 flew back, propelled by the tremendous force of being hit.

Johnny G went for the shotgun. Skinny fired a round toward Horace's position. Before Johnny reached the tree, I stepped from the bushes and fired a shot above his head.

"Freeze!" I shouted.

He ducked low and began fast-footing it away as more gunshots to my right fractured the night.

I hurdled the bench, going after Johnny. Behind me, the .45 roared again and hot lead whizzed by my head. Lightning lit the sky as Johnny G hauled ass toward the Ford.

"Stop, Johnny!" I screamed above the thunder, lining him up in my sight as more rain began to fall.

He ran past the old Ford, spun and fired his silver pistol twice. I hit the ground, rolled and got to my feet as Horace's cannon went off again.

When I next got a bead on Johnny, he had a half block lead. His long, leather coat was trailing in his wake. I set out faster, trying to make up lost ground when he cut a corner without looking back.

In the distance, sirens assailed the night.

When I cut the same slippery corner, I caught a glimpse of Johnny just before he disappeared from view. Even before I reached the mouth of a dark alleyway, I heard his footsteps echoing off the walls. I ran after him as the sirens grew louder. With a quick furtive look over his shoulder, he tossed a garbage can aside to slow me down.

Then he crossed an avenue and ducked into a hallway. A speeding car missed me by inches, as I ran across the street to crash through the door of the same apartment building. I heard Johnny's footsteps racing up the staircase, sucked in a deep breath of air and went after him.

Crouched on the fourth floor landing, he fired two rounds at me. Both shots missed by inches. Again, Johnny was up and running with me behind him on the stairs.

When I eased the door to the roof open, I peeked out and caught a glimpse of Johnny leaping to the next rooftop. He landed safely, then glanced over his shoulder to spot me coming after him.

Three rooftops later I was closing the distance between us. Another leap and I spied him slide over the edge of the building. Thunder sounded nearer, as I spotted him clattering down the fire escape. I followed.

Near the second-floor landing, I took aim with the .38, as he broke across a well-lit street corner. At the instant I was about to squeeze off a shot, a truck rumbled by blocking my aim. Tucking the gun away, I clambered down the fire escape until I was low enough to hang from a rail and land safely on the ground.

I could only guess which direction Johnny had taken.

Down a dark alley that separated a warehouse from a line of tenement buildings, I trained my ears to pick up his fleeing footsteps. But all I heard was falling rain. I figured he might be laying in wait to ambush me from behind a trash bin where the alley came to an end a half block away.

While inching deeper into the alley, I heard a faint grating sound above me. I looked up and spotted him climbing to the top of another fire escape. Again I aimed my .38 and waited for the right moment. When he attempted to climb onto the rooftop, I squeezed the trigger. He screamed and disappeared from sight over the edge of the rooftop.

I ducked into the building's rear door and started up the stairwell, sucking deeply for each breath of air, legs and chest on fire. At the top of the stairwell I stopped to catch my breath.

The door to the roof flapped open and closed in the wind. When I finally braved easing out onto the roof, I could hear Johnny above the patter of rain but could not see him. He was cursing in a pained voice. I followed the sound to spot him lying on his side, holding a bleeding thigh. He was aiming his piece toward the fire escape.

By the time he heard me creeping up on him it was too late.

"Drop it, Johnny!" I put the working end of my rod close to his head. We were both still breathing hard, as I said, "Lay it down nice and easy or I'll scatter your junkie brains all over this rooftop."

He stuck his tongue out of his mouth, flicked it, cackled and let his piece fall from his grip.

"I had a hunch you were undercover."

"You should've listened to your hunch."

Kicking his piece aside, I made sure I didn't get too close to him. Even though he was on the ground bleeding I detected no surrender in his eyes.

"What now, Slick?" he asked.

"I'm dropping you off at the nearest precinct," I said, trying to catch my breath while a quandary of emotions swirled around inside of me. "You should be thankful that's all I'm going to do."

"Thank you!" He spat at my feet and licked his lips. "Like hell, man! You ain't shit to me. Never was and never will be!"

He grimaced and pushed himself up onto one knee, then struggled to a standing position while still clutching onto his bleeding thigh.

"Tell you what, Johnny," I said, lowering my gun and patting the handcuffs in my jacket pocket to make sure they hadn't fallen out. "Answer one question truthfully. Then maybe I'll let you walk."

"One question?" he said, indecisively, squinting his eyes until his dark pupils became pinpoints of concentrated light. "Like, I'm supposed to believe that shit. Who do you take me for, some jive-punk, like the ones who work for me? Well, for your information I'm much smarter than that, Mr. Know-Nothing Cash."

"What have you got to lose?" I motioned my head toward the roof door that was flapping in the wind. "Answer one question, Johnny. Then you can go."

The rain had lessened somewhat but thunder rumbled above the constant shrill of NYPD sirens drawing nearer.

"What do you wanna know?" he asked.

"Who put the bad dope on the street that killed a half dozen junkies about two weeks ago?" I raised the gun back to his head. "And don't you lie."

"I don't know, man! I— I—"

Cocking my .38, I pressed the cold barrel to his wet forehead. "Who did it, Johnny? Was it you?"

"Yeah, man!" He stared cross-eyed at the muzzle and dropped to his good knee, whimpering with tears pouring from his eyes. "Yeah! It was me. But I was just following orders. Please don't kill me."

"If I wanted to kill you I could have done that a quarter-of-a-mile ago. Stand up!"

He struggled to his feet. I reached into my jacket pocket and pulled out the big bag of dope I'd bought from him two nights before.

"I'm giving this back to you at no charge, Johnny."

"What?" He looked both leery and hopeful. "Why? I don't get what—"

"Stick it in your pocket," I said, handing him the bag.

He started to comply, paused in mid motion, and said, "You can't be for real, man. You got something else in mind. Don't you?"

Tentatively, he opened the bag, licked a forefinger and jammed it into the white powder. Pulling his coated finger from the bag, he stuck it in his mouth, then sucked and licked it greedily.

"It's the real shit, all right."

"You should know."

"What happens when I put the stuff in my pocket?"

"Me and you are going to take a hike over to the police station. I'll handcuff you to a street sign, walk a few blocks away and report where you are by phone. Then you can proudly show off what a big time businessman you are."

"Huh?" His eyes widened and bulged. "You said you were going let me go."

"So…I lied. Sue me!"

The full force of my words hit him in an instant.

"You don't know what a big operation you're screwing with," he said, foaming at the mouth. "The cats running it will chew you up and spit you out like a bad taste."

"What cats?" I demanded.

"You wouldn't believe me if I told you how high up the ladder my pull goes, Jack. But I'd never be dumb enough to tell the real deal to an old punk like you."

"Okay, Johnny, you win." I shrugged. "Time for you to see the proper authorities. They'll know exactly how to handle you."

"Big deal." He threw both his hands in the air. "Take me in then, big shot. I'm ready. Let's go. I'll even lead the way."

Before I could react right, he struck a sharp left hand to my jaw.

Stumbling back, I tripped over a steam duct and landed hard on an elbow. My rod fell from my grasp. In a flash, Johnny kicked me in the ribs. Another kick sent the .38 sliding across the wet rooftop.

I scrambled on all fours to reach the gun before Johnny could beat me to it. But even with his gunshot leg hampering him, Johnny still had running on his mind.

I got to my feet in time to see him as he jumped from the rooftop toward an adjacent one. His lead foot fell a few inches short, but he somehow managed to cling to the edge of the roof with one desperate arm.

Ironically enough, his other hand still clutched the plastic bag of white powder. The bag slipped from his grasp first, then his other hand lost its grip on the roof. A flash of lightning lit the sky when he let out a piercing high-pitched wail that didn't end until he hit the sidewalk with a sickening thud.

I made it down to the street like I was Jesse Owens and tossed my jacket and hat into a pile of trash. Then I ducked my head low and started fast stepping. A block away I took cover behind a parked car when two prowl cars turned a corner and raced by me.

When I finally turned onto Lennox Avenue, I lifted my head and walked at a less conspicuous pace. Crossing 126th Street and Morningside Avenue, Horace pulled the Mercury to a stop beside me.

Wet and cold to the bone, I slid into the heated car.

"Glad to see you in one piece," I murmured.

"Likewise," he said, in a shaken voice as he pulled the car into the flow of traffic. "I been driving around for the last half hour hoping to find you."

"With cops everywhere?"

"They didn't pay me no mind."

"I hope you're right."

"Not one of them even glanced my way. I swear."

As the windshield wipers clicked methodically, the street-lights melded with blinking neon signs and the headlights and taillights of other cars created a blur of bleeding colors.

"Tell me what happened, Nate. And please don't tell me Johnny got away."

"No," I said, sinking into the comfort of the leather seats. "I went after him. He died trying to jump a roof. But he confessed before that happened. So you can rest easy. We got the right man."

Then it was Horace's turn to bring me up to snuff.

"Before all the shooting broke loose, one guy came up near where I was hiding, trying to move closer to Johnny and that skinny guy. A squirrel, a rat, a pigeon or something was flopping around in the bush right next to me. Then this one cat stops and draws his gun and starts coming closer. He fired off a couple of rounds. I think he hit whatever it was in the bush. But when he came closer, he must've seen light hit my Peacemaker or something. Anyway, I had to take him out."

"That's about when I set out after Johnny. What happened next?"

Horace sighed long and spoke with a low uneven quaking voice.

"They kept coming at me, Nate. Like zombies coming and coming, popping off those little peashooters of theirs. They couldn't shoot a lick either." He cursed. "All...I mean, all... I ever I wanted was Johnny dead. They gave me no choice, though."

"Johnny was all either one of us wanted," I reminded him. "When I had him, though, I decided I was going to turn him in. That's when he died trying to get away."

We rode along for a bit in silence. Then raindrops the size of hailstones began pelting the roof and windshield, ending their assault as suddenly as they'd begun.

I asked Horace to pull over and let me out.

"We only got two more blocks to go," he said.

"That's okay. I want to walk from here."

As I was about to step into the rain he put a hand on my shoulder.

"Would you hear me out first?" he asked. "One more minute before you go."

"Okay." Uneasily, I shut the door.

"I'm just glad you listened to my cry for help."

"I guess you would have done the same for me. That's why you could ask."

"I suppose you're right. I just hope what we did was right."

"Right or wrong, it's done now."

"I know that." Horace's shoulders sagged and his eyes looked both skittish and tired. "But it was like a nightmare. Me blasting away with my Peacemaker. Them like moths drawn to a flame, coming and coming like they wanted me to put them out of their misery. I had to empty all six rounds to do it. All the time, in the back of my mind, I'm thinking under different circumstances any one of them could've just as well been my son Rudy."

I thought about how to reply, then opted to say as little as possible.

"I think we've both learned a lot tonight."

Again I was about to step out of the car when I decided otherwise and pulled the door shut again.

"Horace. Do you know why I didn't hesitate too long before I agreed to help you?"

"Why, Nate?"

"Because of the kind of man you are. You're a decent and upright, hardworking, family man. So I trusted that no matter what went down, not a soul would ever hear about it from your lips."

"You're sure right about that, Nate." He put a hand on my shoulder again. "But there's one more thing I need to say before you go."

"Make it quick."

"I am a veteran. That part's true enough. But I never saw no action. Most of the time I worked in the mess hall at Fort Bragg. And before tonight I never killed nobody."

CHAPTER 11

Lillian scheduled our open house party for a Friday evening exactly one week after the shootout in Morningside Park. We invited all of our best friends and some folks from the musical production she was working on. Though it was to be a major celebration, she told me to leave all of the planning to her.

Meanwhile, Horace's parting words the night of the shootout kept echoing through my mind. As hard as I tried to shut out the events of that night, I realized I'd taken a big step into the unknown. While I tried to justify being a major part of taking so many lives, it was difficult to brush off the fact and move on. Guilt plagued me even though I kept reminding myself that the gang planned to kill us. Yet the fact that they were all dead, as part of my doing, made every minute of my life a new experience that was racked with mental anguish and a loss of appetite.

Whenever Lillian questioned me about my detached grim moods, I conveniently played my state of mind off with a certain amount of truth, saying I was concerned for Joe Weathersby's upcoming trial. Then I'd tell her all that I had learned speaking to his attorney, Lucas Haynes.

Distraught as my jumbled thinking was, I was lucky whenever I could cram more than two hours of untroubled sleep into any given night. My dreams kept returning me to Morningside Park, or on the roof with Johnny G. In one nightmare I saw the dead faces and eyes of the five junkies Horace put to rest. Those vivid images stayed with me long after I woke up in a cold sweat. Furthermore, nightmares about the war began to trouble my sleep as they had for so many years after I was safe and sound stateside.

The evening of the open house I was ramrod tense by the end of my shift. I had several stops to make on the way home, so I called gypsy cab driver Leroy Grimes. When he pulled to the front of Wally's in his new Ford Fairlane, I had him help me load the trunk with a case of expensive champagne, a dozen bottles of wine and several bottles of top-shelf liquor that I'd ordered from one of the tavern's distributors. Then I joined him in the front seat.

Leroy was a frail, smallish, dark man who I often called on for long hauls and occasionally when I wanted to tail someone.

"I'm going to make a couple of stops and hit Ray's barbershop on Lexington," I told him, as he pulled into traffic without bothering to ask where I was going. "Wait for me and metaphorically leave the meter running the whole time."

"That works for me, brother man," he said.

I stopped at a little florist shop on Broadway and picked up a dozen red roses and a like number of pink and white ones. Back in the cab, during a serious bog in traffic due to an accident, I found myself reviewing the previous week.

All the major newspapers broke banner stories about the five junkies who were gunned down in Morningside Park. The local print media, TV news shows, radio talk show hosts, along with politicians, were all scraping their knees to climb onto the bandwagon. Updates and new opinions seemed to pour in with each passing hour. The history of the phantom junkie killer also came to light. Even the deadly spreading of the poison dope was now common knowledge. All over the five boroughs, most citizens were getting their first undisguised peek into the dark underbelly of the city's drug problem.

The governor, the mayor, the police commissioner, Captain Owen Frye, who was the top man at the local precinct, and everyone under their command was feeling the heat. Some of the questions still being asked were: How could so many murders be committed prior to the big shootout without the public being informed? If the morgue had not gotten such a big run on lead-filled junkies in one night, would the public have ever been alerted? Who was responsible for the cover-up, and whose heads would roll? These were the biggest questions that were left unanswered.

Later that evening, on the barbershop's portable TV, I'd had the privilege of watching Captain Owen Frye in full uniform, studded with ribbons of commendations. I was hoping to see him break into a cold sweat under the pressure of about a dozen cameras focused on him. But that did not happen.

The captain was a slight-built man, about fifty-five years old, and had a hawk-like face with a beak of nose, furtive eyes and hunched shoulders. All of which, combined, gave him a predatory look. Adding to the image, his eyes darted to and fro as he spoke in harsh defensive tones while his body remained rigid.

"These investigations, not surprisingly, have brought on a lot of derogatory name calling, witch hunts, and even more political grandstanding than I've ever seen in my long years of public service."

He paused a brief moment before going on.

"But I won't let any of that interfere with, or compromise in the least, the job I have sworn to uphold. Everybody wants immediate results. Well, so do I. And I'll tell you right here and now, my men are working day and night, sometimes putting in twenty-four-hour shifts. And none of us will sleep peacefully until we get to the bottom of all this mess. I'll also be the first to tell you that I'm glad the media has finally decided to focus on the problems that my dedicated men and I face up here in Harlem every single day of the week. With the limited manpower we have at our disposal, it's vital that you know and believe the best is what we give to our jobs, and nothing less!"

When the last word was arrogantly spoken, he parted the crowd on his way inside the 30th Precinct. I recognized the building. The outside façade hadn't changed a bit since my days on the force.

"All them words and he ain't really said jack shit," Ray, the barbershop owner, said while clipping my hair.

"He ain't gonna say nothin' worth repeatin' neither," said a plump well-dressed woman sitting between her young twin sons dressed in identical sailor outfits. "They had this white woman reporter on some television news show last night. She was talkin' about spendin' one night in Harlem to see what it was like. She sounded like she had just survived a twelve-year war. And she kept going on and on about how she didn't get a wink of sleep because of all the racket of sirens and guns goin' off all night long."

"One night for most of them is just about all they could take," Ray commented.

"Maybe," a nattily dressed customer with processed hair added. "But a whole weekend of partying hearty up here, with the right people showing 'em how, and they wouldn't want to ever go back home to the life they knew before."

There was a good round of laughter.

"One whole night, uh!" The plump woman spoke again in a no-nonsense manner. "She ought to try living up here for a generation and then she might have something to say worth me listening to."

Two people tried to speak at once, but Ray excitedly pointed at the TV. Mouth agape, he shushed everyone quiet, saying, "I know him. That's the guy who calls himself Pudding."

We all turned our attention to the 12-inch TV screen mounted high enough for all to see. A middle-aged, white, male reporter was standing beside Pudding.

"Now they're interviewing junkies?" the plump woman exclaimed.

"Quiet!" Ray ordered.

No one had heard the question but the reporter, ready for a response, was holding the microphone close to Pudding's mouth.

"We can't get no jobs downtown. Can we? So some folks, like, replace hope with dope. See? We're all just trying to survive on the little piece of the pie we're left with. Just like you, mister TV man, we're all doing the best we can. If hustling dope and breaking the law stood between you and starving to death," Pudding jabbed a forefinger at the reporter, "you tell me what you'd do in our shoes."

The cameraman took Pudding's last words as an opportunity to grab a quick shot of his unique footwear with his toes hanging over the front rims of the soles. We all laughed at that but quieted down in time to catch more of what was happening on the TV.

"But what about the recent rash of murders?" the reporter asked. "Don't you, personally, fear for your life every day?"

"Hell no!" Pudding blurted. "People die up here in Harlem all the time. Like, there's a million and one ways to die up here. So people dying never surprises me or nobody in their right mind living on this side of town. In fact, if I were to die right here, while I'm talking to you, like, it wouldn't surprise me none."

The reporter winced and looked into the camera as though he would rather be somewhere else.

The barbershop rocked with laughter.

"Lordy, Lord, for crying out loud." Ray chuckled. "What's this crazy old world amounting to these days?"

~

The open house party turned out to be a big and enjoyable success. Wine, champagne and liquor flowed freely, and Lillian had hired a caterer to lay out an exorbitant buffet spread. As part of his tip I invited Leroy to come back to join the party with his cute, plump, pale-skinned wife, Shirley. They were both dressed in similar black and gray outfits. Shirley complimented Lillian several times on the fine food she readily sampled.

"Good people. Good food. What more could anyone ask for?" Lillian said, raising a glass of champagne.

Chris Wilkins, the Bronx veteran from my old squad during the war, even showed up for the first time to anything I'd invited him to attend. Wearing a prosthetic leg, he moved about in an almost natural manner. He and old man Wally, both sports fanatics, found plenty to discuss and debate in a contentiously friendly manner.

Early in the party I had a stack of 45s from my extensive record collection on the turntable, spinning some old boogie-woogie tunes. Before long Lillian and I took to the dance floor to join some young folks from the play who were shaking a leg. Lillian had taught me a few fancy dance steps, and we had a routine that required little of me as she did most of the work. But gradually I became more animated.

After prancing about for two songs, a slow doo-wop number by the Flamingoes, "If I Had You," fell to the turntable. We embraced during the intro and did a two-step. At one point I felt obese Harry Swayne's eyes on us while he was taking up the full breadth of a love seat. I could not begin to imagine what his thoughts were like. But I'd have bet he would have paid handsomely to attend the party just to be in such close proximity with so many of the fine young women from the cast of the play. Then, of course, there was Lillian to make the landlord's heart ache.

"They used to call me Coffee because I grind so fine," I whispered in her ear during the song.

"If you ask me, you still grind just fine," she whispered back. "But now that they don't call you Coffee, what do they call you?"

"Now they call me Mr. Lucky in Love."

"Do they now?"

"That's right, baby. You heard me."

"I can tell you're going to talk to me real sweet later tonight, Mr. Lucky in Love."

"I'm gonna do a whole lot more than talk to you, baby cakes." I dropped both my hands to caress her rear cheeks for emphasis.

"But you know how much I love the way you talk that talk."

"I'll talk to you but, like I said, I'm going to do a whole lot more than talk."

"Oh? Like what more, for instance?"

"I'm going to make you squirm."

"Oh, well, you know how much I love squirming." She ground her pelvic region into me to emphasize her point.

"Can you beg, too?" I asked.

"I'll be happy to beg as long as you promise to deliver the goods."

When the second slow record ended we parted company to allow ourselves time to cool down.

I refilled my champagne glass and found myself listening to a roundhouse discussion that soon became a lecture taking place in the kitchen. I joined the circle of about six people and stood beside Brownie's partner, Vince. He was with a stylish beauty that had Ethiopian-like features. She held onto his arm while listening to Allen Bowen, the executive producer of the play Lillian was involved with.

He was a sophisticated looking, trim man of medium height, about sixty-five years of age, and he wore a formal black suit with a red ascot and held his drinking glass close to his heart, tapping on it with a large, gold and diamond ring.

"The Harlem Renaissance was absolutely something to behold," he said. "It was an unprecedented time the world had not seen before and has yet to see again. It was a time I'll always remember with a great deal of fondness, too. Which is exactly the essence of what we are trying to evoke in the play your lovely hostess Lillian and I are putting together."

Bowen smoked a meerschaum pipe and enunciated each word pedantically. I had just met him that night and immediately found him a little too officious and stuck on himself.

"During that time we had the great Paul Robeson, The Krigwa Players of Harlem and Bert Williams, all doing lavish productions of shows like: *Shuffle Along, Emperor Jones* and *All God's Chillun Got Wings*." He puffed dreamily on his pipe, blew a cloud of aromatic smoke toward the ceiling and continued. "Some of those productions ran for over a year."

"What finally put an end to the renaissance?" Vince asked.

"I'd say," Bowen responded, "it was the long lean years of the Depression. You see, the renaissance began shortly after the end of World War I. At the time there were countless reasons for hope and faith in the minds of most colored folks. We felt we were on our way to becoming bona fide beneficiaries of the American dream of prosperity for anyone willing to work hard."

He cleared his throat before continuing.

"Erroneously, as it turned out, we thought that our participation in the war effort would end some of the discrimination problems we faced. Problems such as being shut out of the trade unions, school and housing segregation, and being literally cut off from the rewards offered in the wake of the Industrial Revolution. For a while, short as it may have been, the dream did hold the promise of better days."

"Those must have been wonderful times," the pretty, petite woman with Vince said, in a wistful manner. "I often wish I'd lived during those days."

As Bowen went on, everyone except Vince, his girlfriend, and I drifted away. Then I decided to join the conversation by putting my two cents in.

"Those were also unprecedented times for African American literature, as well. Poets like Langston Hughes and Claude McKay; novelists and writers like Countee Lee, Nella Larsen, W. E. B. Dubois, and a host of others were making their presence known. Not only were many of them getting book deals, there were black newspapers and periodicals galore publishing their works along with many other brothers and sisters' writings at the time."

"The way you talk about those days," Bowen spoke with measured tones, "it almost sounds as though you personally knew all of those writers."

"I've read their books," I said. "So in a way I do feel as though I know them even now. Unlike many of the stage plays of that era, which would cost a fortune to reproduce, most of the books I'm speaking about are still available no farther away than the nearest library. And they are available to everyone, even if they can't afford to see your play or any others."

"It's interesting to hear someone put things in perspective like that," Vince's girlfriend said, as she offered her hand to me. "Hi, Nate. I'm Florence. Florence Hawkins. You and Lillian have a wonderful place here."

"It's a pleasure to meet you, Florence. I'm glad you could come."

"Nate's a writer," Vince interjected. "He does a lot of stuff for *The Uptown Beat.*"

"Occasional music reviews," I amended.

"He's real good, though," Vince said with a coy smile. "And he never splits his infinitives."

"Actually, I split them once in awhile. But only if they need splitting."

"Have you ever done any acting?" Bowen inquired, peering over the rim of his eyeglasses.

"Only as a last resort," I quipped.

He laughed politely.

When Brownie pulled Vince aside, and into the dining room, Florence addressed me again.

"The reason I'm so interested in what you're saying is that I am a school teacher. And you can't imagine how difficult it is to get children to show any appreciation for the written word."

"That is something I've noticed."

"I blame that on two things: parents who don't read themselves, and even more, there's that insidious device I call the idiot box, television, they spend so much time in front of nowadays."

"You're definitely right on both counts. I believe there's another reason, too. The books they're assigned to read, mostly by dead, white, male writers, don't reflect the children or the world they see around them. Those books are about people who, as far as the kids can relate, may as well come from Mars."

"You know," she said, with a bright smile, "I like the way you put things."

Allen Bowen smiled at me sheepishly, did a slight bow and exited the kitchen.

"Good writing, nonfiction, as well as fiction and poetry, should be an integral part of our culture," I went on. "Take it away from a society of people and they're destined to lose a major part of their identity and their heritage. It's bad enough that we're so poorly represented in movies and on that idiot box you mentioned. But that's a horse of another color I don't even want to get started on. That would take me all night long."

While Florence and I continued our conversation, I studied her in greater detail. She had chestnut colored skin and naturally rosy tinted cheeks, long eyelashes accentuating bright eyes and keen features contrasting a set of full lips.

"Beyond my job as a teacher," she told me, "I work with the school board inviting people from as many backgrounds as I can find to come in to give inspirational talks to the children. Vincent came in once and told them what it's like to be a police officer. We're also lucky enough now and then to get well-known people like Adam Clayton Powell and Harry Belafonte to contribute their time." She frowned. "But it's so hard getting enough of our folks to commit any of their time to the kids' welfare."

"That's a pity."

"How about you?" she asked enthusiastically.

"How about me, meaning?"

"How about if I arrange for you to come into one of the neighborhood schools to give an inspirational speech?"

"About what?"

"Books, naturally. You've made a good case with me already. You could talk about the things we try so hard to impress on them: the adventure, the beauty, the romance and intrigue that can be found between the covers of a good book."

"If you can't reach them, why would you expect them to listen to me?"

"Because you're a man. Some of the kids never have the opportunity to hear a strong, confident brother who lives in the community show any sign of caring about them."

"Thanks for the compliment."

"Well, are we on?"

"I'll give it some thought and let Vince know," I said, as I saw Brownie trying to get my attention. "But for now, please excuse me."

"I'll write down the phone number where you can reach me at work," she said in haste. "I'll give it to you before I leave."

"Do that, Florence. It has been a pleasure conversing with you."

As I stepped into the dining room, I caught Lillian giving me the evil eye from the buffet table. From her vantage point, I imagined her having closely watched the verbal exchange I'd just had with Florence.

Vince was right behind me when Brownie and I stepped out of the apartment and into the hallway.

"Walk us to the elevator," Brownie said.

"What's cooking?"

"I've got something I want to run by you. I don't think it can wait."

"Florence seems to like you," Vince said casually, as he fell in step beside me.

"I like her, too."

"That's cool by me, Nate," he said with a shrug. "She's just a friend. Nothing more. So if you want to see her—"

"Thanks, Vince. But I don't think it would be too cool with Lillian."

"Screw the polite jibber jabber, guys," Brownie said, as he poked the down elevator button. "That's why I didn't want to show up here tonight anyway."

"Why's that?" I asked.

"I've got too much on my mind to be exercising my social skills. For instance, you're on Lieutenant McKellerhan's shit list, you know? When I was leaving the station house tonight he even went so far as to tell me that it would be wise for me to stop associating with you."

"Did he, now?"

"Honest injun." Brownie snarled. "I told him what I do and who I see during my off-hours is none of his damn business."

"Did he tell you why I'm persona non grata?"

"That's what really bothers me. I mean, spill it out to me, Nate. What the hell have you done that's got McKellerhan so itchy around the collar?"

"I told you about looking for Freddie Tucker and not being able to find him."

"You told me that. But what haven't you told me? There's got to be more to it than that."

"Your guess is as good as mine." As an afterthought I added, "Except, I did talk to a friend in the DA's office to get permission to visit Joe Weathersby."

"Aha! Going to the DA, that'd do it. McKellerhan would definitely see a move like that as going against the grain. He'd expect you to go through him."

"I really don't give a shit. If there's anything else I can do to help Weathersby, I'll do that, too."

As Brownie and I glared at each other as though we were about to step into a ring at the 125th Street gym, Vince interjected, "There's something else."

The elevator came and the doors opened, but they ignored it.

"The lieutenant has a new protégé he's playing rabbi to," Vince went on, "a guy named Tommy O'Brien. The two of them've been acting real chummy and spending a lot of time behind closed doors. That makes G. B. and me wonder what they might be cooking up. Straight off the bat, I never liked O'Brien's looks from day one. If you ask me, he dresses too much like a pimp to do anything but work vice."

"It's more than the way he dresses," Brownie added. "O'Brien's the newest member on the team. He's only been with us for a little over two months."

"About the same time the phantom killings got started," I mused aloud.

"Exactly! With that being the case, I took the liberty to do some checking into his background."

"What did you come up with?"

"He was transferred over from Brooklyn. Flatbush to be exact. Seems as though he was pulled in on the carpet regularly for using excessive force."

"We're talking regularly as in very often," Vince said. "Black, white or brown, he wasn't prejudiced about who he jacked up. It's like he thought his badge gave him a license to put the stranglehold on anybody he felt like putting the heat on."

"After the fourth incident they suspended him," Brownie took over. "And he ended up spending six months on a shrink's couch. Finally, he got a clean bill of health and was reinstated. Now this basket case turns up here as McKellerhan's right hand man and confidant. That's what bothers me."

"Plus," Vince said, "while we were having a briefing this morning, I got a peek at a little revolver he wears in an ankle holster. When he noticed me checking it out, he seemed to get a bit nervous and pulled his trouser leg down to cover the piece. It was a shiny little number that looked like a thirty-two Beretta."

"The initial junkie killings were done with a thirty-two that used hollow point shells," Brownie explained. "But Freddie Tucker was offed with a forty-five. To complicate matters more, another forty-five is what blew away the five suspected dealers in Morningside Park. One gun is what ballistics tells us, and five armed junkies dead."

"Strange," I said. "That adds up to at least three killers or the same killer using three different weapons."

"Maybe," Vince said. "But dig this. The night that the five cats got theirs in the park, about four blocks away their top man, Johnny Garrison, was found dead at the bottom of a five-story drop. And he had a fresh gunshot wound that passed through his left thigh."

"My, my," I said. "Did you guys get a make on the slug or the shell casing, the caliber and what not?"

"Nope," Vince said, "because no slugs or casings were found. And like I said, the bullet went straight through his thigh."

"Too bad," I replied. "Who's handling that investigation? The papers say Brisco."

"He was first up," Brownie said. "Then they put Taylor on it until yesterday. Now it's back on Brisco's desk again. After all, it was his squeal that came up right after the one for Morningside Park."

"Is he still working alone?"

"Yep," Vince piped in. "That's another strange thing. O'Brien was supposed to be Brisco's new partner. Then McKellerhan snatched O'Brien to work with him. Sam's been back to freewheeling ever since."

"Whatever happened to Sam's old partner, Kenny?" I asked.

"He got transferred after getting a promotion," Vince answered. "He's on the Lower East Side now."

"Anything else strange about Garrison's death?" I asked, cautiously, wondering what happened to the big bag of dope that had taken the five-story fall with Johnny G. "Besides him getting it so far away from the rest of his gang?"

"Nope." Brownie primped his mustache pensively. "Why? Is there something else we should know about?"

"No." I shrugged. "I just thought there might be more."

"You're not holding anything back you might have heard going around, are you?" Brownie scrutinized me intensely.

"What more could I possibly know that you don't?"

"So anyway," Brownie said, once he'd taken his hard gaze off me. "I've warned you. That's the best I can do. But try not to get any further into McKellerhan's doghouse. If you do, there's no telling what might happen. And I'm not too anxious to start looking for a new sparring partner."

He laughed and gave me a pat on the back and repeated a line I'd heard numerous times, "I been too spoiled knocking you silly once a week."

"To hear you tell it," I said. "So where are you guys off to in such a hurry?"

"Over to Brooklyn," Brownie answered, "to see if there's any more dirt we can dig up on O'Brien. So let's put off the gym routine until Wednesday."

"That sounds about right to me. With the way the party's going there's no telling what time I'll get to bed."

CHAPTER 12

Saturday night Lillian and I went down to the Village to catch a young, promising, new group I'd heard good things about. We got to the small MacDougal Street club just in time to catch their last set. The joint was a Bohemian type haunt. On each tiny round table an empty wine bottle served as a candle-holder. The tablecloths were oilcloth red-and-white checkered jobs with ample wax stains on them. The walls were old brick with hardened cement oozing from each separation and layer, and abstract paintings hung here and there. Exposed wooden beams supported the high ceiling and the cracked concrete floor was strewn with sawdust. Although little more than half of the seats in the smoke-hazed joint were occupied, the audience was thoroughly engrossed by the tight sounds of the quintet.

The group's keyboard man and leader, Elliot Sands, had great range and timing. Reginald Harley did the reeds and flute arrangements. Playing a Les Paul guitar, a young white cat, Billy Kant, demonstrated some very innovative licks while showing he also knew when to lay back. The upright bass player was plugged into a large amplifier and kept the beat in a creative and impressive style. The young drummer, however, was the glue that held it all together. And he and Sands communicated often with their eyes.

Two of the tunes they performed were traditional jazz in origin, but the band lifted the familiar melodies into funkier rhythms, something that the audience could pat their feet to. With all the amplification at their command, however, they never abused the power. As a testimonial to their restraint and range, a slow ballad they performed, "When Sunny Gets

Blue," was as wistful as ever I'd heard it. The applause they received between tunes, and at the end of the set, was genuinely enthusiastic.

Most of the crowd left, but Lillian and I stuck around and ordered more wine. Later, when the keyboard man was alone at a rear table, I went back and introduced myself. We exchanged pleasantries. Then I told him I wrote for *The Uptown Beat* and invited him to have a drink at the table with Lillian and me.

Elliot Sands appeared to be in his mid-twenties, but he had a cosmopolitan air about him and spoke with a jazzman's sense of wit and cynicism. He sipped his wine sparingly. Following each sip, he dabbed a handkerchief at his pencil thin mustache. When we began discussing the history and the future of black music, he became animated and impassioned.

"Twenty to thirty years from now," he said, "I believe all of our music will have a much wider audience. Jazz, however, will always have a very select appeal because it's the classical form of our music. But I still think a lot of squares who haven't caught on yet, especially the critics, will be coming around and saying they were always hip and down with our sounds."

"When you say *our* sounds, could you be a little more specific?" Lillian asked.

"I'll try." Elliot smiled politely. "That's something I'm still trying to put a finger on. But I'll try." He took another sip of wine and dabbed at his mustache before going on. "The roots to *our* music can be traced to the old-time Negro work songs, the blues, spirituals and the sounds from the islands, too. But the bottom line is that they are all of African origin. Everything from the country sound, to swing and bebop, too, all have the same roots. Now modern jazz, which my band plays, is an amalgamation of the whole spectrum. It's a different slant, a new emphasis that comes with the passing of time and the world that surrounds us. In fact, I've been working on a standard polka arrangement and adding some funk up in it."

"What inspired you to try that?" I asked.

"All over Europe our music is accepted with a lot more appreciation and respect than it is here in the States. The people over there are far more open-minded, shall we say, than our average honky. That's why I'm working on the polka thing. It's still in the playful stage of development. But—"

"Why do you think that is, in Europe?" Lillian interrupted him.

"Because race is not such a big deal over there," Elliot answered as though he'd expected the question. "They accept the fact that *our* music is the only cultural contribution this country has ever given the world. Left up to the white man, we'd still be listening and dancing to oakie-from fanooky music."

"Why does everything always come down to race when *our* music is the subject of conversation?" Lillian stiffened. "I believe if people constantly look at the world with that kind of attitude they can't help but fail."

"Pardon me, Miss," Elliot said, "but what I'm saying isn't some uneducated rant. It's an economic reality."

"For example," Lillian demanded.

"Let's talk about popular music. LaVerne Baker made a buck or two off songs like "Tweedle Dee" and "Dance with Me Henry." But Georgia Gibbs, a white woman, became famous and later made a fortune when she did covers of the same songs. You see, they play her covers on all the major radio stations. So mainstream America is allowed to tune into Georgia and know what to ask for when they make a trip to the record store. But LaVerne can never expect the same kind of recognition or the same financial success. But that's only one example. If you want, though, I can name fifty cover songs that illustrate the same point."

"What are cover songs?" Lillian asked me.

"They're remakes of original music. For years, black music was labeled and characterized as *race music* and taboo. Another example of a cover song is June Valli's "Crying in the Chapel," which was originally done by Sunny Till and the Orioles."

"Sh-Boom," Elliot added, "is credited with being the first rock 'n' roll hit. But the Crew Cuts got it from the Chords."

"I still believe we all have to make our own way in life," Lillian said, "each of us as individuals not hiding behind lame, color-related excuses."

"I agree with you, baby." I gave her an affectionate pat on the thigh. "However, until we have our own record labels and more black-owned radio stations, we're going to have to put up with being discriminated against by the old boy network. Historically speaking, the last thing those in control want to do is relinquish their control."

"Well said." The keyboard man tipped his glass in a salute to me. "I think I'd enjoy being interviewed by you."

Lillian stiffened even more and then directed another question to him. "If you think jazz music is such a dead-end street, why don't you play something else?"

Elliot thought her question over before answering.

"Because I love what I do. For richer or poorer, it runs in my blood. As a kid, it was the first music I ever heard playing in my parents' house. And if I'm ever going to know any kind of professional satisfaction, I have no choice but to do what I do. I believe that goes for any true artist."

I felt an urge to tell Lillian to think about the way she feels when she is dancing. I resisted and changed the subject by asking Elliot if he'd ever heard of Joe Weathersby.

"That was the first name I heard when I hit town a week ago. But I never heard him blow. Have you?"

"Once. He's as good as advertised, too."

"Too bad," Elliot shook his head remorsefully. "I heard he got all jammed up and busted."

"That's true. Don't worry, though. I hear he has some solid people looking out for his best interest."

~

Before we left Elliot Sands at the club, I got the phone number of the friend he was staying with so we could schedule time to do an in-depth interview. Outside the air was nippy, especially for early May. I started to hail a cab, but Lillian suggested we save the fare and catch the subway.

"It's not like you're J. Paul Getty," she reminded me.

As we walked in silence toward the closest subway stop, her high heels clicked a steady staccato rhythm on the gritty sidewalks. All the shops along the way were closed. The streets were virtually deserted of pedestrians and the traffic was sparse. One look at her profile when we first walked out of the club and I could see that she was steaming with resentment. I knew that if I placated her foul mood everything would be copacetic. But I refused to speak first.

The late night wind heaved at our backs and she clutched a gloved hand to the collar of her coat. Even when we reached an intersection to cross, she kept her distance, never accepting the hand I offered more than once.

While waiting on the train platform she finally broke the silence.

"Sometimes I wonder about you, Nathaniel."

"Wonder what?"

"I think hate destroys whoever carries it in their heart more than anyone it's directed at. That's what I'd teach any children I bear."

"I agree, but what's that got to do with me?"

"The way you went along with the self-pitying act that guy was putting on made my skin crawl. And all to get an interview? That's what's wrong."

"The young man made a few good points."

"Do you mean to tell me you can't see a better future for *our* people? All our problems can't be explained away as white against black with us as victims. Don't you see that things are improving? Maybe just a little, but you have to admit things are getting somewhat better."

"A little," I conceded. "Even you have to admit, though, Harlem has gotten worse in just the last few years. Don't you remember we were talking about some of the problems last month?"

"I'm talking about what's going on for colored people all over the country. Not just what's happening in Harlem."

"What's happening in Harlem could happen anywhere."

"I doubt it." She moved a step away from me on the platform as a train pulled up on the other side of the tracks, kicking up wind and dust. "In fact, I truly doubt that."

"All I'm saying is that I can relate with what the fella said."

After another lengthy silence and the train had pulled away, I spoke again.

"Record companies have taken rock 'n' roll and made millions of dollars with guys such as Pat Boone singing cover songs like Little Richard's 'Long Tall Sally.' Meanwhile, someone like John Lee Hooker has written countless songs that get played on only a few radio stations. It's the record companies that decide who gets air time. If the deejay's hands aren't greased, it's like *no ticky no washy*. They make stars out of the likes of Elvis and Fabian because they promote them with lots of cash. They accept their music in preference to having their teenagers' dollars ending up in the pockets of Bo-Diddly, Chuck Berry or Fats Domino."

She dropped her eyes, took my hand, stepped closer to me and leaned her head against my shoulder.

"It wasn't just what he said."

"Then what was it?"

"Something about him reminded me of someone I never liked."

"Someone, like who?"

"Way back when," she sighed at length, "a guy I knew in high school up in the Bronx. He was a few years older and always hitting on me, even though I wouldn't give him the time of day. Talk about being egotistical, one time he told me that he was the best thing to ever happen to colored women since the invention of the hair straightening comb. He was one of those slicksters who thought he knew it all and was always complaining about how the white man's system was holding him down."

I squared up to face her with our eyes locked and our noses mere inches apart.

"That sounds almost like the way you used to describe me."

"Well…" she smiled, "in some ways I'm still not too sure about you. The jury is still out on that count."

"Is that right?" I smiled back at her, and said, "Reminds me of what we went through last night about that school teacher, Florence, when all we were doing was having a decent conversation."

"You're not going to bring her up again, are you?"

"Why not?" I laughed but cut the mirth short. "It seems she was worth talking about for an hour or more last night after everybody left."

"Which is why I thought that subject was history after the way we made up," Lillian said, sullenly.

"It's the same old story, Lil. You've got to learn to stop jumping to such hasty conclusions about people or their intentions. Most people are just not that shallow and easy to read without giving them some time."

"What if you find out you're wrong and they cause you pain, then what?"

"You dust yourself off, pick yourself up and get back in the race."

"That might be a workable philosophy for you." She frowned and turned her head toward the rising racket of an oncoming train. "Unfortunately, though, I'm not the tough guy you are. I've learned to be protective, to be skeptical, and to look past the fronts people put on so well. As much as I hate to admit it, I've got to be more sensitive to possible repercussions than you. My skin's too thin, and I can't take the wear and tear of being wrong too often. I've been hurt enough."

I didn't respond verbally, but her last statement prompted a lot of thoughts to flood my mind. She'd told me about a few of the bad relationships she'd been in before we got together.

However, uppermost in my mind were the many risks I'd taken since we'd been together that she had no clue about, culminating with showing up in Morningside Park with Horace Yancy.

~

On the northbound train, I noticed the drummer, Pee Wee Merkins, sitting at the front end of our car. After two stops, I excused myself from Lillian.

"I'll be right back. I see someone I need to talk to."

I approached Merkins and sat beside him. He looked up and acknowledged me with a smile, appearing much healthier than when I'd last seen him

"Hey, jack of all trades," he said jovially. "Fancy running into you again."

"What's shaking beside the bacon this time, Pee Wee?" I asked, as the train hit top speed.

"I'm hanging in there. Feeling my Ps and Qs and trying not to complain since I started cleaning that filthy skag out of my system."

"Good for you," I spoke above the crescendo of the train's wheels. "How long have you been clean?"

"It's been a couple of weeks now. But quitting ain't so hard. I must have done it at least twelve times."

I laughed with him, then said, "It sure is a rotten shame about young Weathersby, isn't it?"

"You bet." Pee Wee dropped his eyes to the train's floor. "I feel for him every single day, brother. The cat has a lot of talent that don't come easy."

"No shit."

"But it's funny you should bring him up now."

"How so?"

"Because I heard something through the grapevine the other day that might be useful to you. That is, if you're still trying to help him out."

"Run it by me," I said, as the train doors hissed open at a stop.

"That gray chick that was with Freddie the night Joe decked him."

"Yeah?"

"She might have had something to do with him getting blasted."

"Can you be a little more specific?"

"Well," he said, as the train began rolling again, "word is one of Freddie's flunkies talked her into slipping Fred a mickey. When he was out cold, so the story goes, she let this same dude, Wayne Wesley, into the flat. Then according to the word on the street, he blasted a .45 cap in Freddie's head. Then he and the bitch ripped off Tucker's life savings and his stash, too. More word of mouth is that same night the two of them absconded to Detroit."

"Very interesting, Pee Wee. Very interesting indeed. Do you happen to know the gray chick's name?"

With the interior lights rapidly blinking on and off, the train lurched and screeched forward.

"Let me think." Pee Wee scratched his chin. "I believe her name was Dottie something-or-other."

"And this guy, Wayne Wesley, any chance he looks a little like Weathersby?"

"Hmm...." His eyes widened. "Matter-of-fact, now that you mention it, they could pass for brothers."

~

With every step I took, as Lillian and I walked to our building holding hands, Pee Wee's story made more and more sense. It confirmed a long-standing belief I had that more criminals would elude arrest if they kept their dirty deeds a secret.

However, the temptation to brag about their exploits was obviously too great for many of them to resist. Given the distance between New York and Detroit, and the time that had elapsed since the discovery of Freddie Tucker's body, the time for the grapevine to pass the word seemed apropos.

~

Early Monday morning, I got my friend Howard Katz from the district attorney's office on the line. We bantered to and fro like old friends sometimes do, then I got down to business.

"It's common knowledge," I said, "that Tucker died of a gunshot wound. What I'd like to know is, was it a forty-five caliber bullet that killed him?"

"That could be the case," Katz stalled. "But what's that got to do with you?"

"I've got some information I want to pass your way. First, I need your solemn oath that my sources, whoever they might be, and I remain anonymous."

"The state versus Weathersby is not even on my calendar," he said, irritably. "Besides, this office feels we've already built a substantial case against your friend and we're ready to prosecute."

"If you look over the evidence, you'd probably change your mind, quick. As you know, Lucas Haynes is defending him. We've talked a few times and I've learned that the one eyewitness who said he got a peek at the alleged gunman said it was a fast peek through a cracked doorway, Howie," I emphasized his name sharply. "While the eyewitness is not particularly old, he does wear very thick eyeglasses. Without them he'd probably be considered legally blind. Which means this case may end up getting tossed out of court by any reasonably thinking judge before it even goes to trial."

"I know enough about the case," Katz blurted, "to know that the eyewitness says he was wearing his eyeglasses at the time."

"He claims that, yes. But everything you've got is circumstantial except for his testimony. Lucas Haynes is a sharp attorney. We all know that. He also knows his way around a courtroom and has a knack for winning the respect of jurors. Should the case actually go to trial, believe me, he'll create plenty enough reasonable doubt for any jury to mull over. He'll also be sure to emphasize that we're talking about possibly convicting a college student of cold-blooded murder, a clean-cut young man who comes from a respectable family and has a father who's a doctor."

Katz remained silent.

"Compare him to your eyewitness, a guy in his late sixties, who hasn't held a steady job in ten years and is living on disability handouts. Furthermore, it was well after midnight and the man, who admits to having been asleep at the time, heard a gunshot. According to him, he hopped up from his bed, peeked through a cracked door and claims to have seen Weathersby and a white woman running down the steps. Says he saw him, particularly, clear enough to be 100 percent certain of his identity."

I paused, relishing the silence on the other end of the line before going on.

"So why didn't he call the cops right then and there? His explanation is that he was afraid to get involved, and chalked the incident up to thinking that since he was sound asleep, maybe what he thought was a gunshot could have been something falling on the floor above where he was sleeping. All of that, I believe, would be enough reasonable doubt to drop this case and go after the real killer. Wouldn't you say?"

"We still have the fact that the kid did have an altercation with the deceased the night before."

"I'm glad you brought that up. I'd like you to see how the prosecution is going to explain how Joe got into Tucker's flat to shoot him square in the head while he was lying in his bed."

I wore a grin, trying to imagine what Katz would say next.

"So what have you come up with that's so earth shattering?" he finally asked.

"First things first. Do I have your solemn word on my anonymity?"

"That goes without saying, Nate," he replied, clearly annoyed. "Now fill me in on what you know."

I passed on the rumors I'd gotten from Pee Wee Merkins.

CHAPTER 13

Right before noon on Tuesday, the phone rang at Wally's. I picked up the receiver during the third jingle.

"Wally's."

"Nate," a very familiar voice said. "This is Horace."

A tinge of anxiety curled up in the center of my gut and the place near my spine where the slug used to be burned red hot.

"Okay. Now that I know who it is, what do you want?"

"We need to talk."

"It's your nickel."

"No," he quickly replied. "Better we do it face to face and as casual as possible, if you get my drift."

"Any suggestions?"

"Last time I was in there, I noticed the trap on the sink in back of the bar and the one in the men's john were corroded. I promised Wally I'd take care of replacing them. So I thought I'd mosey on over there right now and do the job."

"I'll be here."

Ten minutes later, Horace pulled in front of the joint driving his company truck. He parked the dark blue vehicle with yellow lettering, then made a big show of gathering his tools from the side of the panel truck.

When he walked through the door, he carried a large wrench in one hand and a toolbox in the other. Hooked under one arm was a large galvanized bucket. While I went about my duties, he came around the bar, hunched down and placed the bucket under the elbow of the corroded trap.

"You can go right on working like I'm not even here," he said.

"Fine," I responded, polishing a section of the bar top that didn't need the attention. "So tell me what's up."

"I thought you should know two cops came around to the house to question me," he said, while fitting the wrench around a huge nut.

"When?"

"Just a couple of days after the big night." He paused and began to loosen the rusty joint. "Sunday morning when the missus and I got back from church they were parked out front, waiting."

I refilled two orders, waited on a new customer and also took his lottery bets for the next day. Then I positioned myself near Horace again.

"Go on."

"They asked if they could come in and sit down. Said they had something new to report to us."

"Uh-huh."

"Soon as we got inside, the one called Brisco told us about them suspecting Johnny G to be the punk responsible for poisoning Rudy. Then he went on to say that Johnny G, himself, had been killed. He started off talking real friendly. Almost like me and him and the missus were old friends from way back and he was just making a social call."

"And—"

"He told me how a lot of Johnny G's boys got murdered the same night."

Horace undid the old elbow, which was orange with rust and dropped it into the galvanized bucket.

"He said all but Johnny were done in by the same forty-five caliber gun. I said, 'Good riddance to bad rubbish.' Then he asked if I had a big forty-five pistol registered to me. That's when I told him that I used to have one but it must've gotten stolen out of my truck and that I know I should have reported it. But I said it kept slipping my mind."

"Then what?"

"He asked if they could take a look around my place," Horace said, gazing up from his squatting position. "So I say, 'Go ahead,' like it didn't bother me none they didn't have a search warrant. They looked. I mean, they looked everywhere real good. But I knew they wouldn't find my Peacemaker. I'd dumped it straight in the Hudson first thing after I dropped you off that night."

"That's good news. Did my name come up?"

"You bet it did. That's why I stayed away from you for so long. I got the feeling they've been tailing me now and then. I'm not even sure if they finally stopped."

"What did they want to know about me?"

"Mostly, how I got to know you and how good did I know you."

"What'd you tell them?"

"That I know Wally. I said my business was with him. You, I said, I hardly speak to and know mostly by sight."

"Sounds like Brisco made it clear he suspects you killed Johnny and his boys."

"Oh yeah. Without a doubt, he made his suspicions clear. But my old lady stuck behind my alibi. She said I was home at midnight that night like every other night of the week."

"All that's good."

He shrugged again, as he greased a new nut and began to tighten it.

"He still had more questions, though, and went back to the fact I let a registered gun get stolen and not report it. He didn't like that story at all. But I knew he couldn't prove I was lying or whether I was speaking gospel."

I left him and went to deal with a gay couple who had just entered.

When Horace finished his work under the sink, he changed the trap in the men's room. I paid him out of petty cash and he left without us exchanging another word.

Learning that Detective Brisco had questioned Horace Yancy had me alarmed. Yet after mulling things over I reasoned that

Brisco's suspicions were only a natural outcome of the events that had transpired. If I were handling the case, I told myself, I would have proceeded similarly.

The bereaved father would be a prime suspect and one of the first people questioned. Fortunately, Horace had disposed of the traceable gun. Another fear that had nagged me was all the driving around after the shooting that Horace had done before he picked me up. But if anyone had reported seeing him, after he and his wife had sworn that he was home, Brisco would have used that information long ago when it had first surfaced. At such a late date, therefore, I felt I could rest easy about that coming to light.

Also, as I'd learned talking to Brownie and Vince, no slug or shell casings were found near Johnny G's corpse, which might have linked me to the scene of the crime. Nevertheless, I knew since Brisco was suspicious of me being involved, he'd do his best to make my life uncomfortable as possible or worse.

~

Although Lieutenant McKellerhan had failed to show up the last week for his payoff, I knew eventually I'd see his bulky, bear-like frame darken the doorway. With all the hoopla surrounding the shootout in Morningside Park, the subsequent news and pressure the media was putting on the precinct, McKellerhan's absence didn't surprise me. Nonetheless, I was betting he wouldn't let another week go by without collecting his due.

When I had just about given up on him showing up, a trimly built ofay guy about five-feet-nine with undercover cop written all over him, sauntered through the front door dressed like a pimp might. He was about thirty-five years old, sported a green Alpine hat, a pair of fancy sunglasses and a dark iridescent suit. Under the stingy brim hat, his dark red-tinged hair appeared to be slicked back. Ten years ago, he'd probably been described as baby-faced. However, time and cynicism had hardened his features and the description no longer applied.

Insolently popping chewing gum, he strolled up to the bar, leaned against it and slammed an open palm down on the old, wooden bar top.

"Nate Holt," he announced belligerently. "I hear that's your name."

"So who the hell are you?"

"A new acquaintance of yours," he said, smiling crookedly, as he offered me a hand to shake. "Tommy O'Brien's the name."

"Am I supposed to be impressed?" I asked, ignoring his hand.

"Be that way then." He dropped the proffered hand to his side and laughed. "It's okay by me, if that's how you want to play it. But I'm sure you know why I'm here."

"Refresh my memory."

"You really want to go this route, huh?"

"Why not?"

I looked up and down the bar, and across at the booths to cover more than a dozen patrons, looking to see if anyone needed service. They all avoided my eyes and maintained their tense, almost frozen-like positions. Although they didn't know exactly what was going on, they knew O'Brien smelled of trouble and my actions weren't making things any better.

In dramatic fashion, O'Brien reached into the breast pocket of his iridescent jacket and produced his shield, which was pinned in his wallet next to his photo ID card. He slammed the wallet down on the bar top.

"Detective Thomas O'Brien is what the ID reads. And that's none other than my badge to go with it. Got that, pally?"

I paid more attention to his shield and ID than I needed to ascertain its authenticity. Then I pushed his wallet back to him.

"You're a cop. So what? I still don't understand why you think I'd be expecting you. No one in here called for you guys that I know of."

He blew a gum bubble until it popped, chewed at some remnants which had stuck to his bottom lip, gathered the whole wad in his mouth and then spat it on the floor. Then he pulled his sunglasses off, tucked them in his jacket pocket and smiled with a curled-up lip as he straddled a stool.

"You want to make this tough going, huh?" He glared at me with hostile green eyes. "McKellerhan sent me for what you owe him. As you can probably imagine, if you've been keeping up with the news lately, he's been too busy to drop by himself."

Momentarily, I thought about relenting, giving him the two payments without further fuss. But something in my reckless nature refused to acquiesce.

"McKellerhan?"

"When're we going to get past the dumb act, Holt?" his voice rose a notch. "I'm the man you'll be dealing with from now on. Any objections?"

"Plenty!" I said, feeling as though some of Wally's obstinacy had rubbed off on me. "Number one: any business I have with the lieutenant is strictly between me and him. Number two: I don't like you."

"Make the call." He pointed at the phone behind the bar. "The lieutenant will verify he sent me. But as far as you liking me goes, I can't see how or why that should mean an ounce of bird shit to me. I'm not here to win no popularity contest. The question you should be concerned with is whether or not I like you."

"If McKellerhan's got something to say to me, he knows how to get in touch."

O'Brien lowered his head and buried it in the crook of his arms, which were splayed out on the bar. His shoulders rocked like he was either crying or laughing himself to death.

I was calmly pouring myself a double Courvoisier when O'Brien finally lifted his head. He wiped his eyes and smiled at me as though I were Sammy Davis Jr. doing his best impersonation of Jerry Lewis on the *Ed Sullivan Show*.

Still chuckling, he got up from the stool and made his way to the pay phone, dropped a coin in the slot and dialed. Soon I could hear his end of the conversation.

"Hell," he said, "I don't know what's wrong with the jackass. He says his business is with you." He paused. "Yeah, I'm still here. I told him all of that already."

With a faint smile creasing his lips, he swaggered back to the bar and leaned against it directly across from the private line.

I grabbed the phone on the first ring.

"Wally's."

"What the hell's going on over there, Nate?" McKellerhan blared.

"A guy named O'Brien's here," I said casually. "And he claims to represent you."

"That's right! He does. So what's your problem?"

"The problem is no one told me."

"Didn't he just tell you?"

"Yeah, but—"

"And he showed you his shield?"

"These days anybody could be carrying a badge."

"Well, he's on the up-and-up. So don't keep him tied up there any longer than necessary. Hear?"

The line disconnected abruptly, but I held it to my ear like McKellerhan was still on the line.

"He just doesn't look like a cop to me," I said, loud enough for everyone in the joint to hear. "Just tell him, or the next joker you send over here, to act like they've got some good sense and everything will be just fine from now on."

I slammed the receiver back into its cradle. Mimicking the crooked smile O'Brien had previously worn, I slipped two envelopes from my raincoat and slapped them down on the bar top.

"It's okay now. McKellerhan cleared everything for you," I said.

O'Brien had lost his cynical smile. Instead, his lips were puckered into a severe grimace. He grabbed the envelopes and stuck them into his rear pants pocket.

"I was told I might expect a lot of high-falooting shenanigans from you," he snarled. "But I guess I didn't expect so much monkey business from a citizen with so much to lose."

"You got McKellerhan's take. So why don't you scram?"

Again he tried to muster up a cocky smile but wasn't up to the challenge. The best he could do was leer.

"I got news for you," he said in a low, steely voice, "screwing with me is inviting big trouble your way."

"That ain't news," I shrugged. "I've known trouble all my life."

"You can bet it'll be news before I'm done with you." He leaned across the bar and whispered in a foreboding tone. "I'll blow both your lousy kneecaps clean off and see you rolling down this same street on a makeshift skateboard with a tin cup in your hand. Then, just for fun, I'll kick your mangy butt into the middle of traffic every chance I get."

"You'd do all that for me?" I asked, facetiously.

He glared at me for a long moment before trying to get the last word, "I promise we'll meet again, and next time you won't find it so goddamn funny."

"Like I said, Tommy, you got what you came for. Now beat it so I can get back to work."

With a final smirk he strutted out of Wally's, slamming the door behind him. A tangible air of relief swept over me and the rest of the joint.

CHAPTER 14

The next morning, Wednesday, I arrived at the 125th Street gym a few minutes before nine. Bud Garnet, the old guy who ran the place, called out to me as I came out of the locker room in my workout duds. He motioned a finger for me to come over to where he was mopping the floor.

"Got a message for you," the old, tar-black, ex-pug said.

"What?"

"Your cop pal, Garret, called about fifteen minutes ago. Said he was running late."

"Thanks, Bud."

A half hour later I was punching on the heavy bag while a lightweight held it. By that time I had completely given up on Brownie making an appearance.

His absence troubled me, though. For close to four years he had never missed a workout. Furthermore, he had never even been late. With the complexities surrounding the phantom shooter, Brownie and Vince sniffing into Tommy O'Brien's shady background in Brooklyn, and Detective Brisco openly suspicious about my involvement in the Morningside Park massacre, I had a lot to mull over.

In connection with Morningside Park, Horace had acted as though we were off the hook because he had tossed away the dirty weapon. But it would not surprise me if Brisco chose to drag him into an interrogation room one day for a more extensive questioning session. Even as stoic and closemouthed as Horace was, I knew he'd be no match for Detective Brisco, who had a wealth of experience when it came to confronting liars and unearthing the underlying truth behind their lies.

Also notable, Lieutenant McKellerhan had recently warned Brownie about associating with me. In addition, McKellerhan had disassociated himself from me by sending O'Brien for his weekly payoff.

It seemed as though I was shrinking into a no man's land with the known world closing in rapidly to squeeze me further and further into a corner. Digging my way out without some informative observations from Brownie was a scenario that did not appeal to me. When I added O'Brien's boldface threats of yesterday to the growing list of my concerns, the picture took on an even grimmer complexion that bordered on the macabre.

~

Even after the workout, my body was still uncommonly tense, almost wound as tight as my mind. Then the customers in Wally's later that day seemed more demanding, trifling and eager for me to listen to their petty woes and tipped less. The numbers runner, Syd Barnes, ran late and all the bettors in the house, nursing their drinks, became even more objectionable. They all felt certain that if Syd didn't pick up the day's betting slips in time to get them to the banker it would be the very day their numbers hit.

"He'll be here soon," I kept repeating.

In the nick of time, snappy-dressing Syd rushed through the front door like a pony express agent, grabbing my slips and cash on the run.

When the phone jingled during a hectic after-work rush, I jumped as if someone had jabbed me with a hot poker. I expected more bad news.

"Wally's!"

"Good news," a cheerful voice said just above the jukebox and the joint's din.

"You have to speak up louder."

"Nate! It's Howard Katz."

"Oh...What's up?"

"Good news. That's what's up. Can you hear me?"

"Barely. The place is jumping. Can you make it fast?"

"Should I call you back? Or do you want to—"

"No, no!" I said, turning my back to the room and covering my free ear. "Just make it fast."

"The story about Wayne Wesley and Dottie proved to be a winner."

"You don't say?"

"I do say." He laughed. "We sent the authorities in the Detroit area a wire. They responded by busting Wayne Wesley and Dorothy Blaine soon after."

"And?"

"They were dirty, Nate. They were caught holing up in some fleabag hotel with a big bag of uncut smack." He whistled. "Eight whole ounces."

"That's great!"

"Your information was right on the money. When the FBI agents finally got their mitts on them they threw in a few questions about how Freddie Tucker died. I guess you can figure out what happened next without a road map."

"The woman made a deal?"

"Bingo!" he said. "Her story, almost word for word, verifies what you heard through the grapevine. There was one notable exception, however. The way she tells it, the guy sprung the plot to kill Tucker on her by surprise. After pulling off the hit and grabbing Tucker's stash, she also claims he dragged her along with him at gun point. She says he threatened to have her mother and her baby back in Brooklyn killed, if she tried getting away."

"She's just trying to protect herself."

"That hypothesis is highly probable."

Glancing at the reflection in the mirror behind the tavern's well-stocked shelves, I could see my thirsty customers were beginning to look like inmates on the verge of springing a riot. Still, there was one more question I needed an answer to.

"How soon until Joe Weathersby gets released?"

Katz promised to pull a few strings and do his best to get Joe released as quickly as possible.

~

Perhaps Katz had done exactly as promised, but it wasn't until later that evening that Joe got to walk away from Riker's Island as a free man. Blinky borrowed a girlfriend's car and picked him up. At a quarter to eight, the two of them walked through my front door. Weathersby's father was due to come for Joe the next morning, and Blinky decided that my place would be the best spot to rendezvous. He felt that if Mr. Weathersby saw the dump where he lived he would have a long-lasting negative opinion of all New Yorkers.

When I answered the door for Blinky and Joe, Lillian rushed past me and gave Joe a big hug, as though he were a long-lost relative. Next it was my turn to embrace the young man and give him a few commiserating pats on the back. His wounded eye was still somewhat discolored, but otherwise he didn't look the worse for wear.

"Thanks for all you did," he said. "Blinky told me how much I owe you."

"I'm just glad I was able to help work things out."

"Are you hungry?" Lillian directed her question to both of them once they were seated in the living room.

"I'm okay," Joe responded. "Don't go out of your way for me."

"Or me," Blinky muttered a trifle uncertainly.

"I'll take both answers as a yes," Lillian said, before turning to head for the kitchen.

While she was busy rustling up something to eat, Joe concentrated his attention on my many shelves of records.

"Man, you got quite a collection here," he said, with awe.

"Especially those stacks of seventy-eights. They're my pride and joy. Some of them are very rare. Pick out something, anything, and I'll put it on the turntable."

After mulling at length he selected Thelonius Monk's "Ask Me Now," which was one of my favorite ballads by him. While we sat sipping cold brews, digging the sounds and the delectable aroma coming from the kitchen, Joe noticed the alto saxophone case which sat half hidden in a corner of the room.

"Is that what I think it is?" He pointed toward the case.

"Take a look."

He got up from the couch, picked up the case, sat down again with it on his lap and opened it. Inside was a slightly battered and tarnished alto saxophone.

"This sweet baby's old," he said, fingering the keys. "The action is pretty good, considering. Do you blow some?"

"Naw! I waited too late in life to start. I was twenty when I picked it up for the first time. Then I was too impatient, wanting to sound like Bird when I couldn't even get past 'Old Folks at Home.'"

Joe laughed and hummed a couple of bars of the song, and said, "I remember learning that tune when I first started taking lessons."

"I'm sure learning it came easier for you."

"Maybe." He sipped at his beer, then added, "It's really all about learning the twelve scales and how to improvise off them; that's the key to playing well. If I were going to be around, in no time I'd have you blowing like you've been at it for years."

A little later, Lillian called us into the kitchen and the four of us sat down to a nice spread of broiled salmon, scalloped potatoes, green beans and hot buttered biscuits. We talked casually while scarfing up the food.

"So what are your plans?" I asked Joe.

"His father wants him to become a doctor now," Blinky answered for Joe.

"He figures I tried the nightlife, as he calls it," Joe picked up the conversation. "Now he expects me to go the scholastic route. I can't really blame him. I mean, it would be hard to argue with him after the way things turned out."

"That's a shame," Lillian said. "Nate tells me you have a
tremendous amount of talent."

He smiled modestly, dropped his eyes and went back to the
act of putting his fork to good use.

Blinky jumped on the silence.

"I've been telling Joe that even if he wanted to get back into
Julliard, or some other music school outside the war zone, he
wouldn't be able to start until September anyway. That's more
than four long months from now. Maybe by then he can change
his father's mind."

Joe looked as though he was about to speak, but instead
smiled awkwardly and went back to eating. It was midnight
when we called it a night. Joe went off to the spare bedroom,
and Blinky curled up on the living room couch with a pillow
and some blankets Lillian had given him.

~

Joe's parents arrived the next morning promptly at eight
o'clock while I was still in the shower. Lillian took them on a
tour of the apartment and down to her dance studio on the second floor. Later, Lillian made a big pot of coffee and we all sat
down in the living room.

The Weathersbys were a fair-skinned couple, tall and trim.
They resembled each other enough to be brother and sister and
appeared to be in their early fifties. They were dressed conservatively, as though they were on their way to or from church.
Mrs. Weathersby even wore a blue bonnet with a pair of fake
carnations on it. They were both excited by Lillian's mention
of the play she was working on which was opening that coming
Friday night.

"We'll have to come back up and see it one weekend," Mrs.
Weathersby promised.

Soon the conversation turned on a more serious note.

"I want to thank you again, Nate," Mr. Weathersby said, nodding his head in Blinky's direction. "Mr. Carlson has filled me in on all the trouble you went through to help us out. If there is—"

"Think nothing of it," I said. "Us Philly folks have to stick together."

"You being from Philadelphia is one thing," he said, "but beyond that I'm prepared to show my appreciation in a monetary way. Name a figure. I trust your judgment."

"No money needs to change hands. It's not like I'm starving." I said with a smile. "I was happy to help. It was just a matter of making a few phone calls. That's all."

"If you insist," he said, with a shrug.

"I presume you like New York better than Philly?" Mrs. Weathersby asked me.

"I like the pace. Philly's a little too slow for my taste, especially on Sundays."

We talked about the changing complexion of North Philadelphia and Harlem. Then Mr. Weathersby squirmed in his seat and picked up his hat from his lap.

"We hate to run," he said, "but we've got to drive over to Joe's old apartment to meet the superintendent to pick up his belongings and hit the road for home. I'd liked to get back soon after noon to open up the office. Today's the first time I've missed even an hour of looking after the folks who come to me."

"Mr. Weathersby," Blinky spoke up with his face twitching dramatically. "I know because of the way things went down that you have a good right to be bummed out on the music scene. But you should know your son has a lot of God-given talent that many people would sell their souls to possess."

"I realize that," Mr. Weathersby said. "And he had a chance to follow that dream. The way I look at it, maybe what happened was God's way of steering him toward a profession in which he can be helpful to others and not have to worry about his soul."

"Music is important, too," Blinky countered. "Imagine a world without music."

"I'm not slighting the importance of music," Joe's father said. "I just think he should give medical school a chance. He's got a bright mind and he learns fast. And if he has any trouble with specific areas of study, I'll be right there to help him. He should have no trouble enrolling at the University of Pennsylvania." He cleared his throat. "Anyway, that's what my wife and I have decided would be best."

Mrs. Weathersby nodded assent.

"I'm not suggesting that he wouldn't make a good doctor," Blinky replied. "It's only that as a musician I think he'd be destined for greatness."

"That may be true, but he has another opportunity awaiting him that is not always available to our people. We need doctors, lawyers, scientists, teachers and other educated people to help advance our cause if we hope to make the future better for the generations to come. Joe happens to be in a position to go further with his schooling, and I intend to make sure he does exactly that."

Blinky started to speak again, but Mr. Weathersby held up a hand to silence him.

"So you'll better understand me, let me tell you a bit about my life, Mr. Carlson." His eyes were focused above Blinky's head. "My father was a Baptist minister. He wanted me to follow in his footsteps. Somewhere along the line, though, I decided I wanted to major in medicine. He gave me his blessings. In fact, he was tickled pink by my decision. However, when it came time to start college he didn't have the money to pay for my full tuition. Scholarships were available and my grades would have qualified me. But my father told me that if I accepted a scholarship I would always be beholden to someone else's generosity."

He paused at length. We all waited through the prevailing silence.

"His views were not mine at the time. Even now I think of them as being old-fashioned. Nevertheless, I respected his wisdom and took his advice. In the end I worked my way all the way through college, pre-med and medical school. It took me ten years, but I've never regretted the road I took. After all, I earned my degrees by the sweat of my own brow. Best of all, my father lived long enough to see that happen."

As the Weathersbys and Blinky filed out the front door, Joe lingered behind long enough to hand me some musical notations that he'd penned on notebook paper.

"I wrote down the twelve scales," he said. "Study them and don't be too surprised if you hear I've found another music school to attend by September. Hard-headed people run in my family. But if my mother ever comes around she'll help me convince my dad to see things differently."

"Sounds like a familiar scenario."

"Yeah," he looked boyishly shy as he replied. "It's always been that way."

CHAPTER 15

I had not seen tall and handsome Andre Goode inside of Wally's or in the neighborhood for more than a year. I'd heard a rumor that his absence from the scene was due to a jail sentence that sent him up to Attica on some unknown charges. Shortly after he arrived, a fair-skinned, jittery sister with dyed-blonde hair walked into the joint to sit with him in the rear booth, joining the late Friday afternoon regulars.

She wore a retail clerk's uniform, had a moon-shaped face, large breasts, thin hips and bird-like legs. From the moment she sat down with Andre, the animosity between them was evident. They held a heated conversation for more than ten minutes before Andre tore himself away to replenish his drink and order one for her.

As he leaned on the bar awaiting my service, I scoped him out from the corner of my eye. Andre was in his late twenties, I guessed, and of black and Hispanic heritage. He had a swashbuckler's profile, like a young Errol Flynn. Yet he seemed to lack the know-how or self-confidence to complement his looks, like a man always under a dark ever-present cloud, faking the necessary bravado.

"What can I get you, Andre?" I asked, when time allowed.

"Advice and two gin and tonic on the rocks."

"The drinks are no problem, but the advice may not be worth ten dead flies." I went through the automatic motions of filling his order.

"Don't short change yourself," he said, with a smile. "We all know you're a man of wisdom. So tell me, Nate, what do you do when you're a handsome young, mack-daddy, like me, and the women won't leave you alone?" His smile gleamed, almost convinced of his own words. "Tell me that."

I laughed and said, "That reminds me of an old joke a jazzman once told me. What is the key to life?" I set the two drinks in front of him while he pondered the curve I'd thrown him.

"I don't know." He scratched his clean-shaven chin.

"B-natural."

"Not bad," he said, without cracking a smile. "I got a better one, though. Check it out. What's the difference between a two-hundred-dollar call girl and a ten-dollar street walker?"

"You tell me."

"A hundred and ninety dollars." He chuckled, grabbed the two drinks and gave me an over the shoulder wide-toothed grin.

About fifteen minutes later, a burly guy with nappy disarranged hair staggered through the front door. He wore paint-stained coveralls and his face was twisted into a distraught mask of anger and confusion. The woman with Andre grimaced and made a move to duck under the table the moment she saw him. Before she could perform the act, though, the burly man turned his attention toward the rear corner of the bar and saw her.

"You bitch, you!" he bellowed.

As he stormed toward her with his arms outstretched in a murderous mode, the woman shrieked and made an effort to elude him but failed. I grabbed the baseball bat I kept for such occasions and vaulted the bar.

Before I could intercede, the monster had Andre's frail companion by the throat, shaking her like a rag doll. Gertie's shrill screams filled my ears, and Andre looked on perplexed, yet removed, as if the whole drama was being staged for his entertainment.

I held the big man up in a headlock and wrestled him away from the petrified woman. Then I released him and waved the baseball bat threateningly.

"I don't know where the hell you think you are, but I don't stand for no dumb-ass shit in here."

"She's my wife!" the burly man shouted. "Don't you understand? Ask her." He pointed an accusatory finger at the frightened woman, who had shrunk up against the rear wall.

"What I understand is that you better get the hell out of here." I menacingly raised the Louisville slugger.

When he made a sudden move toward me in anger, I swiped the bat across his left shin. He collapsed to the floor. Holding his leg, he wailed in pain.

"Get out!" I shouted.

"My leg!" he whimpered. "I can't walk."

"Then crawl!"

He managed to climb to his feet, then limped out the front door and turned to his left. Still shrieking hysterically, the woman disappeared after him, turning in the opposite direction. I then directed my anger toward Andre.

"You, too, Andre. Out!"

"Why?" He was still seated at the booth. "I didn't do nothing, Nate."

"I said out!"

"Don't blame me. I was just sitting here minding my own business. I didn't know the bitch was married," he said, telling an obvious lie.

"I don't care whether you knew she was married or not. Take your business somewhere else from now on."

I grabbed him by his shirt and jerked him to his feet. As I was leading him, protesting, toward the front door, the woman's husband burst back into the joint. With his eyes burning he held a small pistol pointed at Andre. Before either Andre or I could react, the gun discharged in quick succession. Once, twice, then a third time it spat.

All three shots found their mark. Andre groaned and clutched at his stomach with all color draining from his face. Everyone in the place, including me, stood frozen, bug-eyed, as a blood curdling scream rose from somewhere in the crowd.

When Andre fell on his face, the man stepped closer, aiming down at Andre's prone body. Before he could pull the trigger again I laid a forceful strike with the baseball bat across the back of his head and his knees buckled. The gun clattered to the floor as he collapsed face down on top of Andre.

Awhile later, I stood outside the joint as the crime scene technicians performed the last of their duties. In the refreshing warmth of a pleasant spring day, a gathering crowd of onlookers grew larger by the minute.

The shooter had regained consciousness shortly after two blue uniforms arrived on the scene, whereupon he'd been handcuffed and taken into custody. A man from the coroner's office had pronounced Andre dead, and his body had been hauled off to the morgue.

While obtaining statements from the eyewitnesses, along with another detective, Detective Sam Brisco completed a list of names, addresses and phone numbers. Then the tall, stout detective strolled up to me with his thumbs tucked under his suspender straps.

"I want to see you around the corner at the precinct for your statement."

"If you say so," I replied. "When?"

"Right now!" he said, combatively. "You didn't think I was talking about next week, did you?"

"I'll head over there as soon as the night man shows." I glanced at my wristwatch. "He should be here any minute now."

~

Twenty minutes later, the desk sergeant asked my purpose for being there, took my name and told me to have a seat. The hard worn bench I sat on faced the pebbled glass window of Brisco's office door. Five minutes later the door opened and old Gertie came out in a hurry, blowing her nose into a handkerchief. She was so flustered as she rushed toward the exit that she failed to notice me sitting so close I could have reached out and grabbed her blouse sleeve as she fast-stepped past me in a daze.

Sam stood in the doorway of his office lighting a cigarette and studying me with a malevolent expression on his face. I started to rise from the bench, but he stopped me, signaling with the palm of his hand. He took another long draw on his cigarette, turned on a heel and disappeared back into his office.

A few moments later he reappeared carrying an empty coffee mug down at his side with a finger curled through the handle and entered the busy duty room. When he came out with a full cup of coffee, he nodded at me in passing and pointed his chin toward the open door of his office.

I followed him into the room and took a seat across from an old cluttered desk. He shut the door with his foot and languidly crossed in front of me and sat on the edge of his desk, looking down at me while biting his bottom lip and crushed his cigarette out in a large ceramic ashtray that contained at least a dozen butts.

"Want to tell me what went down?" he drawled in a bored manner.

I related the facts as he sat listening with his eyes half closed. I went on with my statement while he sipped from his steaming cup and fading sunlight slanted through the Venetian blinds of the window behind him. When I was done he yawned and scratched the scar that ran from his bottom lip to well below his chin.

"I wish all my cases were this easy to close." He grunted an aborted laugh that flashed purple gums. "But I have to take some statements anyway. Procedure and all. I'm sure you understand."

"I do."

"This two-bit squirt, Andre, getting bumped off is not the real reason I wanted to talk to you anyway. I've got another matter concerning you that's been troubling me for far too long."

"What's the beef?"

Studying me like I was a microscopic specimen under glass, he stood and grimaced as though what he had to say was too profound to say while sitting.

"Remember the talk we had a couple of Saturdays ago?" Without waiting for a response, he went on, "I was trying my best to let you know where you stood. Obviously, though, you can't take a hint. Either that or you just want to make things tough on yourself. That I don't know because I'm not a mind reader. Get me?"

"Not entirely." I stretched my legs out in front of me and folded my hands in my lap ready for the long haul.

Before speaking again he paced out of view behind me.

"I tried to remind you then what a good life you've got going. A numbers writer, making good bucks. An upstanding citizen with respect in the community. A gorgeous woman, who most men would risk dying just to get close to." He guffawed.

"And?" I said.

"And you've got your friends on the force, too. I warned you to go ahead and play it cool. But what did that mean to you? Nothing, it seems. I guess you've got a death wish. Is that it, Nate?"

He came back into view wearing a smirk that seemed to elongate his face as he ran a slow hand across his shaved head.

"It's not that I don't like you or anything." His smirk widened into a sadistic, gum-exposed grin. "But I still have a job to do. And I take a dim view of so-called friends withholding information that could make my life easier. Now do you understand me?"

"So far," I measured each word carefully, "I hear you. I even told Lieutenant McKellerhan I was sorry to have been so evasive when you asked me about Freddie Tucker. The truth be known, I was seeking him out. Doing it only to make sure that a friend of the family, a talented young sax man, Joe Weathersby, didn't get abused by some bastard like Freddie. But, when you asked me about Tucker, I was unaware that someone had already blown him away. So I made the mistake of being what I call discreet. That was my mistake."

"So instead of coming to the department to get permission to talk with the kid, you decided to go straight to the DA's office?"

"I didn't mean to ruffle any feathers. I just wanted results."

He clicked on the overhead light to illuminate the darkening room and flopped down heavily in a squeaky, swivel chair behind his desk.

"Given time I knew we would be having this conversation." He smiled with a self-satisfied gleam in his dark eyes. "So talk to me."

"There ain't much else to tell."

"Really?" His nostrils flared and his mouth puckered. Suddenly, he was on his feet again, leaning over the desk with his pink lips baring predatory teeth. "How well do you know Horace Yancy?"

"He's the plumber for Wally's," I answered, with a shrug, "What else should I know about him?"

"Did he tell you that his son had been killed by some bad dope?"

"I didn't know anything about that until I read it in the paper after everything came out. Why?"

"I could spell it out for you."

"Then, please do."

"With a little help from you, Horace Yancy killed a junkie named Johnny G and five of his boys."

I leaned back in my chair, threw my head back and put on a good belly laugh show. When I was done he walked around the desk and squatted close to me.

"I'll tell you how it went down," he whispered in my nearest ear, his breath smelling of garlic and tobacco. "Yancy comes into the bar asking for your help in tracking down who was responsible for killing his son Rudy. See?"

"Yancy," I said, "and me committing murder? That's really a big stretch. Isn't it, detective?"

"Not at all. Horace Yancy was once the owner of a registered forty-five caliber gun. He now claims the gun was ripped off from his truck a week before the shootout in question. But he never reported the gun stolen. So I say he got rid of the gun only after he got revenge for his son's death." He wore a smug expression while the silence extended itself. Then he stood. "How's that sound so far, Nathaniel?"

"I suppose you have proof of these allegations?"

"Enough to speculate." He walked around the desk and sat down in the swivel chair again. "Want to hear me out?"

"Go ahead. It's your show."

"Wally's plumber comes to you and tells you his son was poisoned by bad drugs. Right?"

"You're repeating yourself. Like I told you, that was news which only came to my attention after everyone else in the city was reading about it."

Outside, the sky had darkened considerably and only a few splinters of slanted light pierced through to fall on the desk.

"So, like I was repeating," he said, "Horace recruited you. Together the two of you wiped out those five punks in Morningside Park. Then you got to Johnny Garrison, too." He leered at me. "How am I doing so far?"

"Get real!" I said confidently, almost convinced of my own lies.

"I am real!"

"What do you base your theory on?"

"Experience," he spoke the word explicitly. "Twelve years of experience. Add to that a strong gut feeling and word I'm picking up every day from the street. Seems there's a lot to learn about you, Nathaniel, that I didn't know before. You see, there are a lot of folks around here who think you picture yourself as some kind of chocolate-covered white knight who can come charging out to rescue whoever you want anytime the feeling moves you to climb up on your charger."

I responded with raw emotion, raising my voice for the first time.

"Take off the blinders, Sam. Can't you see there's something really funky going on here? So either you're part of the cover-up or too dumb to see what's really happening right under your nose. But answer me this, who's investigating the phantom shooter? Please tell me that. Is it you, Sam? Because as far as I'm concerned all these drug cases somehow relate."

"McKellerhan and his partner have that case," he answered, calmly. "But there's no relationship. Completely different guns. Nice try, though."

"I'll bring my gun in. Run it through ballistics. Whoever killed any of these junkies wasn't me, Sam."

"That's funny. You see, I've got witnesses who saw two dudes, who fit both your description and Yancy's. They were making business arrangements with Johnny Garrison and his boys a couple of nights before they got blown away. Further investigation has given me reason to believe that a big deal was supposed to go down in Morningside Park the very same night when all the shooting took place."

"Sounds like a lot of hearsay to me."

"Perhaps. But I have a strong hunch that given time the truth will make its presence known. Given that presumption, I plan to know you better than your very own shadow does."

"You can spend the rest of your life trying to implicate me in this mess and still come up wringing your hands dry. These so-called witnesses you're talking about are probably so shady in nature you wouldn't dare bring them forward to face a jury in a court of law."

"Uh-huh. See!" he said. "Then you have an idea of who some of these witnesses might be?"

"Hell, no! I just know if they were credible you wouldn't be wasting your time with all of this half-baked nonsense you're running by me now. If you had anything to back up your theories, I would already be charged with murder. I know that much, and you know that, too."

"Sounds like you've been thinking about my position for quite awhile to come up with that conclusion."

"Call it my gut feeling, Sam!" I said with more gumption than I'd intended. "As I said earlier, I apologize for going to the DA's office instead of working things out with you or McKellerhan first. Other than that, I have no more to say."

"Is that so?" He picked up a pack of cigarettes from his desk and stuck one in his mouth but didn't light it. "I guarantee you I'll find some way to shake Yancy's alibi. When the time is right I'll grill him like a Christmas turkey. Before long he'll tell me everything I need to know. So enjoy your freedom while you can. From the way I see things, though, it won't be lasting too much longer."

"Sorry to hear you're so confident in my guilt."

"I'll push till I hit the right buttons…because it looks as though you've gone too far to turn back. One slip is all I need." He smiled, then added, "By the way, I guess I don't have to tell you that you better not leave town without telling me."

"You can save your breath on that. I'm not going anywhere." I pushed up from the seat.

Pinching the cigarette with his sickly pale lips, he leaned further back in the squeaky, swivel chair. I made it to the office door with quick purposeful strides, exited and slammed the door forcibly.

CHAPTER 16

It was 7:20 p.m. when I arrived at my flat, still highly agitated, and found a note from Lillian on the kitchen table. She'd heard about the shooting at Wally's and knew I'd been summoned to the station house to make a statement. The note went on to remind me of something already on my mind. The play she'd worked on so hard was debuting that evening and the showtime was scheduled for 8:15.

"Hope you can make it. Love, Lil," she had signed.

After a quick shower I laid out my best suit, a black, three-piece, pinstripe job, shined a pair of my favorite Stacey Adams comforts and grabbed a gray fedora. I was about to rush out and try to hail a gypsy cab when the phone rang. For a moment I considered ignoring it. On second thought I snatched up the receiver.

"We better get together soon," Brownie said.

"That's impossible tonight. Lillian's play opens in ten minutes. I'm running out the door now."

"What time will you be back?"

"Let's say," I estimated, "about twelve. We'll probably go out for drinks after the show."

"I'll call you then," he said in a constrained voice. "Until then, brother, watch your step."

Again, I was about to close the apartment door behind me when I had another change of heart. Stepping back into the flat, I went into the master bedroom and opened my sock drawer. From the far rear corner I located my .38 Detective Special laying snugly in its shoulder holster. I slipped out of my jacket and strapped the piece on. While straightening my jacket I wondered what explanation I'd give Lillian if she noticed I was packing heat.

The play had already begun when I arrived at the off-Broadway theater. I chose a seat near the rear of the packed house. From the moment I sat down I looked forward to the intermission, planning to find Lillian so we could sit together.

As I was led to expect, the play was a lavish production. The basic story line followed the efforts of a fictional Harlem man who was trying to start a theatrical company during the roaring twenties. The lead actress, whose amorous attention he sought, kept giving him the cold shoulder. Meanwhile, a young and talented chorus girl, who was in love with the main character, could not get to first base with him.

The costumes were very reminiscent of the times. The music, choreography and songs were nothing less than stunning. I found myself feeling proud of Lillian and the work she had done to help pull the show together.

Yet as colorful and lively as the play was, my mind kept wandering back to my talk with Detective Brisco. His theories were too tight, too right on the money. Again, I tried picturing Horace Yancy not breaking under an extensive interrogation. One slip of the tongue from him, and I was a goner, too. Fortunately, the junkies, who had obviously placed Yancy and me on 116th Street, were not the kind of witnesses a jury would take seriously. Still, Sam's determination to charge us with murder was frighteningly apparent.

Also clouding my thoughts were visions of being on the rooftop with Johnny G moments before he had taken the long fall to his death. He'd made veiled insinuations about the powers that backed his play. At the time I saw his posturing as a vain attempt to talk his way out of my threat of dropping him off at the nearest police station. Now I wasn't so certain. Perhaps there was a ring of truth to his frothing at the mouth accusations.

Also, Brownie had pointed out that Brisco was investigating Johnny G's death and had arrived at the scene without a partner.

I wondered if he'd gotten there before any squad cars had arrived. After all, no mention had been made about the big bag of dope, which should have been found near Johnny's body. Prowl cars had begun arriving only moments after I had slipped away from the scene. Therefore, it was doubtful that someone other than a cop had accidentally stumbled across Johnny's body and decided to grab the bag of dope for themselves.

My mind was still in an active whirl of mental gymnastics when intermission came. In the mezzanine, I spotted Lillian. She was dressed tastefully in a low-cut green satin dress and a rented mink stole. She hurried up to me, all smiles.

"Nate, I'm so glad you made it."

"Me, too, even though I was late."

"Did you miss much?"

"Whatever I missed I'll see another night."

"I heard about what happened at Wally's," she said. "How awful."

"True," I shrugged. "But I guess it's par for the course in a dive like Wally's. You know the saying, life in the big city and all that. So why don't we forget what happened for tonight and simply enjoy the play? There'll be plenty of time for us to talk about that crap later."

"You've got a deal," she said, as she rose on her tiptoes and planted a polite kiss on my nearest cheek.

After the intermission, sitting beside her helped me concentrate more on the play. When the grand finale came, the audience rose and applauded with gusto. Several curtain calls later the packed house was still showing their appreciation and filing out of the theater with smiles on their faces.

Later, Lillian and I joined most of the cast and crew at a nearby nightclub. She introduced me to the principal players who I had not already met at the open house seven days ago. I bought a few of them drinks while I tried my best to enjoy the celebration unencumbered by my own concerns.

The show's producer, Allen Bowen, noticed me in the crowd and approached me with a drink in hand.

"So what did you think of our production?" he asked.

"It was quite stunning. Although I missed the beginning, I'm looking forward to checking it out from the beginning."

"Too bad you're not a stage critic." He laughed and added, "We could use all the favorable publicity we can get."

"You'll get it. Everyone in the audience enjoyed it, and I'm sure they'll be telling all of their friends what a good time they had."

"I hope you're right," he said, before drifting back into the crowd, puffing on his meerschaum pipe.

Somewhere around midnight I could see the strain of getting the show ready had taken its toll on Lillian. So I suggested we call it a night. Outside the club I insisted we catch a taxi home. Rather than face the distinct possibility of being turned down by a white driver afraid to make a trip up to Harlem, I approached a gypsy cab parked at the curb a block away.

"If you don't mind taking us up to 137th," I said, "there's a two dollar tip in it for you."

"Juan Morales at your service," the young Hispanic driver said. "Wherever you want to go just hop into my chariot and we'll be on our way."

It was a comfortable 1955 Plymouth Belvedere, clean and roomy, and Juan took Eighth Avenue. The night was warm and both front windows were rolled halfway down. Soon the earthy smell of Central Park crept on the wind blowing through the open windows. Lillian leaned and snuggled close beside me.

"Cigarette?" Juan offered an open pack of Camels in my direction.

"No, thank you," I said, "but could you find some hip music on the radio?"

"Si." He tuned to a jazz station. "You like?"

Sassy Sarah Vaughn's voice came across the airwaves singing "Words Can't Describe."

"You're happening, Juan."

Lillian nestled even closer, listening to Sarah's sentimental lyrics. As we neared the north end of the park, her exquisite profile smiled dreamily. I felt so proud to be her man. Then her shoulder evidently edged against my piece. Suddenly, she sat erect and faced me, no longer smiling.

"Why are you wearing that?" she demanded.

"A few incidents don't add up."

"So you had to wear a gun to the opening of my play?"

"Maybe I'm just being overly cautious."

"I hope so," she said, rolling her eyes upward. "But please tell me what the hell's going on, Nathaniel."

"Can we talk about this at home?"

She turned her head away, looking out the window, fuming. Then she swung her head back around with her eyes blazing.

"I need to know what's happening now!"

"Okay." I sighed, then spoke in a subdued voice. "Do you know Horace Yancy, Wally's plumber?"

"Yes. You pointed him out to me once."

"His son was poisoned by some bad dope about four weeks ago. He asked me to ask around to find out who might've sold it to him. Then it turned out the guys who may have been responsible were the same junkies who got mowed down in Morningside Park."

Sassy Sarah ended the song, as the tires hummed through the open windows. An instrumental began on the radio that I had heard before but I could not think of the title or bandleader's name.

"So?" Lillian's eyes were moist.

"Of all the people out there who might have done it, well, in Detective Brisco's mind, I'm the alleged perpetrator."

"You!" She appeared confused, then said, "I still don't understand the gun. How's that fit into what you're telling me?"

"It's simple, dear. I don't trust Brisco."

While she was evaluating that, I noticed an old Caddy tooling along beside us. There were two rough-looking hooligans in the front seat. Their eyes looked past Lillian and fell on me. I noticed another dude in the rear. Our eyes met and I saw a deadly gleam register as he raised something in our direction.

Within a fraction of a second the object in his hands became identifiable as the double barrels of a shotgun jutting from an open window. A moment before one of the barrels thundered and glass shattered, I pulled Lillian toward me twisting my body to shield her.

She screamed as I pushed her to the floor with me on top. Shock filled her eyes and I spotted blood on the side of her face.

Tires screeched as the Belvedere swerved and Juan cursed in Spanish. As the car lurched forward faster, another blast shattered the rear window and sprayed us with a thousand splintered shards of glass.

Lillian shivered in my arms but didn't scream this time. I assessed the damage done to her. She had one deep scratch on the side of her forehead, and I felt blood seeping from the back of her head.

But all the wounds appeared to be superficial, coming from flying glass.

"Did you take a direct hit?" I shouted above the roar of the two car engines and their racing tires.

"I don't think so," she said, between frightened gasps for air.

The sound of a smaller gunfire punctuated the air and bullets thumped along the side of the Belvedere.

Juan cursed in Spanish again as the fenders of the two cars clashed. Then the Belvedere fishtailed, skidded and straightened out. Pulling my piece out I got up from the floor and peeked out the shattered rear window. The Caddy was about five feet behind us.

The driver was trying to maneuver alongside us again. But Juan zigzagged cutting in and out of traffic. Then the Caddy jumped into the oncoming traffic lane making up distance fast as a host of horns blared. The front gunman leaned most of his body out of the window. He aimed a small caliber handgun as the guy in the rear appeared to be reloading the shotgun.

"Lose 'em!" I yelled to Juan.

As the Caddy closed on us I leaned out the side window and fired two quick shots at the driver's face. The windshield exploded and the Caddy careened and screeched and seemed to pick up speed as the front gunman grabbed for the wheel.

Again fenders clashed with an ear splitting sound.

I ducked to the floor as the shotgun once again roared above the chaos. That's when I assume one of the tires on the Belvedere blew. Amidst the clashing of nickel-plated bumpers there was a sudden hard crashing jolt. Then we spun around like a manic merry-go-round sliding sideways along the Avenue.

Nearby, the Caddy slammed headlong into a telephone pole. The Belvedere's forward motion ceased when its right side crashed into a parked car.

Lillian and I were crumpled together on the floor. She wrapped her arms around me, sobbing, with blood now streaming down the side of her face. Sirens rent the air.

I pulled myself upright and away from her. Behind us an immense explosion lit the night sky. Through the front window of the Belvedere, now turned south, I saw one of the gunmen staggering away from the blazing Caddy.

Quickly I clambered from the wreckage. The man was a good hundred feet away and a ball of orange flames silhouetted him.

The gunman staggered farther from the blazing car as I ran toward him. He spotted me then turned his head to see the flashing lights of a prowl car speeding from the opposite direction up Lennox Avenue.

Still running, about thirty feet away from him, I slowed to a stop and aimed my .38. He made a few quick steps toward an alley.

"Stop!" I yelled.

He screamed something unintelligible and jerked his gun in my direction and fired a reckless shot. Three times I fired back until he rocked, tilted and fell over backwards. On the way down his gun discharged once more toward the sky.

I closed the distance between us with long strides. Kneeling beside him I saw his eyes roll back in his head and blood gushing from his mouth.

"Who sent you?" I screamed in his face.

As the hood's fading eyes strained to focus on me, a prowl car screeched to a halt at the curb. The dying paddy tried to spit up at me but died trying. Two cops in blue were out of their squad car, inching forward, tense, with their guns drawn and trained on me.

"Drop the gun!" one of them commanded.

CHAPTER 17

With my head throbbing incessantly, I slipped back into the conscious world. It took awhile to orient myself and put together the events that found me waking up alone in a cell inside the 30th Precinct. Oddly enough, the first thing I remembered was the name of the bandleader whose song came on the radio after Sassy Sarah's song and before the shooting started. In the darkness, without my wristwatch, I had no idea what time it was or how long I'd been unconscious. I did know that one side of my face was caked with dried blood.

After the shootout, when the two cops approached me on Lennox Avenue, I dropped my gun as ordered. However, my desperation in pointing out Lillian's need for an ambulance caused them to start manhandling me. Within a matter of a few minutes the entire scene had transformed into something that resembled a cop's convention. Meanwhile, I kept shouting for one of them to call for medical assistance while jostling with the two cops who were holding me.

Shortly after that the world went black.

It was almost 8:00 a.m., I discovered much later, when two officers in blue appeared at the cell door. When one of them called my name I was still woozy as I got to my feet. A sergeant opened the cell door and handcuffed me while his partner held a gun trained on me. Then they led me upstairs to Lieutenant McKellerhan's office. One of them knocked on the door.

"Bring him in," McKellerhan's booming voice commanded.

I stepped into the room to find him and Detective Tommy O'Brien. McKellerhan was at a desk so small it made the bulky man appear even larger. O'Brien was standing at a side window smoking a cigarette with a cocky grin on his face.

"You can take those off." McKellerhan pointed to the cuffs I was wearing.

"Yes, sir," the sergeant complied.

"That will be all," McKellerhan dismissed the men in blue.

When they stepped out of the room and closed the door, McKellerhan motioned for me to have a seat across the desk from him. Weak and dizzy from the short walk up the stairs, I slumped down in the seat straining to keep my head erect.

"Want to tell us what happened?" McKellerhan asked.

"First," I spoke through parched lips, "how's my girlfriend?"

"You're the one here to answer questions," O'Brien said, while mashing his cigarette butt in an ashtray on the corner of McKellerhan's desk.

"Not until I find out about my girlfriend."

Before O'Brien could respond, McKellerhan barked, "Shut up, Tommy! Make yourself useful. Go get him a wet towel for his head."

O'Brien stiffened, paused a moment, then walked toward the door.

"And bring him some coffee."

O'Brien exited the room, shutting the door behind him.

"Now," I said, "about Lillian?"

"She was rushed over to Harlem Hospital. Although she's in pretty good shape, she did suffer some bruises. And they had to shave her head to stitch it up right."

"Dammit." I grimaced at the thought.

"To be on the safe side the doctor in charge said they'd be keeping her overnight for observation."

"How about her state of mind? Can you tell me that?"

"I did talk with her for a few minutes," he said, dropping his eyes. "But I didn't want to press her. You should know, though, she's extremely pissed off. She was even ready to walk out of there after they put in the stitches. It took awhile for the doctor to convince her to stay the night."

"Thanks for passing the word on," I said, unable to shake myself free of knowing how much harm I'd caused to the one person I truly loved.

"Not a problem." His blue eyes narrowed, as he leaned closer across the desk. "Now, back to the business at hand. Mind telling me how you ended up involved in a major shootout on my turf?"

"One more thing. How did the driver of the Plymouth come out?"

"He was out cold for a while but came around before long. He's at Harlem, too. They think he may have a slight concussion. However, with the jam you're in, I wouldn't worry too much about him."

O'Brien came back into the office and set a mug of coffee on the desk and handed me a damp towel, which I put to immediate use.

"You can make yourself useful elsewhere, Tommy," McKellerhan said in a low rumble. "I'll handle this."

"Whatever you say, sir."

O'Brien left the two of us alone again while I continued wiping dried blood from my face, after which I dropped the towel to the floor. Then I washed down the cobwebs in my mouth with a few sips of bitter, lukewarm coffee.

"Now, Nate," McKellerhan leaned back in his chair with hands behind his bulging neck, "about the shooting."

"Lillian had a play open near 42nd Street," I said, letting the words tumble freely from my lips. "After the show we went for cocktails around the corner to a place called—"

"All that I know already. What happened after is what I'm interested in finding out."

"Around about twelve o'clock I asked Juan for a ride. We were heading home, having a peaceful ride along the avenue. Then all hell broke loose."

"And you just happened to be packing iron?"

"Thank God I was!" I took another sip of the horrible coffee and pushed the mug aside.

"That so?" Another scowl lined his forehead. "That's unusual, though, isn't it, for you to be packing?"

"I have a permit to carry as I'm sure you know by now. And the way things have been shaping up lately it seemed like a good idea."

"What things?"

"You probably heard about some of it." I cleared my throat. "I was in here yesterday."

"The incident in the bar, huh? A jealous husband thing, wasn't it?"

"Exactly. All I was expecting was to come in and make the usual statement. It wasn't the first shooting I witnessed."

"That I know about." He rotated two fingers in an impatient circle. "So what else happened?"

"Brisco happened," I said, harshly, but McKellerhan registered no reaction. "He listened to my report politely for about three whole minutes. Then he began to cook up some notion to pin his entire caseload of murders on me."

"What murders?" He leaned forward placing his elbows on the desk, making a tent of his fingers, locking his cold, blue eyes onto mine.

"The Morningside Park massacre."

Noticing his eyes widen slightly, it was apparent that Brisco's theory was not one he had shared with the lieutenant or the bear-like man was a far better actor than I gave him credit for.

"Pretty wild, huh?" I chuckled.

"Well," he said, with one bushy eyebrow raised, "Sam's been under a lot of pressure lately. We all have. As preposterous as his notion might sound to you, or me for the matter, I'm sure Sam must've had good cause to question you along those lines."

"That's easy for you to say. No one tried to gun you and your lady down last night."

"True," he scoffed. "But I still don't get the connection. Exactly what role did Sam see you playing over there in the park?"

"Why don't you ask him?"

"Because I'm asking you," he said, with a gentle purr that sounded dangerous.

I sipped more coffee to discourage the cobwebs that were clamming up my mouth again.

"Horace Yancy is the plumber for Wally's. His son was one of the users who was killed by some bad junk awhile back."

"Go on."

"According to Brisco's brilliant theory, Yancy and I set up the cats in the park. Then we blew them away."

"Uh-huh!" McKellerhan grunted and began to chew his bottom lip, as his restless eyes settled on me. "Still, I'm not following your angle. Why were you carrying your thirty-eight last night?"

"Who, with a gun, wouldn't pack it after being told some street hustling junkies were passing rumors about them killing some of their boys?"

"I see." He scratched the deep cleft in his chin. "So that's what you think this attack boils down to?"

"Maybe. But maybe you can tell me better. You've had plenty of time to get a make on the palooka I took down."

McKellerhan grimaced wide enough for his faulty dental work to show.

"That's asking a lot of confidential information from me, Nate."

"Let me remind you again, Lieutenant," I said, straining to keep my composure, "my lady and I were shot at last night by bona fide hit men if I ever saw any. And one of them was wielding a sawed-off shotgun. If I'd been a fraction of a second slower ducking us out of the way, my woman and I would both be dead."

"Okay!" He relented after a long, thoughtful silence. "Against my better judgment I'll give you something to fill your pipe with. Not that it will do you much good except to know what you might be up against."

He pushed away from the desk, stood, cracked his knuckles and walked to a slender side window to stare out toward the sound of the traffic passing below.

The new silence was filled with a gruff laugh from the duty room, the hunt-and-peck of a typewriter, a pair of heavy footsteps passing the lieutenant's door. All of that blended with McKellerhan breathing as though the oxygen in the room was running low.

"You've heard of the Donzani family, of course?" He turned and ambled back to his desk with his eyes downcast and his hands clutched behind his back.

"Their names make the papers regularly."

"That's right."

A harsh rasping sound escaped his throat. Then he smiled wryly with a slight growl, sat and pulled the lower left-hand corner of his desk drawer open. He dug inside of it and grabbed a near empty pint bottle of rye and set it down on the scarred desk covered with reports. From the same desk drawer, he came up with a stack of Dixie cups, pulled two of them free and placed one in front of me.

"You could probably use one of these. I know I sure as hell can."

He poured the dark amber liquid with a practiced hand and screwed the top on with a half twist and set the bottle down between us. We touched cups and threw the shots down.

"What I'm about to tell you is off the record, naturally. But it's information you'd probably find out in due time anyway." He winked. "The Donzani family fought tooth and nail for years to maintain their stranglehold on the Lower East Side in a war with the Altamares. Carmen Altamare, his brother Alphonso, and their boys, are the ones I'm talking about. But Joe Donzani and his clan came out on top. They had the guns. See? Guys from Philly and Detroit stepped in to give him a hand. Believe me, it was one big bloody mess before the dust settled. About six months ago, or thereabouts, is when this all went down."

"I recall reading something about it."

"Now for the last couple of months there have been a lot of back stabbings and squabblings between everybody and their grandmother, trying to get on the good side of the victors. Enter those three punks who tried to gun you down."

Equally, he poured the last corner of his pint into the waiting paper cups.

"So far I'm following you," I said.

"The two bodies in the Caddy were fried to a fine crisp, and we haven't been able to identify them as of yet. The one shooter, though, the guy you popped—"

"Yeah?"

"That was Jake O'Shaughnessy."

I reached for the cup of rye and lifted it in a salutory manner. He did the same, and we threw two more shots down our gullets.

I cleared my throat and asked, "Tell me about this guy, O'Shaughnessy."

"He's your typical thug from around Tenth Street and Avenue A. He was thirty-two years old with a long criminal history. Murder-one before he was seventeen. That was just one of the raps he beat. Whatever we busted him on he walked away from. In other words, he had a long habit of beating the law and laughing about it afterwards. The stuff legends down there in that neighborhood are built on."

"But where does this Jake O'Shaughnessy fit in with the Italian mob?"

"Until recently," he said, as he snatched the empty pint from the desktop and dropped it into a waste basket, "he fit in no-where. But things have changed now that heroin has become such a profitable business venture. The Tenth Street boys are obviously bullying their way in to pull off the muscle jobs or acting as couriers. A piece in the action is what they want. Exactly who they represent and where they really stand in the grand scheme of things, that's what nobody on our side of the fence can figure. Not yet, at least, because the picture seems to be changing from day-to-day."

"It's all about the drug trade," I said, almost to myself, "isn't it?"

"That's not it entirely." McKellerhan slapped his thick, chaffed hands and rubbed them together and stood up wearing a wan smile mixed with a tinge of what looked to me like regret. "It's not all about the drugs, son."

The big man walked back to the morning-lit window and leaned his hands on the dusty sill of the filmy, barred aperture.

"It's about all the rackets, per se," he said, in a low, almost strangled voice that echoed off the window. "What brings in a healthy profit? That's the question. See? That's what brings out the predators, the scavengers, the bloodsuckers and other parasites. Say it's a sex thrill, a high some folks get that puffing reefer gives them. Or when it comes to gambling, say, a chance to bet on a prizefight, a horse race, a ballgame, an eight ball in the corner pocket. You name it."

He turned back to face me, wearing a sentimental-like expression that looked out of place on him or in the room, and went on.

"Then you got the numbers racket, the same game you front for in that dive around the corner where you work. Folks hoping to win a hundred dollars or more. It might as well be the promise of a trip to the moon. Nevertheless, they keep lining up to take their chances, don't they? But I don't make the rules, Nate. I just enforce the will of the status quo and do my best to protect them as much as I can. That's all, pal. Because, well... um...that's what I get paid to do. It's my job."

"I see," I said, more to myself than to him.

CHAPTER 18

I collected my personal belongings along with my gun. When I walked out of the precinct, there was only one goal on my mind, which was to get Lillian out of the city as fast as possible. The hazy morning sunlight hit my eyes with a laser-like intensity. It caused my aching head to throb more with each heartbeat. I felt hungry, worn out and grubby in my wrinkled blood-caked clothes. In the face of more pressing concerns, however, I immediately dismissed my discomfort, including the fact that I had not eaten anything since noon the day before.

I picked up a copy of *Daily News* at a candy store and hopped a bus. Most of the people, especially the bus driver, gave me a double-take as though I were a leper in my bloody clothes.

On page one of the newspaper there was a photograph of the gunman, Jake O'Shaughnessy, lying dead in the middle of the sidewalk on Lennox Avenue. I turned my attention to the accompanying story and read the text quickly. Lillian's name had been omitted but I was tagged. I left the newspaper behind when I jumped off the bus near Harlem Hospital.

Lillian was in a private room. She sat on the side of the bed dressed in a green hospital gown with surgical gauze shrouding her head. When she looked up to see me standing in front of her, her eyes looked vacuous. Even though McKellerhan had given me an idea of what to expect, I still wasn't prepared to see her looking the way she did. She smiled weakly as silent and pained inquiries begged at the corners of her eyes. They blinked nervously a few times, then seethed with anger and frustration.

"Hold me for a minute," she said in a whispered voice.

She sat there stiffly, not resisting, yet not returning my embrace.

"I…I'm so sorry, Lillian." I held her closer, feeling like dog shit. "Truly sorry."

"You don't look too good yourself."

"I've been at the station house all night."

Still holding her, I tried to will away her fear and confusion.

"They had to give me a sedative last night," she informed me.

A middle-aged nurse, who was all smiles, marched into the room with a swish of her starched uniform.

"Look who's all ready to go home," she said. "And your boyfriend's here, too."

"Yes," Lillian answered, absently. "How soon can I go?"

"I just talked to your doctor," the nurse said, eyeing me dubiously after checking out the condition I was in. "He'll be here soon. He wants to take another look at you before you're released."

"I want to go now," Lillian insisted.

"Just be patient, sweetie. We're only talking a little longer. After all, you've got your whole young and glorious life ahead of you."

"If I want to go right now," Lillian said, "you can't stop me. Can you?"

"Technically speaking, you should wait for the doctor to release you. He might want to prescribe some painkillers you may need. But fear not, my child, we won't hold you against your will. Although, as a matter of precaution, you would have to sign a statement saying you chose to leave against the hospital's recommendation."

"Could you give us a minute?" I asked the nurse.

"Certainly," she said, then strutted from the room.

Lillian curled her legs under the covers of the bedclothes and sat up with her back against the headboard.

"What is it, Nate?"

"I think it might be a good idea if you went somewhere to stay for a couple days."

"I don't want to hear that." She closed her eyes and exhaled. "I want to go home."

"Just a few days to be on the safe side. I need time to check things out."

"What about the dance studio?"

"You're not even supposed to be there today. Remember?"

"That's right. Betty's covering for me." Her voice was listless. "Since you seem to have everything all figured out, where would I stay?"

"How about with your friend, Vera, on the island? We haven't been out there in over a year."

She finally agreed, but it took considerably longer to convince her that I should go to the flat alone to pack a suitcase for her.

"You wait here. I'll borrow Wally's car and be back within the hour."

She was about to protest, but I put a finger to her lips.

"Shush, lie back, close your eyes and relax. I'll be back in a flash."

I gathered her clothes from the night before and took them with me. Bloodstains on the rented mink stole and her pretty green dress were further reminders of how close she'd come to being snuffed out.

From a phone booth in the hospital lobby, I reached Wally at home. He'd already read the morning paper and caught TV coverage of the shooting. So when I asked to borrow his Pontiac, he agreed without hesitation. I got a long distance operator to look up and dial Lillian's friend, Vera Branch, who lived way out in the sticks on Long Island.

"I was just about to step out and do my Saturday morning shopping," she said, bubbling with life. "How was the play last night? I'm hoping I—"

"Vera!" I cut her off. "Lillian needs a place to stay for a couple of days. Things have turned ugly here."

"Don't tell me you two had a fight."

"That's not it. But it'd be better if we explain everything once we get there."

"Oh, of course," she said, sounding perplexed. "In case you've forgotten, let me give you directions."

~

I picked up Wally's new aqua-green Pontiac Bonneville and made a stop at the flat. The most difficult decisions of the morning came figuring out what to pack for Lillian. After that guessing game was done, I threw some water on my face and slipped into a casual outfit. As an afterthought, I opened one of the two suitcases I'd packed and tossed in a wig that Lillian sometimes wore.

Satisfied that I had done my best, I made it back to the hospital, parked in a space reserved for a doctor, grabbed both suitcases and rushed up to meet Lillian. After a bit of fussing around she decided on an outfit that was suitable and changed into it. Then she donned the wig, a long, black frizzy job. She blanched when she saw her reflection in the mirror and had to turn the wig just right so the gauze wrapping didn't show beneath it. Lastly, she covered her eyes with a pair of oversized sunglasses.

While driving away from the hospital I checked the rearview mirror often. When I was certain we weren't being tailed I jumped on the Harlem River Drive heading north to the Cross Bronx Expressway. Soon we were crossing the long expanse of the Whitestone Bridge. With the city fading behind us I began to relax a bit.

It was an overcast morning with low drifting clouds turning the sky to a cotton candy gray. And before long we were rolling east on Route 25, also known as the Jericho Turnpike.

"I still feel like I'm in a daze," Lillian remarked. "I guess it's the medication they gave me."

"I'd say, under the circumstances, you're doing fine."

Thirty minutes or so later, on the secondary rural highway, we rolled through one of those ready-made communities that were popping up all over the island. It had been completed since our last drive to Vera's.

Dozens of tree-lined streets sat at the foot of a bluff side. Shafts of sunlight cut through the clouds and glittered on rows and rows of freshly painted pastel-colored houses. The black-top asphalt was so new it looked as though it had been poured that morning, and a tall steeple of a church marked the sky.

A mile or two later we came close to the grounds of a new high school. Traffic was slowed by a mass of cars entering the parking lot. Judging by all the pom-poms I saw, and the festive mood of the folks in their cars, I assumed they were attending a track meet or a baseball game. Traffic opened up again a couple of hundred feet past the school grounds.

Then sprawling shopping centers, service stations and restaurants dotted the highway. I couldn't help noticing that all the white faces I saw looked freshly scrubbed and carefree. Appraising them in swift passing, it was hard to imagine any one of them with troubling thoughts that might keep them awake at night like Lillian and me.

"How about some coffee?" I suggested when my stomach growled loud enough for her to hear.

"Sounds like you could use some breakfast, and a bit of food sounds good to me."

While we were waiting for our meals in a rustic, roadside diner, Lillian called Vera to tell her more about the true nature for our visit and to make sure that she would not be too shocked by her appearance. When we were done eating we lingered in the diner over more coffee. That's when I told her about my talk with Lieutenant McKellerhan, the O'Shaughnessy link and the implied mob ties.

"For some reason," I explained, "I must be on their shit list."

"Did McKellerhan offer you any advice?"

"No. But in so many words he did practically justify all the rackets as something that came with big city life."

She shook her head as though thinking along those lines was too much for her to comprehend at the moment.

"What's your next move going to be?" she eventually asked. "Drop me off, then what?"

Sipping the bland coffee, I thought about how to answer.

"Damn if I know where to start. Brownie was trying to tell me something important the other night when I was running out to catch the play. I told him to hold up until we could talk later."

"And," Lillian said, "I guess you haven't had much spare time since then."

"To say the least."

"Still," Lillian frowned, "I can't spend the rest of my life hiding out at Vera's."

"A talk with Brownie should help clear up a few things. The local dealers are all probably connected somehow. It's about finding the common denominator."

"What I'd like to know is how Lieutenant McKellerhan reacted when you told him about the case Brisco was trying to build against you."

"It seemed as though he was hearing that line of reasoning for the first time. Either that or he's a better actor than I give him credit for. But I definitely got the impression he could run with Sam's line if it cleared the case off the docket. After all, he still has a job to hold onto. Without the power that gives him, he couldn't bum a dime."

I almost shared a hunch that the only thing McKellerhan seemed surprised about was the fact I was armed at the time of the attack. However, I held that back, figuring Lillian had enough to worry about without hearing that.

"So…besides meeting with Brownie," she said, "what do you intend to do?"

"I'm not sure, but I don't want you to worry."

She frowned more severely, making a sad sight of herself with the wig and what I knew it was covering.

"Isn't it a little too late to try keeping me in the dark?"

"Right now I'm only concerned with getting you out of town. I haven't really thought too far beyond that. However, I think the next best move for me to make is to get in touch with my friend Howard Katz with the district attorney's office. If McKellerhan and Brisco are on the take, there's no telling how high the corruption goes. I need someone independent and far removed from their control. I can only hope Howie's that man."

Lillian started to say something then took off her sunglasses and folded her hands on the table in front of her.

"There's one thing more I need to know." Her eyes were penetrating.

"What's that?"

"Did you really have anything, I mean…anything at all to do with what happened in Morningside Park?" She interrupted me as I was about to respond. "That's something I need to know, Nate. So please, tell me the truth."

"What kind of question is that? "

"Don't answer a question with a question this time around."

"You think I'm cold blooded enough to—"

She blinked her eyes several times before demanding, "Were you involved or not?"

"You're almost as bad as Sam Brisco." I shook my head and looked out of the diner at the passing traffic. "If I did have anything to do with Morningside Park, do you think I would tell anyone?"

"I wish you'd stop avoiding the question. Yes or no?"

Staring her straight in the eyes, I said, "No! I didn't have anything to do with what happened that night."

I figured our conversation was over for the time being until Lillian reached out and placed a hand on the restaurant receipt as I reached for it.

"There's something you should know about Detective Brisco and why he may be acting the way he is."

"Huh?" Her words were like a kick in the gut. "I don't get it. What about him?"

"Shortly after you and I started going together, he started hitting on me." Before I could respond she went on, "He'd pull over whenever he saw me on the street or come into a store while I was shopping and pick up where he'd left off."

"Isn't that something you should have told me about way before now?"

"I didn't see any reason to do that, because I let him know I wasn't the least bit interested in his advances. The mere thought of me going out with someone as crass and unsophisticated as him makes my stomach turn. As far as me telling you goes, though, what do you expect me to do, Nathaniel, give you a full report every time some guy makes a pass at me? No, I am quite capable of handling situations like that without making a big deal out of them."

"I just wish I'd known. Then I might have understood why he kept bringing your name up so many times."

"Well," she stared at me defiantly, "now you know, like I know so much more about you. Anyway, what would you have done differently if you'd known before?"

I declined to answer, picked up the check and suggested we get back on the road.

~

Vera Branch grew up in the Bronx with Lillian, and they'd been friends since grade school. For the last three years she'd worked as a nurse at Kings Park Psychiatric Center, which was located near the middle of the island. Her house, however, was farther east near Northville.

The private road to her small ranch house ran for a quarter of a mile through a heavily forested area. The house was erected on a cinderblock foundation and was centered on several acres of land. To the rear of the house was her proudest possession, a moderate size greenhouse. It was a good fourteen by twenty feet with a peaked roof that stood about fifteen feet tall at the center. That's where Vera cultivated a variety of exotic trees, plants, flowers, vegetables and herbs.

Vera and her dog Chester, a golden Labrador retriever, emerged from the house as soon as we pulled into the circular driveway that cut through a stand of pine and scrub oaks.

She was a rosy chocolate-skinned woman, who was almost as tall as me, full-bodied with a vibrant personality and an out-spoken nature. Wagging his tail, Chester barked and growled, sniffed at Lillian and me and then went off running hither and thither, still wagging his tail. After Vera greeted Lillian, and led her toward the house, I retrieved the suitcases from the trunk of the car.

Later, Lillian and Vera both insisted that I stay for dinner. While they prepared the meal, talking over old times, I took a walk in the woods at the rear of the property. By a standing ar-rangement, Chester accompanied me.

A foot-worn path curved through brittle oak and pines with fallen limbs scattered here and there. Chester disappeared from view now and then, but I stuck to the path. Vera had warned me more than once that yellow jackets build their nest in the ground but not along the path.

About a quarter of a mile into the woods I reached a high spot located near enough to see the northern shore overlooking the Long Island Sound. In the fading light of day I could see the vague landmass and twinkling haze of lights coming from Connecticut across the wide span of water.

On past occasions, that was where I'd always turned around to head back to the house. But following Chester's lead, as though he were trying to show me something new, I decided to go farther. Before long, off the path and cutting through the woods on a different angle, I soon heard the hum of sparse traffic. A short hike later Chester and I came to the edge of a two-lane bypass.

From there I could make out a fork in the road to my left and the familiar landmark of a church not far from the entrance to Vera's private road. Chester seemed proud of the fact that he had introduced this new discovery to me, as though he were saying by mental telepathy, "See where you are now?"

"Good boy. Good boy."

He wagged his tail and licked at my face while I affectionately rubbed his shoulders and back.

"You're a far better sidekick than the Chester that Marshall Dillon has on TV. Plus, you don't walk with a limp either."

Once again thinking about Vera's warning of yellow jackets, I decided to skirt the church's property yet stay close to the road on the way back to the front of Vera's house. Chester must have assumed I could find my own way, because that was the last I saw of him until I was ready to drive back to the city.

Lillian tried to convince me to stay over for the night, but I insisted on leaving. Around 8 o'clock she accompanied me to the Bonneville. The night sky was filled with dark, fast-shifting clouds and the threat of rain was in the air. She was wrapped up in one of Vera's coats with the hood up.

"Remember who loves you," Lillian said as we embraced.

"I promise. But one thing does bother me."

"Well, don't keep me guessing. What is it?"

"I wonder how you could so easily believe that I might be capable of doing what Brisco claims."

"Not so easily, Nate." She stood back but close enough for me to read her eyes in the dark and shaded by the coat's hood.

"When I first met you, a few of my girlfriends, and even a couple of your so-called friends, implied that you live a kind of daring double life."

She went on ignoring my attempt to interrupt her.

"They were all trying to clue me in, as they put it. But I'm not blind or stupid, Nate. I saw what I wanted to see and assured them that whatever you did when you were not with me was your own business and not mine or theirs. Soon enough, though, I found myself believing exactly what I wanted to believe. All those long walks of yours, in the middle of the night, I trained myself not to worry or even think a lick about. That's because I kept trusting you to always handle whatever came your way. And I left it at that, Nathaniel."

"Until—" I said, thinking about how Brisco seemed to enjoy the discomfort he caused me whenever he used my full first name.

"No, Nate," she said, "don't say anymore. Just go back to the city and do whatever it is you have to do and come back for me as soon as you can."

She rose to her tiptoes and briefly touched my lips with hers. Then abruptly, she turned and hurried away toward the warm inviting glow of Vera's ranch house.

CHAPTER 19

It was close to ten that evening when I parked Wally's Bonneville in the garage near his Seventh Avenue flat. Inside the vestibule of the stately corner building where he and his wife resided, I buzzed him. A long minute later the intercom sizzled with his gruff voice.

"Who's there?"

"Nate, Wally."

When the release button sounded I pushed through the thick entrance door and hit the steps two at a time. Wally was at the door of his third-floor flat when I stepped into the hallway.

"Sorry I'm late." I handed him the car keys.

"No problem, buddy. How'd things go?"

"I got Lillian stuck away somewhere safe. It's too soon to tell about anything."

"I'm sure you'll work things out."

"Thanks for the use of the car. And look for me Monday morning, eh?"

"Wait, Nate." He stepped into the hall and tugged at my retreating sleeve. "Don't run off so fast."

"What's on your mind?"

"I just wanted to tell you something." He eased his apartment door a hair's breath from closed and his voice was tight. "The trouble you're in—"

"What about it?"

He shuffled a step or two and the age lines in his face scowled at me as he flung his hands out to his side.

"In a way I feel responsible for the jam you're in. That's all I'm trying to say."

"Why would you say that?"

"Getting you involved with Yancy." He gave me a dumb-founded look and screwed his old face up into more wrinkled skin than I'd ever seen. "That's what's bothering me."

"How do you mean?"

"C'mon, now. You know what I'm trying to say. When Horace's son got done in, he was crying on my shoulder one day when you were off to speak to that kid in jail. That's when I suggested he should talk to you."

"What were you looking for, a commission?"

"Can the crap, Nate. I'm being serious."

"So you think Horace latched onto me? Did he tell you something like that? Is that it?"

"All I'm trying to say is I told Horace you might be able to help him out. Whether or not he ever followed up on what I suggested is anybody's guess. And whether it would have had anything to do with what happened a couple of Fridays ago is also up in the air, too. Ain't it?"

"I guess—"

"Still and all, if I can help you out of this mess you're caught up in, you know where I am."

"Thanks, Wally. I'll remember that."

"Nothing to it, kid. Want some time off you just say so."

"Naw. What the hell? I've still got all of tonight and tomor-row off. All things considered I should be ready to do my shift come Monday morning."

"Just in case," Wally screwed his face up again, "I'll show up in the morning on Monday. Meantime, why don't you get some rest? You look like a pile of shit warmed over."

"Thanks for the observation."

He jiggled the car keys in a crinkled black hand, slipped his door open, nodded wearily in my direction and disappeared into his flat.

Shortly after I ducked out of Wally's Seventh Avenue build-ing, a hard spring rain began to slash down with a vengeance. Hugging close to the buildings I fast-stepped looking for a gypsy cab driver. Then the roar of a super-charged engine and slicing headlights cut a corner and splayed on me. Looking over a shoulder I recognized the black and red, two-toned Bel Air and Brownie behind the wheel. He threw the passenger-side door open and I slid in beside him.

"About time I found you, super-sport." He revved the engine and sped down the street before asking, "How's Lillian?"

"A little scarred up but taking things far better than I have any right to expect."

"From what I heard, I just missed you at the hospital by about ten minutes. A girl I know at the front desk remembered seeing y'all leaving and the Pontiac you drove off in. I figured it was Wally's."

"I had to get Lillian out of town."

"Smart move. After I missed you at the hospital I swung by your place. Lucky I did too, bro."

"Why?"

"Your flat's bugged. I saw the team leaving as I pulled up. I hung around for a while to warn you. Then it became evident that you had something else in mind."

"Are you sure they bugged me?"

"I know the wire guys, man. Fortunately, they didn't spot me cruising by and checking them coming out of your building. Believe me, though, smart money says it's your flat they bugged. The question is what the hell do they think they're going to learn?"

"Who the hell knows?" I shrugged.

"I've got a spot to put you up in, up in Yonkers. In the meantime let me bring you up to date on what Vince and I've been piecing together since we last saw you."

"Good deal," I said, feeling weary. "I want to swing by my place anyway."

"Come on, man!"

I gave him a look that spoke volumes.

"You'd best run in and out real quick. If you do show up there, I would guess they'll probably be expecting you to stay put. But that's just a guess. There's no telling who might high-tail it over there. And whoever they are, for all we know, they may come in blasting."

"Drop me a block away. I'll go in the back door."

"Maybe I should go up with you. They may have left some-one sitting on the place."

"If they did, whoever it is will find himself in real big trouble."

~

I slid the key into the lock and opened the door gently. Inching inside with my gun drawn, I went through the dark rooms, one at a time. Presently, I gathered I was alone and switched on some light. Next I turned my radio on to mask the sound of my movements. Then I went to a secret cache hidden deep in my closet. I was gratified that the four hundred dollars I'd stashed away in a pair of rundown sneakers was still there.

Upon further inspection it didn't appear that the place had been searched. Nothing seemed disturbed in the slightest. However, though the place looked unchanged, something about it seemed transformed. It was like a house of mirrors with its soul stripped, like a performing arts stage I had starred on that no longer remembered me.

Once more I began gathering clothes—this time, my own. I felt both foolish and reckless coming back to my flat know-ing that it was bugged. But there was a rage churning inside me that relegated logic and reason to secondary considerations. Flashing back to the attempt on my life, which almost took Lillian's as well, ignited a flurry of emotions, not the least of which was a yearning for revenge.

If I'd not seen the gunman at the very moment I spotted him we would both be dead. Now both of us were on the lam, hiding like fugitives. I didn't like it one bit and if I could have brought matters to a showdown, I would have jumped at the opportu-nity without a moment's hesitation.

It was the unknown that spooked me. I was pitted against an enemy with no idea of how many they numbered. The friends of the dead man, O'Shaughnessy, and his two equally dead cohorts, plus Joe Donzani and the five borough families, were enough of a menace to make me feel jittery and increasingly desperate.

But there was also the nagging threat that Brisco was trying to nail me as the mastermind and accomplice involved in six homicides. Moreover, if the police were in cahoots with the drug lords, how deep did the pack go and how far up the ladder did the corruption extend? Even more distressing was the realization that if a rogue cop was indeed the phantom shooter, he could easily set me up, put a bullet or two in me, drop a dirty gun in my hand and become an overnight hero.

I thought about all that and more as I crammed a suitcase full. The last item I grabbed was a box of .38 shells. On the spot I reloaded the empty chambers of my Detective Special and stuck the half-filled box in my jacket pocket.

As I climbed down the stairwell and reached the fourth floor, another door below whooshed open and then bolted shut with a loud reverberating clank. I peeked over the rail and saw the shoulders, arms and legs of two blues and someone in plainclothes ascending the stairs. Their footsteps echoed off the walls like small caliber gunfire.

I slipped into the hallway and gently eased the thick, metal door shut with a muffled whoosh and a quiet click. Tensely, I waited as the marching footsteps reached the fourth floor and sighed with relief as the footsteps climbed past me. When the top floor door clanged and echoed shut I eased back into the stairwell and raced to the bottom floor.

The first floor hall was empty when I shot out the back door into the rain. About fifty feet away I glanced over my shoulder in time to see the back door of my building spring open. Before I could see who came through the door, or whoever it was had a chance to spot me, I crouched low and cut a corner.

Through a vacant lot I fast-stepped on broken glass, over tin cans and around mounds of burned out mattresses and other debris. A big dog behind a flimsy, wooden fence barked at my passing. Another dog nearby joined in to bark and growl in a deep-throated challenge.

Relief swept over me when I climbed into the Chevy with Brownie, waiting with the engine still running.

During the wet ride to Yonkers he briefed me.

"I got the lowdown on Tommy O'Brien from a cat who worked the same precinct when he was across the river. Seems as though, like I told you, Tommy had a well-known rep for having a quick temper. He wasn't bad news only to civilians, the cats he worked with didn't dig him too much either. At one point he was suspected of having too many questionable associates and the brass decided to investigate him."

"And?"

"That's when he flipped again and got another excessive force charge launched against him. But it wasn't just any citizen he roughhoused this time around. No, the guy he picked on turned out to be Lionel Worth, a young city councilman." Brownie chuckled. "The way I hear it, most people who know the obnoxious bastard, Worth, would have paid big bucks to see him get the crap stomped out of him. Anyway, that's how O'Brien earned his suspension and a six-month date on a shrink's couch."

"That's interesting. But what do you think that has to do with the people who came after me?"

"Don't rush me, bro. I'm trying to give it to you in chronological order."

"Screw that. I want to know who the people are who sent O'Shaughnessy and his boys after me."

"Simmer down some. I had to cross a few lines and promise a few favors to get the real skinny."

The rain had slackened to a misty drizzle as he rolled the car to a stop at a red traffic light where he paused, looked both ways and accelerated across the street.

"Jake O'Shaughnessy was a terror to behold long before he met up with you," Brownie said, and clucked his tongue. "He had a long rep for doing goon work for the highest bidder. Mostly, though, I hear he was one of Michael Tanner's boys."

"Tanner? I think I recall the name."

"He runs the neighborhood around Avenue A and Tenth. So technically speaking, everybody around there works for him one way or another. That's why I'm beginning to see a possible tie-in that would explain O'Brien's motive for being the phantom killer."

"I suspected him being the guy, too. But when I honestly thought about everything I've heard so far, O'Brien being the rogue shooter doesn't add up."

"Why not?"

"The description doesn't fit. I mean, didn't you tell me the shooter's a tall, heavy-set guy? O'Brien's not quite tall enough to fit the height requirements and he's too thin in the ass to win the booby prize."

"So," Brownie glanced at me sidewise, "you two have met then?"

"That we did." I rolled my window down and spat out into the rain. "He popped in Wally's the other day to collect for McKellerhan."

"Nice guy, huh?"

"One of the best," I said, acidly. "But I don't think he's the shooter."

"Maybe not," Brownie conceded. "Still don't let the physical description throw you too much. There's no way of telling how much validity we can place on the eyewitness accounts."

"Why not?"

"We have three witnesses who gave a general description of the perpetrator. They were all far enough away to place doubt on what they said they saw as hard facts. One woman was looking out of a seventh-story window when she heard shots and saw a man walking away from the alley where the first dealer met his fate."

Brownie darted around a slow moving car before continuing.

"Another witness was standing in a doorway a half block away. The other guy was rolling by in his car on his way from a birthday party where he'd downed more than his fair share of liquor. He was still lit up when he stumbled into the station house to report what he'd seen."

"All that would make a difference."

"And don't forget in each instance it was the middle of the night. Given the circumstances, lots of shadows and all that, it's easy to see how they all might've seen a lean man as looking taller and heavier than he actually is. You know how the night can play tricks on a frightened mind."

"All right. Let's forget O'Brien for a while. Back to this guy Michael Tanner. You think he's behind running drugs into Harlem?"

"It's a good bet, Nate. But proving it is a horse of another color."

"What would it take to get a real make on him?"

"More manpower than we've got. That's for damn sure." He shrugged, hands off the wheel for a beat. "I know cats, down-to-earth members of the club, from every precinct in town. You know a couple of them, too. So I can ask generalized off-the-record questions and get some results. But them being brothers or not, I can't actually have Tanner or any of his boys tailed or put under twenty-four hour surveillance. I mean, as you already know, all of this is way out of my jurisdiction to begin with."

"But you have learned more, right?"

"I know that Michael Tanner's about sixty years old, a respected businessman with plenty of political clout. He owns a restaurant, a fancy nightclub, several bars and a funeral parlor, all in the same neighborhood."

"A funeral parlor?" I mused. "That's intriguing."

"Yeah." Brownie grinned. "Imagine him filling his clientele up with liquor, drugs and arsenic laced dinners. That could add up to a huge fortune for an undertaker. The way I see it, he could get them coming and going."

"Uh-huh, You're right. We need more manpower."

"I agree, brother, but," he brightened, "if we can't get what we want right away we have to make the very best of what we do have."

"And what is it that we do have?"

"Well, actually, good buddy, it's not what we have." He smiled and winked. "It's who we have that counts."

CHAPTER 20

The Casa Bella Hotel was on the dilapidated far edge of Yonkers. In better times, the neon sign that once advertised the hotel's name was now burnt dead, bent crooked and groaned on its support with the howling wind. Only a couple of dingy windows in the five-story chipped paint building glowed with illumination. A half block away, Brownie parked at the head of an alleyway on a parallel street. The rain had ceased but the gutters were still awash. We climbed out of the car as a foghorn sounded nearby, and I followed Brownie's lead.

The double doors of the dimly lit hotel were closed but unlocked. He pushed through them with a sense of familiarity. Behind the barred windows of an office cage, an old olive-skinned codger's wide-eyed gaze relaxed with recognition. Then he nodded, acquiescing to Brownie's authority. A sawed-off shotgun lay on top of the small desk in front of him.

"How's it been, Gus?" Brownie curtly asked without missing a step. "Quiet, I hope."

"Real quiet," Gus chirped, his eyes taking everything in, especially me. "Real quiet so far, sir."

We climbed three flights of creaking stairs. As we proceeded down the hallway, a strange sound comparable to a chained casket being dragged across a hardwood floor came from somewhere at the rear of the hall. It grew louder with each step we took. The door to the last room on the right side was ajar. Like all the other doors on the floor, it had no lock and no doorknob and faint light shone from within.

Inside the small, dank room the junkie Pudding lay naked and gagged, spread-eagled and handcuffed by both wrists and ankles to the ancient iron bed that he was rocking to and fro with all his strength. There was a house painter's drop cloth covering the mattress and bunched up beneath him.

A dark-complexioned, round-faced man with gray hair, a new growth of beard and an overcoat that matched his hair, sat in a worn wingback chair near the bed. His eyes and demeanor were meek. A scuffed up doctor's bag and three or four clean towels were near his feet.

Pudding continued writhing and twisting violently against his restraints, cursing something which was muffled by the gag stuffed in his frothing mouth.

"How long's this nonsense been going on, Doc?" Brownie asked.

"He's been pretty passive most of the day," answered the man with a rich baritone voice that was hard to read for emotion. "When he heard you coming down the hall, all of a sudden he sort of snapped."

"Well, well, well." Brownie laughed and glared down at the struggling junkie. "You love to put on a show for me. Don't you?"

Pudding began to fatigue from his frantic gyrations. The iron legs and bedposts stopped rocking but the springs still complained.

"I thought you said he volunteered to clean up," I addressed Brownie, as I squatted on a stool beside the man he had called Doc. "He doesn't look like a volunteer to me."

"He's had lots of time for a change of heart since his jones came down on him."

Brownie took off his leather jacket and hung it on a hook behind the door and continued speaking.

"He's been going through a ton of changes since then. You should have been here with me and Vince for some of them. Talk about the theater of the wretched, man, you sure missed quite a show. Take yesterday for instance, he was willing to confess to any and all crimes committed in the neighborhood for the last ten years, if only I would get him one more fix."

The junkie's struggling finally gave way to exhaustion and he lay still except for his skinny chest which heaved up and down as he sucked oxygen through his nose.

"Does he have to be trussed up like that?" I inquired.

"I'm forced to take precautions when I'm not around," Brownie replied. "When he calms down and promises to stay that way, I'll undo him. He knows that."

Pudding glared up at Brownie and then at me while gnawing at the piece of torn sheet stuffed in his mouth.

"I know at first glance this might look kind of extreme," Brownie said to me. "But I gave him my word that if he cooperated with me, I'd help him kick his habit. And I intend to keep my word. Once he's done cold turkey, I'll let him walk away a free man and owing me nothing. Then he can march right out of here and shoot up all the skag he wants. I wouldn't even give a good country damn if he marches straight from here to an OD. But I am keeping my word. He will leave here clean. That, my friend, you can bet the farm on."

He grunted an abrupt belly hoot and went on.

"I told him exactly what he was getting himself into before he agreed to come here with me. This is not the first time he's tried kicking. He's a two-time graduate from that get-well farm they run down there in Kentucky for his kind. So Pudding knew perfectly well what he was getting himself into."

Before I could think of a response he went on.

"So no, Nate, don't weep for him. He should thank God to be here. And believe me, Pudding knows just how true that is. He was in a meat wagon roundup when I came along. He and three other users on their way to be charged and booked. Due to me, and nothing else, he's not kicking his habit locked up on Riker's Island this very minute."

Pudding closed his eyes and began to breathe in a more normal fashion.

"Want me to take the cuffs off now?" Brownie leaned over the bed and asked. "Huh? Make up your mind now. Yes or no?"

Affirmatively the pathetic junkie feebly nodded his head.

Brownie undid the cuffs from his ankles. Then he released one wrist leaving the other one clamped to the metal bedpost. With that done he snatched the gag from Pudding's mouth and dropped it to the filthy floor. Then he picked up one of the towels from the floor, grabbed a pitcher of water from the nightstand, poured a little water from it and began wiping his hands.

Slowly, straining with each movement, the junkie managed to sit up with his chicken-thin legs dangling over the side of the bed. Gazing at the floor he let out a plaintive sigh and began to grumble in a low, unintelligible voice that was heaped with anger.

"Don't start," Brownie warned, "or I'll lock you down again."

The man called Doc poured water from the pitcher into a tall glass and gave it to Pudding. He greedily drained the contents and wiped his mouth with his free arm. Then Doc lit an unfiltered cigarette and handed it to him. Pudding sucked on it as though it was mother's milk and blew a plume of smoke from the side of his parched mouth.

"Officer Brown," Doc said, "I'm really hungry, man."

"You can go ahead and take a break," Brownie told him. "I'll be here for a bit."

"But this time of night there ain't no places open within walking distance. I'm starving, man. And I guess it's about time to see if he's ready for something to eat, too." He looked toward Pudding with a doubtful expression.

"Okay, you win." Brownie grabbed his jacket. Tossing it over a shoulder, he asked me, "Want me to pick up something for you while I'm out there?"

"No. I'm not hungry."

"Fine. Stay put until I get back and then I'll show you the room I've got reserved for you. You'll see that compared to this pig sty it's a presidential suite."

"On second thought," I said, "bring me a half pint of Courvoisier."

Pudding grimaced and shuddered, making a face that implied the mere thought of drinking alcohol was almost enough to make him regurgitate.

Brownie scavenged through a mound of trash in one corner of the room and found the wooden leg of a chair. He smacked the open palm of his left hand with the sturdy leg and then handed it to me. While glaring at Pudding mercilessly, he addressed me.

"I'm going to leave him loose. But if he gives you any trouble at all, lay this stick upside his head a couple of times and he'll calm right down."

The moment Brownie and Doc walked out of the room I tossed the chair leg back in the corner, took the dying cigarette butt from Pudding's lips and ground it out on the grimy floor with a toe. Then I opened my suitcase, which I'd carried in with me. Digging to the bottom of it I pulled out a clean pair of white boxer shorts. I handed them to Pudding and slid my stool closer to an open window, which faced a blank wall, and sat back down.

Trembling noticeably, he slipped into the boxer shorts and stretched out on the bed, staring vacantly at the water-stained, crumbling ceiling directly above him.

"Solid, man," he said, humbly. "I appreciate that."

Once the silence had permeated the room I felt as much like a prisoner as Pudding.

"How long have you been trying to kick?" I finally asked.

"I been here since Tuesday night. Another couple of days and I'll be all right."

For the first time I noticed a washpan with a sponge and soapy water under the bed and a bedpan near it.

"What's the idea of the guy called Doc being here?" I asked.

Pudding let out another woeful sigh and then said, "Who else's going to clean up behind me? All chained up and all."

"I guess the Doc's another guy who owes Detective Brown."

"I guess. He's sure enough paying up, too, huh?"

"I'll say." I chuckled before asking, "Brown tells me you've been real helpful with some of the information you've given him."

"If I don't know nothing else, I sure enough know the streets of Harlem. That's for sure, man."

"Then I suppose you know the skinny on Johnny G and his boys."

Pudding seemed glad to have someone to talk to and launched into answering my question.

"Johnny G had a very big mouth, like. So what he was doing most of the time was no secret. He was just lucky, like, to be erratic enough to be hard to pin down. You know what I mean?" he asked rhetorically and went on, "He didn't show up a few places where he was supposed to, like. If he had've, he would've been history a lot sooner. Dig it?"

"You know who put the contract out on him?"

"That I don't know. But I sure as hell know who killed him."

"That's what I hear."

"No shit!" he exclaimed. "Awhile back he was running around bragging that Freddie Tucker had the man in his back pocket. Then when Freddie got snuffed out, and Johnny took over the top slot, he really started shooting his mouth off." He cackled and slapped his free hand on the oilcloth covering the old, thin, stained mattress. "I warned him that he didn't have the cops in his back pocket, like. I told him they got you, fool. But he was a hardheaded rotten son of a bitch. And believe me, don't a soul out there miss him."

"So you think it was the cops who gunned everybody down in Morningside Park?"

"Absolutely without a doubt and indubitably so. It was the man, all right. Everybody in the know knows they get their share of the action. Guys in the patrol cars do the picking up, but nobody thinks they run things. They're just the errand boys. That's why we call the precinct The Dirty Thirty."

He stretched out on the bed and turned his head to meet my eyes for only the second time since I'd entered the room.

"That still doesn't explain why you're so sure it was cops who did the shooting in the park."

"Five dudes, besides Johnny, in one night!" He counted their names off aloud using his free hand to down a finger on his cuffed hand with each name he recited. "All gunned down in one night, like. Give me a break. If it had been a gang war, where was the fricking opposition? These cats were ace-coon-boon blood brothers, too." He shook his head emphatically. "No, man. They were set up, like. 'Cause, like I told you, word on the street was that the man was trying to lure Johnny into a corner for some time. And I swear on my mother's grave that it was Johnny G's big ass mouth that finally brought the heat down on him and his boys."

"Did you ever hear any actual names of the cops involved?"

"No, sir, and I didn't want to know neither."

He was lying and sensed that I knew it.

"Not even one name, Pudding?" I coaxed gently.

"Not even one."

I half expected him to swear on his mother's grave again. After a beat or two of silence I pressed on.

"So tell me about this other theory of yours, the one about the phantom shooter."

"Wait a minute, man." He crossed his frail legs under him in a squat and cocked his head to one side. "Who the hell do you think you are anyway, Nate? Asking me all these confidential questions, like. Then when I tell you what the real deal is you act like I'm out my cotton-pickin' mind." He spoke, brimming with self-righteousness and barefaced defiance. "Screw you, chump! This ain't Wally's bar we in, like. I mean, how the hell you figure you got any jurisdiction to become involved here with me anyway?"

I smiled, dropped my eyes and shook my head. The exhaustion I felt creeping up on me, the lump on my head that still throbbed, the taut emotions and the tensions of the last two days contributed to my impatience, as I focused back on Pudding.

"We may not be in Wally's, but we are talking about my neighborhood. And I'm tired of you punk ass junkies acting like you've got a built-in immunity to all rules and laws or all the pain you cause other people." I let my words sink in until his eyes lowered. "When necessary I make my own jurisdiction, like I make my own justice when necessary. *Like,* see? And as far as I can tell, with all your big talk, when you come right down to it, you don't know dick from dumplings, Pudding."

"What you mean, man?" His voice shook with timidity.

"I think you're using my man, Brown. Filling his head with doubletalk and a whole lot of plain old bullshit. And that's exactly what I'm going to tell him as soon as he gets back."

"You wouldn't do that. Would you?"

"What do you think I came here for, a picnic?"

"No, man," he whined, shaking his head from side to side. "You can't tell him no jive like that."

"Try me. I mean, what's the big deal anyway? I tell him what I think and you can walk out of here a free man."

"It wouldn't work like that. Brown would probably plant some duji on me and bust me good, and jail ain't the best place to kick."

"Tough shit!"

"Why you so hard on the public, man?" He tried for a smile.

"The public has nothing to do with this. I'm talking to you!"

"No, man. Don't...don't...don't tell him no shit like that."

"Are you threatening me?"

"Can't you see I'm spilling my guts out, Jack? What more you want from me?"

"*Like,* I was asking," I pulled the stool closer to the bed, "tell me what you know about the phantom shooter."

Without any further preamble Pudding gave me the lowdown I was there to hear.

"I saw the mother who gunned Moses Grover down. So this ain't just some bullshit I'm rapping or some fool's gossip I heard somewhere."

I waited silently for him to continue.

"It was early one Saturday morning a couple of hours before sunrise. I can't remember whether it was warm enough for me to decide to sleep outside, or whether I didn't have enough cash for a room, or whether I was just so fried that I didn't care where I slept. What I do remember is waking up in this alley sleeping in a cardboard box." He closed his eyes, hunched himself up clutching his knees to his chest and went on. "It was two gunshots woke me up. I thought I was dreaming at first. But the voice I heard was too real to be a dream."

"What voice?"

"The voice of the shooter. That I'll never forget." Pudding cringed more, saying, "I was about thirty or forty feet away from the mouth of the alley. I was lucky, like, he didn't look my way. I saw him walk up real slow and stand over Grover's dead body. Then he blasted him one more time in the head at close range."

"What did he say?"

"Just two words. Right after he pumped him in the head, he looked down and said, 'Goodbye, Moses!'"

"You saw and heard him?"

"I swear!" Pudding said as he came out of his balled-up position. "Other people have all been saying it's a white dude doing the shooting. But I saw whoever it was wore a mask, a pink Halloween thing over his head. He was wearing gloves, too, so I couldn't see his real skin color. But I do know one thing for sure, man. Even though I only heard those two words he said, it wasn't no ofay man's voice that said them. The shooter's a member for sure!"

"I see." I reflected on what he'd said before saying more. "I have good reason to remember that night, too. As I recall it was real cold out. So I can't imagine anyone sleeping outside in a cardboard box like it was summertime."

"I guess not. But have you ever lived in the street, Nate?"

"No, I can't say I have." I pictured him entering the alley that night I watched him from Freddie Tucker's doorway.

"Then believe me or not. I could care less, like. But I am telling you the truth. The same as I told Detective Brown."

CHAPTER 21

The front room on the second floor of the Casa Bella Hotel that Brownie finally led me to was far from presidential. However, it was much more sanitary than Pudding's. The room also had a little sink, clean sheets and a blanket on the bed and curtains on the window. More importantly, it had a working lock on the door. I rinsed out a small empty jar that sat on the sink and poured myself a couple of shots of Courvoisier diluted with tap water. I got a strong rush and body shiver as the first swallow went down.

"I have to run out and catch up with Vince," Brownie informed me. "Sorry, this place is the best I could do on short notice." He shrugged, sweeping his eyes around the room. "But, as you can see, there's a clean bed just made up for you and a lock on the door. I'll get back with you first thing in the morning."

"I don't know how long I can stay cooped up here."

"Don't be too hasty just yet, brother. Give me a chance to get a line on who's who in this game and who you should avoid coming face to face with."

"Just don't leave me stranded here for long. I might get too edgy for my own good."

"Not to worry," he said. "I gotcha back."

He was about to close the door behind him when I called him back inside to have a seat on a rickety wooden chair.

"How much of what Pudding said do you believe?" I asked, sitting down at the foot of the bed to face him.

"Only about the thirtieth being dirty."

"Then you think he's lying about everything else?"

"Not lying, no. He's just out of touch with the truth. For instance, he doesn't know what we know about only one gun killing the five punks in the park. So that leaves that tale out. No one cop would have tried taking out five men that were armed."

"How about the phantom shooter being a black man wearing a mask?"

"Based on only a few words Pudding says he heard, I say no to that, too. I can't wrap my mind around that being true."

"It would make a lot more sense in some ways."

"How do you figure that?"

"He's a black man and blends into the surroundings. But pulling the trigger with the mask on, he's a white man to anyone who might be near enough to glimpse him committing his dirty deeds. And if he is a cop, like you've suggested, he could casually walk around the nearest corner and pull off the mask. Then presto, he's got his badge to cover his black ass. And even if a prowl car should happen along, all he'd have to do is run up to them and say, 'Which way did he go? Which way did he go?'"

"Interesting theory." Brownie wet a couple of fingers and stroked his mustache while he thought over what I'd said. "But why would this black cop want to shoot drug dealers?"

"For profit."

"I still don't get it."

"Suppose there are some precinct cops in on the distribution of drugs. Let's say it goes all the way to the top, McKellerhan, even Captain Owen Frye, both of them involved. Do you think they would have someone, like, say, Sam Brisco, a member, in on the take with them?"

"Probably not," Brownie granted. "So?"

"So he, the phantom shooter, if he is black, knows he can't make the starting team. So he decides to use muscle to get his cut from the back door. Then let's say the drug dealers get tired of paying him off. Or maybe he raises the stakes beyond what they think is fair and they decide to stop playing his game. Then what does he do?"

"Hmm!"

"Or maybe, being that he's new to the game, let's say he steps in and wipes out the existing competition and installs his own people. That way they'd owe him big time, and he'd practically own them."

"Hmm!" Brownie said again, then he laughed that deep-throated rumble of his. "It's a shame you're not still on the force, Nate. You'd make one hell of a detective. Far as I can see, though, there's only one thing wrong with your theory."

"That is?"

"The dealers could go to their friends inside the precinct and complain about the shooter's style."

"In a pig's eye they would."

"Why not?"

"Because the shooter would have the dealers more afraid of him than of them. If they talked, a vengeful black cop from the hood could track them down ten times faster than the captain with all of his resources."

"Hmm!" Brownie hummed again. "You've got a devious mind on you. But tell me one thing more, what makes you think I might not be the shooter?"

"Who said I don't suspect you?"

"Now I know you've gone too far out on the limb here." There was anger in his voice although he tried to smile. "You've got to be kidding."

"You and Brisco both fit the description."

His eyes got serious, hard-slit. Then he laughed as I reached down to the floor for my bottle to pour another drink.

"You had me going there for a second. Lucky I know you so well."

"Speaking of knowing me so well, maybe you can answer me one more question," I said, getting up to dilute my drink with tap water.

"Wing it by me."

"Since Brisco suspects me of collaborating on the Morningside Park murders, I was wondering why you never asked where I stood on that."

I wet my mouth with another swallow of the cognac and water.

"You disappoint me, Nate," he said, as he stood to zip up his leather jacket. "I've known you a long time, and I feel like I'm a good judge of character. You may be a lot of no-good things that I don't know anything about. But I know you're nobody's fool. Second and lastly, you're not the executioner type. That's why I called you yesterday when I heard Brisco was thinking along those lines. You're just not made that way, buddy."

"I'm touched." I took another big reinforcing chug.

"As you should be." He laughed again. "I understand where you're coming from, though. If I were in your shoes, I'd be suspecting everybody and their grandmothers, too."

He backed toward the door, opened it, gave me a mock salute, and then paused.

"Perhaps you're right. Maybe O'Brien's not the shooter. But I think I'm close to proving he's an errand boy for McKellerhan, who is just following orders from the top man in the precinct, Captain Frye. And who knows how high up it goes from there." He shrugged again and smiled. "Just thought I'd pull your coat to the real agenda."

I watched as he closed the door behind him with a quiet click.

∼

The last time I recalled checking my wristwatch, before drifting off to sleep, it was three thirty-seven in the morning. The Courvoisier bottle was empty and my gun lay in my lap. Then a vivid nightmare soon found me back in France with the 92nd Infantry. I was crouched in a foxhole with mortars lighting up the night sky and the steady sound of gunfire peppering the air with lead.

I tried to convince myself that I was dreaming but that didn't work. Instead, I began wondering how I'd been transformed back in time to the last place I would ever want to be.

Finally, I shook myself awake and sat up in the bed, covered in sweat. It took a few moments to acclimate myself to my shabby surroundings. Then I realized that my present situation was better than the nightmare but not by much compared to the ease of living I'd known until recently. Still, I figured the dream was trying to tell me something. After lots of probing thought, it dawned on me how the war had transformed me in ways I'd never looked at closely until that night.

During the first battle against the Germans, countless bullets per second peppered the air and soil around me, with too many hitting their marks to register as it was actually happening. Nevertheless, seeing the soldiers in my outfit falling dead all around me, and faced with the brand-new horror of it all, I peed on myself. In subsequent battles, however, I won a Congressional Medal of Honor because I didn't want the enemy to be the cause of me peeing on myself ever again.

In reflection, I wondered if I was more afraid of being a coward than I was of dying. I suppose, following the war, I allowed myself to become addicted to the spice called danger, flirting with its intoxication but none of it anywhere was threatening as I'd experienced in France.

Yet, like Pudding needed his heroin, now and then maybe I needed the thrill of pushing life past the realms of ordinary. Still, I never compared my double-life to being anywhere close to what I'd experienced in France or the bullet I took in blue. The so-called favors I did, in comparison, were like child's play.

But now that Lillian was paying a price physically, emotionally and mentally for my reckless actions, everything I'd once thought relevant about my double life fell into the realm of vain self-indulgent motivations. For the first time in years I found myself praying, asking God to deliver Lillian from the situations my carelessness had created. With that thought in mind,

I eventually drifted back to sleep, feeling more hopeful than logic and reason should have allowed.

~

About two hours later I stirred awake, instantly alert, with the light of dawn streaming into the dusty window. I had slept in my clothes, so it didn't take long to throw some water on my face, grab my suitcase and hit the streets with a plan. A few blocks away from the Casa Bella I found a family diner that was open. There was an enclosed phone booth near the rest-rooms. I checked my address book and dialed Howard Katz's home number, hoping that he'd be there and accept my early morning call. His wife informed me that he was at the office. I dialed the DA's number and caught him there.

"Working early on Sunday?"

"Nate," he asked, skeptically. "Is that you?"

"None other. You sound like I'm Casper the Friendly Ghost or something. I mean, are you that surprised to hear from me?"

"It's pretty clear that you've got yourself into a major quag-mire. Haven't you had time to notice?"

"Touché. That's why I'm calling you. I need your help."

"You might need more help than I can give you this time."

"Suppose I tell you I have an inside track on who's run-ning drugs into Harlem with a hand from the local police department."

"I'd say forget it," he spoke adamantly. "I repeat. Forget it!"

"I can't forget it. O'Shaughnessy and his boys almost killed Lillian and me. If I can't count on you, where's that leave us?"

"Where are you?" he asked, after a long pause.

"I'll tell you that when I find out why you want to know."

"I'll have someone pick you up and give you protection un-til we can sort things out."

"That doesn't sound too promising to me. I think I'll stay incognito for the time being. Thanks just the same."

"Don't hang up, Nate, and don't interfere in things you don't know enough about. This office and an FBI task force is in the middle of breaking a case wide open that we've been working our butts off and on for the last two years. And the mess you've found yourself caught up in is connected. So for heaven's sake, realize that you need to stay low. Now, once more, where are you?"

Suddenly I forgot exactly what I expected to gain by calling him.

After I hung up the receiver and dropped another nickel in the slot, I left a message with Leroy Grimes' wife, Shirley, for him to call me back at the pay phone. He called a few minutes later. After a brief conversation he agreed to pick me up in forty-five minutes.

I had finished a big breakfast and was on my second cup of coffee when Grimes joined me at a booth in the rear of the restaurant.

"You don't look so good," he said, as he sat down, puffing on a smoke.

"I don't feel so good either. But that's beside the point."

"So where do you want to go?" he asked. "Or what else do you have in mind?"

"You've tailed people for me in the past, all small-time stuff, though. But as you probably already know, I'm in a tight bind. So what I'm about to ask might be dangerous."

"I figured that much as soon as I heard you called. But I'm here, ain't I? So what do you want done, Nate?"

"I want someone tailed around the clock. His movements, who he sees, what time, and where."

"No problem. Just tell me who you're talking about."

"Someone who may be uptown one minute and downtown the next. The surveillance may need more than one driver. So—"

"Hey, Nate," he interrupted. "Just let me know who you want covered and I'll see to it."

He leaned closer with his elbows on the table.

"A detective with the 30th Precinct. Tommy O'Brien's his name."

Leroy nodded his head solemnly, and asked, "Fifty bucks a day sound all right to you?"

"Fifty's fine. But I'll have to point him out to you in some way."

"I know who the dude is. He drives a souped-up white Chevy, right?"

"I'm not sure what he drives."

"A real cocky guy with red hair, dresses like a pimp?"

"That's him."

"Then there's nothing more I need to know except when and how to report to you."

I could have asked Leroy for a ride into Harlem but decided against that. Instead, I had him drop me at the nearest elevated train stop. Suitcase in hand, I caught the first train that roared up to the stop, undecided as to where I was headed. As the train rumbled along my mind raced in circles at much the same speed as the wheels of the train. My head still ached from the knot caused by a policeman's baton. But what engaged me more was my uncertainty concerning where Brownie stood. In the dubious position I was now in I couldn't afford to trust him with all the doubts that were swirling round in my head.

Reflecting on many of my past conversations with him didn't help relieve my anxieties. Conversely, they made my suspicions even stronger. Most recently it was his eager readiness to implicate O'Brien as the shooter with such absoluteness. That was out of character for Brownie, who was usually pragmatic to a fault. Yet, contrary to the facts, he was still doggedly anxious to tag O'Brien as the rogue killer cop. I also recalled that it was Brownie who first brought my attention to the Harlem shooter on that day at the gym not so long ago. Still, it was hard for me to swallow that he, my best friend, could use me for his own purposes.

Also, stories he'd repeatedly told me about growing up in Mississippi painted a picture of someone who could well be an eligible candidate for stirring up racial divisiveness as a smoke screen to cover his ass. Most memorable was the tale of the white sheriff beating his father to a bloody pulp while he, as a kid, witnessed the beating. That same day after our routine at the gym, he had retold the tale. He'd also cursed his life as a cop and denounced junkies as less than human, comparing them with rats and cockroaches. If those were his deepest, underlying feelings, preying on them might be a natural outgrowth of such ingrained hatred. If the junkies were so deplorable, and less than human, why not capitalize on them?

It did not help that he lacked any suspicion about my having a hand in the Morningside Park shootout. The two people who were closest to me, Lillian and Wally, had expressed some question about the likelihood of my involvement. So why shouldn't Brownie also harbor some suspicions along those lines?

Following a recent pattern, I had many more questions than answers.

~

After aimlessly exploring several transit system routes, I began to feel fed up with the suspense and the unknown, the myriad of nagging questions, the rampant circles my mind chased like a puppy with his tail in his mouth. It had only been a few hours since I'd left the Casa Bella Hotel, but I was already sick of laying low. I headed for home ready for any confrontation that might await me there.

When I walked through the door of my flat, I sensed what later became apparent. Though the place had not been flagrantly tossed, and although nothing had been greatly disturbed, I immediately sensed the apartment had been thoroughly gone over. One or two items stuck out as being misplaced. Inspecting more of the flat, on a search of my own, my eyes soon fell on Lillian's telephone book on a side desk beside the phone.

My heart skipped a beat. Hastily, I flipped through the pages. I was relieved to see that while Vera's first name and phone number appeared in the book, neither her last name or address accompanied the entry. I figured Lillian kept the additional information in the address book she carried with her. But I knew that with a phone number and her last name, her address could be traced through a cross-reference directory. However, I decided that with all the other names in the book it would be unlikely that Vera's would be cause for undue interest.

Besides, I doubted that anyone was searching for Lillian. It was me the thugs wanted dead. I finally concluded that I was being too jumpy, too paranoid, searching for more demons when I already had my hands full of them. I assured myself that as long as Lillian was far away from me, she'd be safe. I also figured the crew coming up the stairs, as I left the night before, were responsible for the search. Moreover, I wondered if they would return once the electronic bug in the flat indicated I was there.

I didn't have long to wait. Shortly after I started the shower running, and was about to step out of my clothes, I heard a forceful rapping on the front door.

Between the insistent pounding, I took a cautious peek through the spy hole with my gun in hand. Seeing who was there I crept quietly back to the bedroom and stashed my piece. Detective Brisco and his backup, two smug guys in blue, a salt-and-pepper team, were at the door when I opened it.

"I had a feeling we'd finally catch up with you." Brisco leered at me.

"Had I known you'd be calling I would have made other plans."

"Can we come in?" he asked, in a pleasant yet irksome manner. "Yes? No?"

"Why not? Seems like you come and go here any other time you please."

"What's that supposed to mean?" he asked, after we had all stepped into the flat and stood in a semicircle.

"Somebody searched here." I examined Brisco's eyes closely. "Between last night and now."

"Is that a fact?" He guffawed, then looked away from me with his eyes roving around the place. "I wonder who the hell might have done that."

His sidekicks smiled, openly defying me to act in anger. And it was anger that was increasingly building inside of me, knowing what Lillian told me about Brisco hitting on her time and time again.

"I'm sure you do wonder about a lot of things, Sam, but not who came in here while I was out. Now, what do you want?"

"The thirty-eight registered to you," he said, reaching for a pack of cigarettes. "I need it."

"Need it for what?"

"To run some tests. That doesn't bother you, does it? I mean, I was surprised McKellerhan let you walk away with it to begin with." He stuck a Kool in his mouth and struck a match.

"Don't light that in here!"

"All right," he consented after considering otherwise and blew out the match. "Now for the gun, where do we stand on that?"

"Wait here. I'll get it."

When I turned to go into the bedroom one of the guys in blue, a tall dark man, blocked my path with his billy club like a tollbooth barrier. As a response to some signal from Brisco, he was just as quick to stand aside and let me pass. When I returned with the unloaded .38, I tossed it flat-wise to Sam.

"Happy hunting," I said. "But don't expect running tests on that baby to put any feathers in your cap."

"When I place you and your friend Yancy in Morningside Park on that deadly Friday night, which I will eventually do, then we'll see what kind of feathers I decorate my cap with."

"Good luck!"

"Luck has nothing to do with anything because luck always runs out."

"Maybe while you're investigating me, I'll busy myself getting the lowdown on placing you at the head of an alley one

Saturday morning, standing over Moses Grover with a smoking gun in your hand and a Halloween mask pulled over your face."

The three of them froze for a second.

"What the heck are you talking about?" Brisco blurted. "You better watch the kind of wild accusations you throw around. Or does major grief appeal to you so much you can't get enough?"

"You speculate and I speculate. I say I'm an innocent man tired of being harassed. What do you say?"

"We'll see." He glared at me through squinted eyes and handed my piece to the white cop. "By the way, I recommend that you don't leave town."

"You did that once already."

He relaxed his tight-knitted brow expression, turned to go, then paused and faced me again. The two blues stood beside him like bookends of diverse size and color.

"I still don't rightly understand you, Nathaniel," he said, shaking his shaved head in a parody of remorse. "Like I told you awhile back, sometimes you have to put foolish pride on the shelf and play it cool and safe. But instead, you stay stuck on pushing your lucky rabbit's foot to the max. Exactly why that is I must find out to get to the bottom of what really makes you tick." He rolled the unlit cigarette between his pink lips and smiled around the filter. "Like I said before, you've got a good job, a real nice pad here, great standing in the community. And, of course, there's that superfine lady of yours, Lillian, who...."

"Shut up!"

"Hold on," the big cop in blue interjected.

Before he could step between us, though, I grabbed Brisco by his cheap suit jacket and pressed him firmly against the wall with my eyes glued to his.

"One more word out of your big, ugly mouth about my lady, and I'll rip your tongue out."

"It's okay," Brisco said to the two cops who were about to make a move on me. "I can handle this."

"Do you understand me?" I screamed in his face.

"Easy now!" The cigarette fell from his lips. "This is not the way I want to see things—"

"Screw what you want, because every time I have to look at your ugly mug you bring up Lillian's name. But all that sissy ass shit stops right here and right now!"

"I…I can forget this happened. Just let me go. If you don't, you die right here. That what you want?"

Heavy breathing filled the room.

Although I could feel their hostile breath hot on the nape of my neck, I was so close to Brisco, seeing vivid reds with such intensity that the guys in blue were no more than mere blurs on either side of me.

Presently, however, I felt cold steel pressed hard against the base of my skull.

"You'd like that, huh?" I demanded, tightening my grip nearer Brisco's throat lifting him higher against the wall.

"Listen, Nate…" he struggled to speak because of the pressure my grip was exerting on his throat. "If you're guilty…I bring you in. That's all I want."

Slowly, I released my grip.

"Get the hell out of my house!"

Brisco straightened his jacket, brushed it smooth, and nodded to his backups.

"Let's walk."

Guns in hand, the blues followed Brisco. I slammed the door behind them.

CHAPTER 22

A second later the phone rang. Apprehensively, I picked it up.

"City Morgue."

"Nate?"

Instantaneously, an electric charge went through me that made me wish I could roll back time to better days.

"Lillian?"

"That City Morgue gag's not funny."

"I know, but I haven't—"

"How are things looking?"

"I can't go into that right now," I said, remembering the bugs Brownie warned me about. "I was just running out the door when the phone rang."

"I called all last night every thirty minutes or so."

"I wasn't here."

"Are you all right, though? Vera and I are both worried silly."

"It's best we not talk right now. I'll explain everything later. But I…I do love you."

"I love you, too."

"Got to run. See you—"

"When can we talk?"

"Soon. I'll call. I promise."

"Real soon?" Her voice quivered.

"Soon," I cooed. "Everything will be all right."

Deciding on going incognito before hitting the streets, I shaved off my mustache and goatee. Then I slipped into the oldest clothes in my closet, put on a reversible raincoat with the black side out, covered my eyes with thick black-framed blue shades and pulled a Navy watch cap down over my head to meet the sunglasses. With that done I climbed the stairs up to the roof, crossed a few buildings and ducked out the back door of another tenement building a half block away.

The unlit cigarette Detective Brisco dropped from his mouth when I assaulted him was now stuck in my mouth. I arrogantly strolled down the avenue, heading south. I assumed the personality of a man on a mission who did not want to be slowed and would maim or kill to get his way. Several people I pass almost every day didn't give me a second glance. About twenty minutes later I reached my destination. Not once during the walk was I accosted or solicited by panhandlers, religious fanatics, shoeshine boys or hookers.

The small dive I slipped into, Vic's Spot, was near 126th off Madison. The dirty, rectangular block-glass front window didn't need any additional help from shades or Venetian blinds to blot out most of the sunlight. A bell above the door clanged and signaled my entrance. Seven people were huddled at the bar. The carpet was damp with spilt drinks and stuck to the soles of my shoes.

The bartender was a big, red-faced, rotund man with freckles and cinnamon-colored, nappy hair. He sported a swollen black eye that did nothing to complement his severely bloodshot, hazel eyes.

"Wha...whaa...do ya want?" he stammered, while stabbing a block of ice with an ice pick.

"Is Vic here?"

"No, he ain't."

"I'm a good friend of his."

"So what do ya want...um...ah...Ivy League cookie...with ah...a bu...buckle in the back?" he said, as he continued chipping the ice.

"I just want to talk to Vic."

A guy sitting next to me came out of his slumped over posture, turned toward me with a quizzical expression creasing his face, and asked, "You Nate, ain't you?"

"You know where I can find Vic?"

He sat up straight and looked toward the front of the dive and back to me. Like most hustlers who haven't made it, he was rail thin and had an impish smile.

"What you need from him?"

"He's a friend I know from way back in the day. What I have to talk to him about, he'll understand."

The tenement building he took me to was four blocks away. We cut down an alley and came to the basement entrance, which was down a short flight of stairs. My guide knocked at the steel door with a sliding spy box at eye level. Soon the aperture slid open and a distrustful eye inspected us.

"I gotta see Vic," the hustler with me said in a hoarse whisper. "Tell him it's me, Terrell, and I got a friend of his with me."

The spy hole slid closed, and a few minutes later the door was unlocked and swung open. As though he were a crime sketch artist and I was a subject to be remembered, the stocky old man behind the door focused his eyes hard on me as we entered.

There was a heated crap game going on in the bare concrete room we stepped into off the vestibule. I stood near the back wall in the smoky room while the man at the door led Terrell past a beaded curtain into the front of the basement.

A fat man with a boisterous mouth, wearing a sweat-stained undershirt, was having his way with the dice. Almost everyone was fading his roll. At the moment his luck ran out, Terrell was pulling on my coat sleeve. He led me to the front of the room and pointed the way through the beaded curtains.

"He's in the corner to the left," Terrell directed me.

I paid him a twenty and entered a dim narrow hallway. It led to a large room which was lit by one dangling light bulb, revealing TV sets, hi-fis, radios, toasters and a host of other hot commercial goods stacked shoulder high. In the far corner of the windowless basement room, Vic Turner sat at a desk in a makeshift office area bordered by more packaged goods.

He was a fashionably slick-looking, hefty block of a man with his feet propped on the desk, smoking a slender cigar with a filtered tip. He wore a light-blue suit, a charcoal silk shirt and a black, stingy-brim hat with a light-blue band that matched his suit.

"Nathaniel Holt," he said, with a guttural laugh. "I thought Terrell was pulling my leg when he described you. Here it is I just read about you in the newspapers yesterday. And now here you are coming around today. So what can I do for you?"

He found himself amusing and laughed some more.

Getting right to the point, I said, "I need a rod or two."

"I had a feeling that was the case." Vic stood, smoothing his pants legs down. "We'll have to go upstairs for that. With the Sullivan Law and all, guys in my business got to be extra careful these days."

We went up to a flat at the back of the first floor. It was a dingy one-room job with a pint-size kitchen, a tiny curtained bath and an unmade Murphy bed. There was a skinny old woman lying in the bed watching a movie on a large TV screen. She looked up briefly at our entrance, then pulled the bedroom covers over her head and turned her back to us. Vic acted as though she wasn't there, crossed the small room and half opened all three drawers of a dresser to display a vast arsenal.

He waved his burning cigar over the lot.

"Pick what you want." He went to the far corner of the room and opened a closet so I could see the contents inside it.

"Need a shotgun or rifle, no problem with that either. I got shells for everything for sale, too."

With several dozen choices at my disposal in the dresser drawers, I picked out a Smith & Wesson .38 snub-nose revolver that fit neatly into my shoulder holster. I also bought a silver-plated Browning .25 auto-loader that held eight rounds. Feeling in a buyer's mood, I also made claim to a .22 short that came with an ankle holster. With that strapped on, the .38 snug near my left armpit and the .25 tucked under my belt near the base of my spine, I felt a strong sense of confidence return to me.

~

My next stop required a trek over to West End Avenue below 94th. It was close to three in the afternoon when the doorman to the ritzy apartment house greeted me with a bewildered expression straining the muscles of his plump, pink face.

"Can I help you, sir?" he asked in a way that suggested the possibility was improbable.

"Miss Virginia Langsford is expecting me," I lied.

"And your name is?"

"Nathaniel."

"Follow me," he said, holding his head aloft. "I'll have to check at the desk. She gives concierge the okay, you can go up."

"That suits me fine." I followed him inside to the elegant, marble-floored interior. After the man at the desk rang Ginny, he gave me an approving nod and I pressed the up button for the elevator.

"Eighth floor, please," I told the black elevator operator.

"Yes, sir," he said, with awe in his voice, staring at me with even more skepticism than the doorman.

Three years ago a mutual friend suggested that Ginny, a successful madam, call me about a problem she was having. A boyfriend had skipped out on her, taking some of her most precious jewelry. After tracking him to the Bronx, and having a short talk with him, the boyfriend and I made an arrangement. First, he had to sell his car, which she had bought for him, to get the jewels out of hock and turn them over to me along with a written apology addressed to Ginny. The amazing part is that all of that took less than four hours of my time.

My dressed-down look gave Ginny a momentary jolt when she swung open the door to her apartment, but she recovered quickly.

"Nate," she greeted me in a singsong voice and invited me in. "What the hell are you doing dressed like that?"

Ginny was a redhead, five-foot-ten or so and even taller in the high heels she wore. Her eyes were emerald, her house dress a lighter shade of green. Exactly as I recalled, she moved with the grace of a screen idol. She was about forty years old and was aging gracefully and her body was as stunning and as compelling as that of a twenty year old.

When we were seated in the living room of her elegantly decorated apartment, cocktails in hand, she picked up her phone and told the switchboard operator to hold all of her calls. Then I explained the reason for my unannounced visit.

"You've probably heard about me on the news or read something in the papers about the jam I'm in."

"I sure have," she said with undisguised curiosity. "What gives anyway?"

"I'm still trying to put two and two together. But I know for sure, if the people who sent those thugs to take pot shots at me and my lady are serious, which I have to assume they are, I'm still in big trouble."

"So how can I help?" she asked, refilling my drink from a serving tray on wheels. "Just name it."

"I think my place is bugged and I need a safe place to make and receive a few calls. I'm afraid to go to any of my known friends, or check into a hotel, for fear of walking into a trap. So I was wandering around trying to think of somewhere to go and you popped into my head."

"I'm glad I did," she said, without a moment's hesitation. "When you recovered my jewels I remember telling you how grateful I was. And what you charged me was veritably nothing to speak of. So I said it then, and I'll say it again, if there's anything I can ever do for you I will. You can stay here as long as you feel the need to. I have a spare bedroom that is hardly ever used."

"It won't be for too long. Just a couple of hours might be all I need. By this evening, at the latest, I should be out of your hair."

"If so, fine," she assured me, "but don't leave unless you're sure you've got everything under control."

"Don't make promises you might regret."

"Don't kid yourself," she quickly added, "I realize what I'm saying. A better friend than me you couldn't hope to find in a month of Sundays, Nate. Like the cliché they often use about classy ladies in my trade, for the right man I've got a heart of gold."

I sighed and relaxed for the first time in what seemed like a year of Sundays.

"You look like the first thing you could use is a little rest," she remarked as she poured fresh drinks for both of us.

"Maybe after I make a couple of calls, I'll do exactly that."

"I'll show you the spare bedroom." She stood. "You can make yourself at home. I'll have the switchboard operator activate the telephone in there. Make all the calls you need to. It's a separate line, so you can give the number out and answer it, too."

The plan that Leroy and I had settled on called for him to leave coded messages for me at Wally's. I spoke with the weekend day man behind the bar, but there were no messages from Leroy or anyone else. I dialed his house and left a message with his wife, using the agreed pseudonym Pete. I also left the number of the phone in the spare bedroom with her.

Ginny went out to a delicatessen and returned with a half pound of lox, assorted bagels, a pack of Philadelphia Cream Cheese, three types of sliced cheese, a jar of sliced dill pickles and another of olives. After eating with her, and listening to her tell me about her recent life, I was beginning to worry about Leroy's whereabouts when the phone in the spare bedroom finally rang.

"I was worried about you," I confessed.

"I'm cool," he replied. "I've just been following your instructions. Before now I didn't have anything worth reporting or the time to call either."

"So what's the skinny?"

"He's back at the 30th now. Most of the day he's been doing what I guess were cop things, like—"

"Cut to the chase."

"Okay." He cleared his throat. "About an hour ago he drove down to a midtown restaurant on the Lower East Side. I checked him park and go in and sit down alone by the front window. I had a hunch he was waiting to meet somebody, because he kept checking his watch every two minutes or so." Leroy giggled in a puckish manner. "So I called another pal, a square looking, white dude. He got there quick and sat down close to your man."

"And?"

"He wasn't a minute too soon either. About the same time, a black Lincoln pulls up. Two rough ass looking paddies, all spiffed up, get out and go in the place."

"Go on." I felt my mouth go dry and my heart beat a little faster.

"My boy, Chuck, the white driver, got to hear a little of what they were saying."

"Run it by me."

"They kept talking about later tonight, later tonight. Then he hears someone say ten o'clock. He heard it twice, real clear, ten o'clock."

"That's when. But did he get a make on where?"

"Only one word of what he heard stuck out like it might be a place."

"What word?"

"Parlor."

"Parlor?"

"As they were pulling by me when they left the restaurant, I got a close-up look at the license plate holder on the Lincoln. It had a name on it, the name of a funeral home, Tanner's Funeral Parlor. See how that might fit."

"Right on! Anything else?"

"At this very minute I've got another man tailing the Lincoln. But I'm still waiting to hear from him."

The hair on my back rose up and tingled.

"Call him off," I said. "Quick as you can."

"But—"

"Just do it! Call him off. I think the funeral parlor's where they intend to meet, and I don't want them suspecting a tail. That might screw things up. Besides, it might not be too healthy for you or your friends to do any more for me right now. So drop the tail on O'Brien, too."

"Whatever you say," Leroy acquiesced. "Call if you need me more."

"You've got it, Leroy. You did a great job and more than earned another fifty as soon as I can get it to you." I hung up and then dialed information to get the phone number and address of the Tanner Funeral Parlor.

Afterwards, I sat there on the side of the bed in Ginny's spare bedroom for a long time before I could will myself to make another move. Then I picked up the phone again to dial Lillian at Vera's. Halfway through dialing, though, I hesitated. What would I tell her?

I have good news. I'm meeting the bad guys later tonight at a funeral parlor!

I placed the phone back in its ornate cradle.

CHAPTER 23

Tanner's Funeral Parlor was located on a side street on the Lower East Side, not too far from the Fulton Street Fish Market. I found an ideal place to keep an eye on the windowless dignified black and white slate building's entrance. There were only a handful of small shops of various descriptions on the street. Due to the late hour, they were all closed.

Across the intersection, down in the basement entrance of a shoe repair shop, I was able to spy through a wrought iron railing. From there I had an unobstructed view of the funeral parlor's front door. I'd staked out the area an hour before and took up my post at nine-thirty. When occasional passersby walked overhead, I crouched, framed in the darkness at the far corner of the basement stairwell.

It was a few minutes before ten when my wait paid off and Leroy's hunch proved to be on the money.

A black Lincoln arrived first. Two big guys jumped out the back doors simultaneously. They both appeared to be in their early thirties and were dressed like undertakers but looking as though they would be more at home in jailhouse duds. They had cautious eyes and moved quickly. The one nearest the curb held the rear door open while an elegantly attired thin man with gray hair climbed from the car a moment before the Lincoln roared away.

The man, who I took to be Michael Tanner, looked up and down the street as though he trusted his instincts more than those of the two men acting as bodyguards. For a fraction of a second it was almost as though our eyes locked across the night. Then he and the other men disappeared into the parlor.

Five minutes later a white '53 souped-up Chevy came along. It slid to the curb on my side of the street, partially blocking my view of the parlor. The engine cut and the ensuing silence was dramatically emphasized. Then Tommy O'Brien stepped out of the ride and slammed the driver's door.

He wore a short brown leather coat, dungarees and suede desert boots. He waited for a slow moving car to roll by. Then he gave the car the finger, tossed a lit cigarette toward the receding taillights and skipped across the street to enter the silver metal doors of the funeral home.

I waited about five minutes to see if anyone else was joining the party. On edge, and unable to stay rooted any longer, I took advantage of a long break in the sporadic traffic and came out of my hiding place to cross the street.

A narrow alcove led to an alley that cut between the funeral home and an adjoining building. A sturdy locked gate was set snugly, three feet deep into the alcove. I tried the handle and put my shoulder against it, but there wasn't the slightest give. After a second's thought, I decided to see if the rear of the place offered easier access.

The glare of headlights from a fast moving car separated me from the ubiquitous shadows. Quick stepping, I reached the nearest corner and turned. Head down, I heard another car slow at the intersection. I breathed easier as it kept rolling.

Overshooting the alley that ran at the rear of the funeral home, I walked an extra half block before retracing my steps. Then deep into the alley, directly behind the funeral parlor, I climbed a high cyclone fence and dropped down into a small, dark, concrete-covered back yard. Light glowed from a high, rectangular, stained glass window that was tilted open. Coming from the open window I heard deep muffled voices engaged in a fervid conversation.

Making as little sound as possible, I moved a nearby trash can directly under the window. With the help of a strut from the porch above, I climbed to stand precariously on the bottom of the upturned trash can. Still, I was too low to see through the slanted window opening.

I reached farther up on the strut with both hands, and supporting my entire body, I inched higher. Feeling like an effigy of some kind I was soon able to pull myself up high enough to peek into the room. From my awkward angle, however, all I could see were two pairs of legs and shoes. Nevertheless, it was a cinch to identify them as belonging to Tanner and O'Brien.

O'Brien paced in a tight, agitated circle, but it didn't sound like his voice I heard speaking. While I was able to determine that much, I was unable to distinguish a single word that drifted my way. I strained to hear better and tried to quiet the distraction of my labored breathing and excited heartbeats that had my temples throbbing.

To my alarm, I became aware of another sound. Furtive footsteps approached from behind me. I twisted my head toward the cyclone fence. On the other side of it a beer-bellied man, wearing a white sleeveless T-shirt, aimed a shotgun in my direction.

"Drop down easy, nigger!" he commanded. "Or I blow you from here all the way back to Timbuktu."

~

Stripped of my guns, with my wrists secured behind me by O'Brien's handcuffs, one of the bodyguards forced me to my knees in the embalming room. Blood from the beating I'd taken at their hands clouded my vision, and I struggled to hold my head upright. Tanner and O'Brien hunched over me. The man who had discovered me peeking in the rear window and the undertaker's two henchmen stood on the periphery of my eyesight. Then O'Brien grabbed me by both of my ears and lifted my head so far back I thought my neck would snap.

"You know who this fellow is?" he asked Tanner.

"Is he the guy we tried to tag the other night?"

"Indeed, he is." O'Brien chuckled and spoke to me, "I promised you we'd meet again and you wouldn't like it."

"What the hell's he doing snooping around here?" Tanner asked, nervously. "It don't make sense he's alone."

"Maybe he's dumber than he looks." O'Brien released his grip on my ears.

"I hope so," Tanner said, as he bent down and lifted me up by the collar. He was close enough for me to smell liquor on his breath, but his grip was sobering and as strong as that of a much younger man. "Want to explain what the hell you were doing snooping around in my back yard?" Tanner asked.

"Looking for my puppy," I said.

"Your puppy?" Tanner's gray eyes appeared dismayed. "Your puppy!"

"He chased a cat down the alley."

He looked at me with increasing disbelief. Then abruptly he began to laugh. The others joined in. Suddenly, the laughter stopped as Tanner smacked me a hard stinger across the face.

"Tubby." He looked toward the beer-bellied man. "How did you know he was out there?"

"I happened to look out my window and saw him creeping around. So I figured I better go check it out. Good thing I did, because I caught him hanging out back there like some kind of goddamn monkey peeking in your back window."

"See anybody else with him?"

"No, sir, Mr. T."

"You can go now."

"Yes, sir. Anytime I can help—"

"Yeah! Yeah!" Tanner snapped. "One of youse take a look up and down the block and come back quick. And somebody call a few more of the boys over on the double."

After the three men left, Tanner bored his eyes into me as he spoke, still holding me by the collar, "What's up your sleeve, Sambo?"

"I thought we might have a sensible little discussion."

"So you came to the back door?"

"Seemed logical at the time."

"Did it, now?" He smacked me again. It stung twice as bad as the first strike. "Make sense when you talk to me or I'll smash your bloody face in until it's soft as putty."

Tanner clinched his teeth tight and growled before punching me. This time the whole side of my face seemed to cave in on itself.

"This floor mops up easily," he remarked. "That comes in real handy sometimes. Now talk to me and make sense."

"I want to make a deal."

"What the hell do you think you could possibly offer me?"

"The truth."

"What do you take me for?" He slugged me again. "All I want to know for now is are you alone?"

As I wobbled on my weakened knees, my head slumped on my chest. The door opened and a pair of footsteps rushed into the room.

"I checked the street, Mr. Tanner. Can't see nothin' out the ordinary. But I got a couple of guys parked out front and in the back, too, just in case."

"Good." Tanner tightened his grip on my collar. "So you are alone. How dare you come anywhere near here after taking out three of my men."

"Doggone spades are getting crazier by the day," O'Brien interjected. "I'm figuring ten to one it's all the roach spray they breathe."

"Well, good riddance to all of them," Tanner said, as he shoved me to the floor.

Face down, I could hear him dusting his hands off.

"So what are we going to do with him?" O'Brien asked.

"I'll settle up. From this night on he sleeps with fish." He boomed, "Paulie!"

"Yes, sir!" came an instantaneous response.

"I want you and Doug on this. Get rid of this garbage."

"Yes, sir." Paulie sounded eager to comply. "I'll go get Dougie."

With the flunky's footsteps gone, an impending silence encompassed the stainless steel and tile room. It was O'Brien who finally spoke.

"Before you turn him over to them, I've got another solution you might like better."

"Like what?"

"I was wondering if you might not give him up to me."

"To arrest?" Tanner testily asked.

"No way." Tommy laughed like a steel wrench grinding. "No, sir, Mr. Tanner, arresting him is not exactly what I had in mind. I have a special interest in this jigaboo. Not only because Jake O'Shaughnessy and I came up pals together. It's more than that."

"So talk to me, Tommy. What is your special interest in him?"

O'Brien walked over to me, rolled me face up and grinned down at me.

"It's a personal thing. I had a run-in with him one day and promised him a lot of pain in the future. But you, Mr. Tanner, can rest assured I'll do a real good job disposing of him."

Sharply, Tanner's leather heels clicked as he paced to and fro for several long seconds. Then the way he laughed to himself it was clear that he liked O'Brien's suggestion.

"Believe me, Mr. T," O'Brien added, "I'd consider it an honor and a favor. While you and your boys have a late night supper somewhere and shoot the breeze in public view, I'll get rid of this louse once and for all."

"All right, Tommy." Tanner's pacing stopped. "I'll let you have him. I'm just concerned as to how he knew we were here. Could he have followed you, perhaps?"

"Not without me noticing. Don't worry about that, though. Before I'm done with him I'll know the answer to that question and many more, or I'll rip his lying head right off at the shoulders."

CHAPTER 24

I refused to go meekly and was conked over the head more than once. When I came to, an impenetrable darkness surrounded me. It took awhile for my head to clear enough to even begin wondering where I was. The constant roar of a souped-up engine and the jolts in the road soon made sense. Then the scene in the funeral home rushed back to me with a startling and frightening clarity.

My hands were still cuffed behind me, my legs tied and my mouth sealed. My head, my ribs and the shoulder that I was lying on ached in unison. Even worse than all of that, it came to me that I was in the trunk of O'Brien's fast moving car. I had no idea how long we had been in transit and not the slightest clue to where I was being taken. I reached down and tried to loosen the ties on my ankles but they were bound too tight.

Presently, the car slowed and made a left turn. A block or two later the road became progressively rougher. Judging from the bumpy ride, I surmised the street we were on was made of cobblestone. Soon the Chevy slowed even more, traversed some large potholes, and then came to a complete and sudden halt. There was a long silence in which my heartbeat doubled.

Then I heard the door of the car open and slam shut and a key slide into the lock of the trunk. I tried to position myself so I could kick up at O'Brien, or whoever opened the trunk. It was O'Brien all right. But he wasn't taking any chances and stood at a safe distance from where my feet were aligned to strike.

Anger had his face twisted into an ugly distorted mask. He grabbed me by the back of my raincoat and strained considerably as he hauled me from the trunk.

Lying face up on the dark cobblestone street, I could make out that we were on the dock of the East River. Except for the distant sounds of traffic crossing the nearby Williamsburg Bridge, and water lapping at the dock, the area was deathly quiet. O'Brien drew his gun, leaned over me and pressed the short barrel into my forehead.

"I been trying to think of one good reason why I shouldn't blow your brains to smithereens and dump you in the goddamn river." His anguish was evident. "Damn you!"

He turned his back on me, walked a few paces, kicked an empty can into the water and bellowed a long stream of obscenities. When he came back to stand over me, surprisingly, he tucked his gun away.

"What a lucky bastard you are," he said. "I guess you just don't realize how lucky you are yet." He leaned down closer this time and ripped the duct tape covering my mouth. "Tell me, if you can, why I shouldn't snuff you out right here and now."

My tongue was thick and coated with fear and my mouth was too dry to speak.

"Damn you!" he said again. "I'm working with an FBI sting team. We've been trying to bring Tanner's clan down for the last two years running. We were this close to bringing them down." He held two fingers a fraction of an inch apart. "This goddamn close to implicating Frye and McKellerhan with them, too. Then you show up and royally screw everything up."

I shut my eyes and tried to grasp the full significance of what he had said.

"All the way while driving over here," he went on, "I was debating with myself. I still have a good mind to put you out of your misery so my cover doesn't get completely blown out the water." He shook his head dejectedly. "Well, what do you have to say for yourself?"

"You're working with the Feds?"

"Big surprise, huh? But the minute Tanner and his people find out that you're still alive and kicking, my cover will be blown for good. So thanks a lot, pally!"

Roughly, he turned me on my side, untied my legs and unlocked the cuffs.

"Again," he said, "I can't emphasize what a lucky son-of-a-bitch you are. If I hadn't done some fast thinking to get you out of that funeral home, you'd be dead at the hands of those two guys who were so anxious to get their mitts on you for a little sadistic fun and games."

With great pain and strain, I stiffly got to my feet.

"I never thought I'd be thanking you, but—"

"Save it! The last thing I want to hear is any kind of thanks from you." He attached the handcuffs onto his belt. "So what are you waiting for? Count your lucky stars and get the hell out of my face before I change my mind."

I'd walked about fifty feet when the Chevy blazed past me. A few blocks later I saw it heading back in my direction. As it came abreast of me, O'Brien steered the car into an about-face and swung the passenger door open.

"Get in," he said, harshly.

"Why?" I stooped down to meet his eyes.

"I've got a plan that just might save both our asses."

I climbed in and we roared away. O'Brien stuffed a wad of gum in his mouth and chewed on it without breaking the silence until we were heading north on East River Drive.

"I'm supposed to meet my boss. He's expecting me to tell him how everything went with Tanner."

"And this plan of yours, how's it go?"

"I'm still toying with the concept. Even if I come up with something that I think'll work, I've got to get the go-ahead from him."

On 54th Street, off Broadway, we entered a multi-level parking structure. O'Brien drove to one of the upper levels, got out and moved a barricade. Then he drove to the next level.

A man of medium height with a craggy face, about forty years old, wearing a trench coat with the collar pulled up, leaned against a Plymouth. He was sucking on a smoke. When he spotted me he tossed the cigarette aside and stepped close to O'Brien's open window and leaned down.

"What the holy hell's going on here, Tommy?" His eyes wavered back and forth from O'Brien to me and back again.

"Bad news is what's up, Jamison," O'Brien said.

"And who the hell is this you got with you?"

"He's the problem." Tommy looked at me.

"The problem?" Jamison asked.

"He's the dude O'Shaughnessy and them tried to take out the other night."

Special Agent Jamison studied me with hard, dark eyes and a perplexed expression on his face. He looked away and glanced around the empty parking lot before climbing into the back seat of the Chevy.

"Talk to me," he demanded. "I need an explanation, fast."

O'Brien told him about the dilemma I'd created. Jamison cursed louder and longer than O'Brien had done on the dock.

"You crazy sum-bitch," he blared at me. "Do you know what a major crimp you've put in our style? Two years down the drain because of some harebrained shenanigans." He threw his hands up in the air. "Oy vey! God save me from assholes like this."

"What would you have done if you were me?" I asked Jamison. "Let someone take pot shots at you and your woman and just let it slide?"

"I thought about finishing him off," O'Brien said, matter-of-factly, "like I told Tanner I would and not mentioning it to you. What do you think of that?"

The special agent thought about the question before answering.

"It might have been the smartest thing you could've done. Maybe one of the best decisions of your life so far. But now, have you any idea where this snafu leaves us? Huh? Jesus, Joseph and Mary! What a grand mess."

"I have a half-baked plan forming in my mind," O'Brien spoke, calmly. "Want to hear it out?"

"Half-baked won't get it," Jamison snapped. "Admit it. Your cover's blown and we'll have to take you off the case and start from scratch. No telling how long it'll take to replace you with someone who can gain their trust to the same degree. I mean—"

"I know!" O'Brien interrupted him. "At least listen to what I have in mind."

"Two years," Jamison lamented. "Two whole years creating your cover."

"So what does it hurt," I interjected, "to hear him out?"

Again Jamison laid his disdain-filled eyes on me. Finally, he shook his head and turned to O'Brien to ask, "So how do you figure we put a tourniquet on this?"

"Well, needless to say, I haven't worked out all the details." O'Brien stuck a cigarette in his mouth and lit it. "But the basic premise goes something like this: Suppose we have Holt, here, get in touch with Tanner to say he got the drop on me and now the tables have turned."

"Yeah?" Jamison said, warming somewhat. "Then what?"

"He tells him that he got me to talk. He knows everything I know. Then he offers to trade me for the assurance that no more trouble comes his way. Meanwhile, we have the meeting bugged. Holt gets Tanner to incriminate himself, Frye and McKellerhan, too."

Jamison took the burning cigarette O'Brien offered and puffed on it in deep meditation. In the confined space the smoke was thick.

"With your testimony against Frye and McKellerhan," Jamison said, "we already have enough evidence to put them away for a lifetime. It's Tanner and his connections in Florida, elsewhere, and with the Italian mob, we wanted to get evidence on."

"I know," O'Brien agreed. "But if we bust Tanner and his boys, I guarantee you someone in his crew will gladly turn state's evidence."

"That's assuming someone in his crew knows who Tanner's connections are. Suppose they don't? Besides that, even with a tape going, what solid grounds do we have for popping him with Frye and McKellerhan?"

"Attempted murder for one. We'll get him to admit giving the order to wipe Holt out. Who knows what else we'll learn if he opens up."

"I see." Jamison squirmed in his seat, inhaled on the smoke and stared at the ceiling of the Chevy for a beat or two before he replied, "I'm not sure it'll work. It's far too risky and most likely I'd never get the okay from upstairs."

"Got any better ideas?" O'Brien asked. "If so, run them by me. I'm just playing the hand we've been dealt. Like a one-eyed man in the valley of the blind, I only see this way out."

Still staring at the car's ceiling, Jamison blew smoke, shook his head morosely. Then he lowered his hardened gaze and rested it on me, studying, searching and questioning.

"Let me get this straight, guy," he finally said, "you're willing to go along with a dim-witted plan like he's talking about trying to pull off?"

"What've I got to lose?"

"Nothing to lose at all, if dying is your cup of tea."

~

It was a little before sunrise when Jamison and I pulled to the curb of a safe house somewhere in the upper Bronx. It was a two-story single dwelling with a screen enclosed front porch. The whole neighborhood had a slight suburban feel to it that made the big city seem distant. Shortly after we walked into the place, Jamison had a pot of coffee brewing.

Soon thereafter, two men he was expecting knocked at the door. Both of them were tall, black men who looked to be in their mid twenties. One was dark skinned, the other chestnut hued. They both were dressed as though they were on their way to run a game of pickup basketball. As they shed their jackets and made themselves at home, it was apparent they were familiar with the layout of the house. Jamison handled the introductions on a first name basis only.

"Fred and Ted," Jamison said, with a wry smile, "meet our friend, Nate."

The dark man was Fred, a wide-shouldered forward in size, who looked as though he'd be great crashing the boards for rebounds. The other man, Ted, looked as though he'd make a good, tall guard, clever at dishing the ball out and pesky on defense.

We shook hands, then followed Jamison's lead into the kitchen and sat at an old wooden table with high-backed chairs. Although the coffee smelled inviting, I passed. I was already feeling shaky and on edge with enough tension and adrenaline running through my body.

Jamison explained the mission. During his longwinded dissertation, Fred and Ted shared furtive glances. It was obvious neither man could believe what they were hearing. They seemed to be waiting for Jamison to laugh and tell them that the whole thing was a ruse.

"So that's why you guys are here," Jamison concluded. "You'll be up front in the show with Nate. Any questions?"

He lit a smoke while the two partners eyed each other dubiously.

"Is this for real?" Ted finally asked. "I mean, you got the okay for this from upstairs?"

"This afternoon," Jamison inhaled, "you'll find out just how real."

"Christ!" Fred said, looking at me. "I was hoping this was all some kind of crazy put-on."

"It's crazy all right," I agreed, "but a put-on, no."

"You two guys are going to have to change up a little." Jamison pointed to Ted and Fred with his burning smoke. "Both of you are dressed too square for the parts. I want a tough, gangster look. Something they'll buy long enough for us to run our game on them. Know what I'm saying?"

"I think I follow you," Ted said, scratching his head. "Real tough thugs, huh?"

"Correct," Jamison said. "But try in some way to look like out-of-towners or it might not work trying to fool the captain and lieutenant. So try to look and carry yourselves like you're hired killers from Philly or something."

Fred and Ted exchanged another bewildered look.

"I could wear an Eagle's sweatshirt," Ted finally said. "No problem. From here on we're hit men from Philly."

After Jamison and his crew split I was left alone in the house with plenty of questionable thoughts to fill the vacuum. A few hours later I eventually stretched out on the living room couch and tried to cast my fears aside long enough to catch a nap.

CHAPTER 25

At three o'clock that afternoon, the hastily planned show-down drew near. The rendezvous was to take place in an abandoned warehouse across the river on the outskirts of Newark, New Jersey, right smack in the middle of a black marshland industrial area complete with huge smoke spewing petroleum plants of megalithic proportions. The day was overcast and the humidity seemed to mute the constant traffic hum from Route One. A gaseous odor mixed with the smell of raw sewage was so thick that it was almost tactile.

The warehouse, set to be our staging area, was a massive block of gunmetal gray. Most of the lower windows were stoned out and a strong wind whistled freely through them. The brisk movement induced a bone-like tinkling from the shredded glass that clung to the wire-reinforced remains of the busted-out windows.

Cavernous storage space and thick steel girders surrounded the bottom floor, which was set in the center of three upper tiers that ran a square perimeter around the main floor. A massive wrench, capable of hoisting tons of payloads, was braced and bolted to the ceiling. Its huge grip appeared to have been frozen in the act of reaching for something on the second tier.

From a third floor window I gazed out at what could have been an apocryphal Hieronymus Bosch painting translated into an industrialized nightmare. Through a pair of binoculars, exactly five minutes before it was due, I focused on Tanner's black Lincoln as it cruised into a gasoline station that had about thirty pumps. Tanner was at the wheel, Captain Frye beside him and Lieutenant McKellerhan in the rear.

I began dialing on the new phone line, which had been especially installed for the occasion. Inspector Jamison stood at another nearby window snapping shots with a long lens camera mounted on a tripod.

McKellerhan lumbered from the car. As the big man made his way toward the correct phone booth, I twirled the last of the seven digits and let the line ring. One of Jamison's men picked up an extension and handed it to him. The inspector jammed it to his ear, holding it in the crook of his neck, as he continued to snap candid shots.

"Yeah," McKellerhan said, gruffly. "How much more of this cat-and-mouse shit do we need to go through, Nate?"

"This is the last call," I assured him.

"Then, what now?"

"Look straight across the highway."

"I'm looking."

"See the long bridge in the background?"

"Which one?"

"The closest one."

"Um…I see it. Sure."

"Right to the left of it, scan down."

"I'm doing that."

"See the gray square building? It's right beside the tall brick one with a water tower on top and a hundred-foot chimney."

"I see it."

"That's where I'm looking at you from."

"If you say so."

"I do say so! Tanner's at the wheel of the Lincoln. You're wearing a cheap, gray suit and your lips are chapped."

"Real funny."

Angrily, Jamison signaled me to speed up the conversation.

"Well, Mac," I said, "try this on for funny. You just wiped your forehead with a dirty white handkerchief."

"Like I already said, what next?"

"Come around to the left side of the building. There's a loading dock. You'll find one of the doors rolled up. That's also where you'll find me and your boy, O'Brien."

"We're on our...."

"And," I cut him off, "don't forget that your every move is being watched. So when you hang the phone up, come straight here and make sure nobody follows you."

As I trampled down the steel steps to the first floor, once again I passed a neatly drawn message that someone had spray-painted on the wall: Bird Lives. Again, my mind reflected on a series of flashbacks, rapidly going through the circumstances that led me to agreeing to help Joe Weathersby to my present situation.

I took up my station as the Lincoln approached at a high rate of speed, kicking up a swirl of black dust. I stood about twenty feet from the open loading dock. Off to either side of me, and out of sight for the moment, Fred and Ted were set in their positions. With the exception of the Eagle's cap that Ted wore, they looked like commandos on loan from some army in the Congo. The Thompson machine guns they were both toting successfully rounded out the illusion.

Not far to my right, Tommy O'Brien, in a sitting position, was roped to a steel girder. His lips were sealed with duct tape and his eyes were wide and focused on the opening I was facing.

When the Lincoln pulled to a stop, the three men climbed from the car casually as though they were on their way to lunch. All three sets of eyes were on me as they approached the steps to the loading dock. Captain Frye, as I'd never seen him before, was wearing civvies. Unlike the other two men, he was without a hat. The wind blew to one side what was left of his receding hair as he walked with his narrow shoulders hunched tightly.

Walking beside him, Tanner's eyes were set hard, staring defiantly at me from under his wide-brimmed, black hat. A white, silk scarf covered his neck and was tucked neatly into the black lapels of his houndstooth overcoat. McKellerhan followed on the heels of Tanner's footsteps like a trained bear on a chain.

Self-assured, they marched into the shadows of the warehouse. The sight of Fred and Ted with machine guns didn't slow them a beat. Neither did the sight of O'Brien roped and gagged. It was as though what they saw, the entire set-up, was exactly what they had expected to greet them.

When they were about ten feet from me I took the safety off the .45 I was holding and aimed it at Captain Owen Frye. Their march halted about six feet from me.

"Why don't you aim that gun somewhere else," Captain Frye said. "Then we can find out what this is all about."

"I'll tell you what it's all about to the letter. For starters, I'm running the show. Two, I set the rules. Understood?"

Fred and Ted moved a few steps closer. Their dark sunglasses hid their eyes and made their presence and movements even more ominous.

"Agreed," Frye finally uttered, eyeing my accomplices warily.

I tucked the .45 into my waistband, took a deep breath and pointed to O'Brien.

"As you already know, your boy here flubbed the job of bumping me off. As you can well imagine, or you wouldn't be here, he also talked a lot."

"Obviously," Tanner said. "So what's the score? I mean, exactly what the hell do you want?"

"What I want is real simple. Whether or not you see it that way remains to be seen."

"Talk to us," McKellerhan growled.

"Not until you personally answer a few questions, Mac." I glared at the lieutenant, going off the carefully prepared script developed by Special Agent Jamison. "Then we go on. Not a second before."

"What is it you want to know?"

"You knew Tanner sicced his dogs on me and that they were gunning to bring me down. Didn't you?"

"Big deal. I knew. Sure. But what was I supposed to do, warn you? Best I could do was tell them I didn't think you were the man they wanted. So don't blame me; I did my best."

"And Lillian?"

"I didn't plan it that way. Honest, Nate."

"It was my call," Tanner spoke up. "I ordered the hit on you. I didn't order anybody else harmed, though. But let's skip the history lesson and finger pointing. O'Shaughnessy and his boys got over exuberant that night. That's all!"

"That's not the question now," Captain Frye interjected. "All three of us want to know where do we go from here?"

"Straight to hell is where you'll go," I snapped. "Unless we come to an agreement right here and now."

"Spell it out," Frye said, cracking his bony knuckles. "What's the deal?"

"I've got the lowdown on your whole operation, a full six-page confession from O'Brien that implicates Frye and McKellerhan. It's signed and sealed. Now you three get to decide whether copies of it are delivered to the proper authorities or not."

In the face of their baited anxiety, I went on with the script.

"As long as nothing happens to me or my girl, you guys are cool and everything's copacetic. You three can go on conning the rest of the world into thinking you're respectable, upstanding Joes. But if something, anything unexpected, takes either one of us to an early grave, you guys better duck for cover."

"Is that it?" McKellerhan asked.

"That's the whole deal. You guys wishing me and my lady a long and healthy life. That's what I am demanding."

"How about him?" Tanner pointed toward O'Brien. "We get to take him back with us just like you promised, right?"

"Why not? I'm done with him," I said. "But before you get any tricky ideas floating around in your heads, I better make another thing clear. I realize that without O'Brien alive to testify against you guys, his written statement will have less impact in a court of law. Maybe it won't even be enough to haul your asses off to jail where you belong. But it sure will put a big damper on your daily operations. Won't it? Eventually, even without O'Brien alive, I bet a strong case could be built to reserve a place in the slammers for all three of you."

"Even with O'Brien alive to testify," Captain Frye, said with predatory eyes gleaming, "I'm not so sure anyone could build a case against us. But what the hell, just to be on the safe side, we'll play it your way, Holt."

"Be sure of this, though," I said, "O'Brien's statement is all down on paper, four copies in the right hands. You and McKellerhan were getting paid big bucks to turn your backs while Tanner's men flooded Harlem with enough smack to sink a battleship. And, for the last two months, you used Detective O'Brien as your go-between."

"Captain Frye's got a good point," Tanner said, flexing his shoulders. "All you got, no matter how true it may be, is nothing but hearsay. As I see it, none of it would be enough to see us in a court of law with the well-heeled attorneys I have on my team."

"Maybe," I conceded. "But do you want to take the chance you'll end up on the stand in front of a jury of your peers?"

Tanner's face turned sour and his keen, gray eyes dropped momentarily.

"We also have to look at another allegation," I said, once again going off Jamison's script. "Not only were you running drugs for the Donzani family into the neighborhood, Tanner, you had your men bumping off every drug dealer who got in your way. Then, I guess, your plan was to use me as a scapegoat, and make me look responsible for what happened in Morningside Park."

"That's horse shit!" Tanner exploded. "Did O'Brien tell you that?"

"What do you think?"

"Why that lying son of a bitch," Tanner said, with his fist balled as he made for O'Brien.

"Not so fast!" I held up both hands. "When we're in total agreement, then you can have him all to yourself."

"Tommy's lying!" Lieutenant McKellerhan interjected. "Tanner had nothing to do with the junkie shootings or the Morningside Park massacre."

"We're still investigating the leads we've got on both cases," Captain Frye added. "From the looks of things it could be a free-lancing cop was trying to cut himself in on the action. The park escapade, well, that's—"

"Oh," I said. "And what cop might that be?"

"Why's that your worry?" McKellerhan asked, with an acid-laced tone. "We're onto who he is. So leave us to handle him in our own way."

"Wait a goddamn minute!" Tanner said, as his wary eyes inspected O'Brien. "Something's not right here. Check it out, guys. He doesn't even look roughed up."

"Sodium pentothal," I said, as I felt my blood rise, "was all he needed to open up."

The three crooks looked skeptically at one another. McKellerhan was the first to voice their collective suspicions.

"Are you sure you're being on the level with us, Nate? I mean, we walk out of here with Tommy and promise to leave you alone, then it's all over, right? A clean slate? No hard feelings carried over?"

Tanner had cleverly positioned himself between Ted's aim and me. Before I could react fast enough to what was happening, he grabbed me in a strong headlock. Using me as a shield he pulled an automatic pistol and fired three shots into O'Brien.

Scuffling feet sounded on the second tier as more of Jamison's gun toting men appeared.

"Unless you want another man dead," Tanner screamed with his gun jammed into my ribs, "all of you back off!"

Jamison leaned over the rail of the second tier with the rest of his men. Frye and McKellerhan raised their hands in surrender.

"It's no use, Tanner!" Jamison shouted from above. "As you can see, we've got a half dozen men covering you and more outside. Give it up, quietly. It's your only chance to walk out of here alive."

Before Tanner could respond I grabbed the wrist of his gun hand and elbowed him in the solar plexus. One harmless shot erupted from his pistol as we struggled for control of the gun. Then in quick succession, a series of shots exploded.

My ears rang as I let go of Tanner's wrist but held onto his overcoat. With our eyes locked he muttered something unintelligible. Then his gray eyes became glazed, rapidly flickering a few times before they froze. A harsh last gasp of breath escaped his lips and he fell away from my hold on him, bleeding from several gunshot wounds.

CHAPTER 26

It was about nine o'clock and low-hanging clouds threatened rain. Not once during our long ride across a series of bridges and through the Holland Tunnel had Jamison asked me anything about Morningside Park or any role I may have played in the massacre. Nor was there any mention of why I had strayed so far off the script during the showdown. Although I was on edge the whole ride, feeling like a whipped dog while anticipating him bringing up those subjects, he drove silently, deep in his own thoughts.

Shortly after the showdown in the warehouse, the New Jersey State Police, in force, hightailed it over to the bloody, highly controversial scene. Two assistant DAs from the big city quickly joined them. My longtime acquaintance, Howard Katz, was one of the DA's men, though he gave no indication that we knew each other. Jamison had ordered his men and me to stand back and keep our mouths shut.

The other concerned parties argued jurisdiction, code violations and other legalities. Meanwhile, the prize catches in contention, Captain Owen Frye and Lieutenant Lyle McKellerhan looked on helplessly, wearing matching handcuffs and waiting to find out who would have the bragging rights of dragging them off to jail.

Presently, a drunken New Jersey coroner, who looked like he had just crawled off a cold slab in the morgue, medically confirmed and pronounced Tommy O'Brien and Michael Tanner dead. With that dutifully performed, he was ushered aside by some other technicians, who stuck around to search and sniff around the bodies.

When a dozen or more members of the press slipped in, they were given a short leash. Nevertheless, they seemed excited by the photos and statements that they did manage to overhear.

Several times over the course of events, my gaze locked with Lieutenant McKellerhan's. He wore a severely disappointed expression on his craggy old face, an expression insinuative of a father whose only son had betrayed him. Though I had no logical reason to pity him, I did. Despite all logic and reason, I did feel badly for him, but for the life of me, I couldn't figure out why.

However, whatever I felt for McKellerhan paled significantly whenever my eyes drifted back to Tommy O'Brien's lifeless body. He was still bound to the steel girder, his mouth still duct-taped and his chin slouched down on his chest with his dark red-tinged hair hanging to one side. All of him limp, sitting in a dark pool of his own blood.

As I thought back to the afternoon when he'd first sauntered into Wally's, I found it ironic that I should end up grieving his death. But even though I had hardly known Tommy O'Brien, I felt a burning hole in my chest big enough to match the three holes that had bled over the rope which bound him.

He could have easily walked away and left me with Tanner's henchmen at the funeral home. If he had, I would probably be fish food at the bottom of the East River and he would still be alive. Instead, he took a big risk, a dear and deadly one. And it didn't help my state of mind knowing that going off the script the way I had by bringing up Morningside Park to protect myself proved to be the one unmistakable spark that fused his death.

Even more incriminating and damaging to my psyche, I'd carelessly allowed Tanner to get the drop on me and fire off the three rounds that had killed him. Consequently, I knew my already overburdened subconscious was going to have to reserve space for more guilt to take up permanent residence alongside the past indiscretions I was already lugging around like dead weight. At that moment, it seemed as though I couldn't win for losing.

When a slovenly dressed technician made a joke while taking a series of flash shots of Tommy, I told him to shut up. Conversely, for all I cared, they could have all spat endless globs of spit on Michael Tanner's well-dressed corpse.

All of this was going through my mind later as I rode in silence with Special Agent Jamison. Then, as we were rolling north on the West Side Expressway, he cleared his throat and glanced over at me.

"I suppose you're beating yourself up pretty bad over the way things went down," he stated.

"Do I have a choice?"

"Overall you did a good job. Maybe things worked out exactly as they were meant to."

"I don't get you," I said, after processing his words. "I screwed up and there's no way of getting around that."

"That's true. However, did you ever wonder why Tommy was so anxious to come up with another plan to keep him actively involved in the picture?"

Before I could respond he went on with his eyes focused straight on the road ahead.

"Tommy was no angel by a long shot, Nate. In fact, the reason he came over to our side two years ago was merely out of self-preservation. But I can't go into details or talk up all the dirt we had on him. Let's suffice it to say that sometimes the agency has to decide on the lesser of evils when we choose who we take on our side and who we choose to put higher on our list as the real enemy."

Hearing those words helped me put together pieces to a larger puzzle. Then I realized that O'Brien's cover had not been fabricated on pure fantasy. He'd obviously been a troubled officer prone to using excessive force and deserving of all his suspensions and the time he'd spent on the shrink's couch. There was no telling what other dastardly deeds he'd done and crimes he may have committed before the FBI struck a deal with him, convincing him to come over to their side of the fence.

Although I longed to know more, I knew probing Jamison was not going to get me what I wanted. Instead, I thanked God he'd taken a great load off my mind with the brief revelation he'd shared with me.

As though reading my mind, Jamison added another thought to cap off his assessment of O'Brien's true nature.

"Like I said, maybe fate was working more than you realized when Tommy went down with Tanner."

By the time he double-parked across from my building, I was feeling tremendously relieved and in a better frame of mind than I could have imagined possible several minutes prior.

"You'll be hearing from us as things develop down the line," Jamison remarked, as I was about to slide out of the Plymouth. "It's not over yet."

"I figured as much. But thanks for taking a burden off my mind by telling me what you did about Tommy."

"I guess you deserved that much, Nate." He tipped two stiff fingers to the brim of his hat in a mock salute and added, "Now do your best to stay out of anymore trouble in the future and we can remain on friendly terms."

As I watched his taillights disappear into the flow of Amsterdam Avenue traffic, an overwhelming sense of well-being washed over me.

I turned on several lights in the flat as soon I entered, hoping to exorcise the demons of the recent past. Then I ran a tub of hot water. All of the aches and pains my body had been subjected to over the last few days begged for a reprieve and a chance to heal. When the water in the tub was at the right temperature and level, a moment before stepping in, I decided to make a call to Lillian.

Unexpectedly, however, as I reached for the phone it rang.

"Hello," I said sprightly, anticipating Lillian on the same vibe.

"Holt!" the male voice was disguised, a hoarse and muffled rendition of its true self. "Listen up!"

"I'm listening," I said, when I'd regained myself.

"Your girl, Lillian, would like to see you tonight."

"Ohh…." I took a deep breath before saying, "I want to see her, too."

"Then you better get your black ass over here real quick."

"I'm on my—"

"Soon! And come alone."

The line clicked dead. I stood there flatfooted like a statue, petrified. Then I dropped the phone receiver and grabbed Lillian's address book from the side table. Rifling through to the right page, I picked up the receiver from where it had fallen. Vera's line rang twelve times before I hung up.

Reflexively, I went for my .38. Then I remembered that he, the last voice I'd heard on the phone, Detective Sam Brisco had taken it the day before.

I threw on some fresh clothes in a hurry, sprinted down to the first floor and pounded heavily on Harry Swayne's door until an eye appeared at the spy hole.

"It's me, Nate. Open up. I need help."

"My help?"

"I need your car. Lillian's in trouble. I've got to get to her quick!"

There was a lengthy silence. I was about to break it, maybe even the door, when Harry finally spoke up.

"Hold on."

His fat footsteps shuffled away and padded back. Then he undid all of his security locks and cracked the door with the safety chain on. I took the keys he handed me.

"I hope she's going to be okay," he said, in a wheezy voice.

"Where're you parked?"

"Right across the street."

His car was an old, pale-blue Nash. I tested how much spunk the small engine had as I raced across the bridge into the Bronx and past Yankee Stadium, cutting in and out of traffic lanes with a reckless abandon. Surprisingly, I wasn't stopped for a host of traffic violations. I sped on, though, wondering what my chances were if it came to outracing a cop car in the tiny Nash.

Putting that fear aside I drove single-mindedly, eyes riveted on the road as an inner voice screamed for explanations as to how I'd gotten Lillian into such a dreadful jam. I imagined her and Vera bound with rope and duct tape covering their mouths, wondering just how crazy Sam Brisco really was. As though it had all happened minutes ago, I recalled every sly innuendo he'd made about how lucky I was to have Lillian. *Be happy. Play it safe.* He had explicitly warned me more than once.

Repeatedly, I tried calming my panicky mind. It was me Brisco wanted, I kept reminding myself. Once he had me, maybe he would let the girls go. I also assumed it was the wisecrack I'd made about him being the phantom junkie killer that had hit home. After all, even if he thought I was really responsible for the Morningside Park massacre, he couldn't pursue that angle without jeopardizing his job with me having suspicions about him being the phantom shooter.

Therefore, arresting me was not what he had in mind. Obviously, instead, he wanted me stone-cold dead as badly as Michael Tanner had.

The way word travels so quickly through the police grapevine, he'd no doubt heard about my hand in bringing down Captain Frye and Lieutenant McKellerhan. I'm sure he thought of that outcome as both good news and bad. Good news that they were busted and bad news that I was still alive.

Then I remembered. Right before the guns went off in the warehouse, McKellerhan had stated that the identity of the phantom shooter was close to being solved. Perhaps they were about to nail Brisco. Maybe Brisco knew he was on the hot seat. Now, with Captain Frye and Lieutenant McKellerhan locked away, fighting for their own skins, and O'Brien dead, there might not be anyone left to reveal him as the phantom shooter except me. Consequently, I understood the call he'd made to lure me to him in a way he knew I could not resist.

Far out on the island, immense booms of thunder rocked the world and jagged lines of lightning streaked the sky. Then a strong solid sheet of rain fell unremittingly. Despite the sluggish windshield wipers, at the last possible moment, I spotted my turnoff on rural Route 25. Skidding through a wet oil-slick turn, the Nash spun out of control and faced the flow of oncoming traffic. With its horn blasting, by mere inches, a tractor-trailer missed ramming into me.

When I had the Nash rolling in the right direction, I estimated that I had about four miles to go. So near yet so far. Following the near collision, I gripped the wheel even tighter, speeding through the rainy night. Then the engine stalled and, cursing, I coasted the car to the side of the road.

For the first time since driving away from Harlem, I checked the gas gauge to find it pointing way below empty. With desperate persistence, one try after another, I finally got the engine to kick over. A short distance later, though, the car stalled again. That's when I spotted the church near the fork in the road near Vera's house.

On foot through the pouring rain, I plunged into the dark and wet woods. Recalling my walk with Chester, I prayed that my sense of direction was on the mark. Unable to locate the foot path I'd followed a few days ago, I kept moving in a southerly direction.

About a quarter of a mile into the tangled darkness my right foot sank up to the ankle, buried in a soft pocket of loosely packed earth. Before I could pull my foot free, I felt the churning of something living beneath me.

Frantically, I drew my foot from the mucky earth, as a furious buzzing became increasingly louder. Enraged yellow jackets were soon in the air all around me. Running a few steps, I tripped over a fallen limb. The cloud of angry yellow jackets began stinging me on every part of my exposed flesh. Back on my feet, I slapped at their persistent stings and fought my way through the dense darkness.

Tree limbs slapped at my face and body. Muffling curses, I finally crushed the last of the tiny stinging beasts against my neck.

Forging ahead, as I tried to get my bearings, I looked up and was surprised to see Vera's greenhouse about a hundred feet away. Using it as a beacon, I soon discovered the foot path. I had almost reached the property's clearing edge when I decided to slow down and proceed with caution.

Too late, I heard a twig snap behind me. Before I could spin completely around, I heard the unmistakable sound of a revolver being cocked.

"What a surprise, huh?" Detective Sam Brisco said.

The tall and stocky shadow he created was only a few feet away in a dark stand of pine. A glint of light from the greenhouse nightlights reflected off the gun he had trained on me. I tried to speak but my mouth was too dry and my brain was moving too fast for words.

"I had a feeling you'd try sneaking up behind. Now walk toward me real slow, like," he directed me with his gun. "Now up with those goddamn hands and turn away from me, slowly."

He frisked me thoroughly with his gun jammed in my spine and discovered I was unarmed.

"Go ahead, step around me." He pointed. "And march on right back the same way you came."

When I was a few feet ahead of him, he slowed and bent down. With his cautious eyes still on me, he picked up a shovel that was lying a few feet off the path.

"Don't walk too fast and don't try nothing stupid."

"You plan to shoot me...then bury me out here. Is that it?"

"Don't talk. Walk! And blame yourself. It was your big mouth on the phone that helped me trace Lillian out here."

Along the path, we trudged on through the wet woods.

"Why me?" I tried to get him to talk. "Because of Morningside Park? That can't be it."

"Because you have a real bad habit of sticking your nose where it don't belong. But you know why. Don't you? So shut up with the fool's play."

"We can work something out, can't we, Sam?"

"It's much too late for that."

"How about Lillian and her friend? Are they okay?"

"They don't even know I'm around, and that's the way I plan to keep it. I cut the phone line long before calling you."

Relief swept over me, and for a moment I didn't feel so bad about dying.

"You've got all the angles figured out, huh?" I said, as we marched on.

"Damn right! I'm looking at early retirement in comfort and to finally stop having to play the poor man act."

"With all the dough you muscled from the junkies you gunned down? What did you do, pretend to be their new source for better drugs at a cheaper price?"

"You got it. So what?"

He pressed the muzzle of his gun against my upper spine. I felt the place the slug previously imbedded in me start to burn.

"Stop slowing down." He jammed me in the back again. "I started a little hole not too far from here. You can have the privilege of finishing it for me. So keep walking with your hands up. That's right. Up higher!"

"But why the Halloween mask?" I asked.

"It worked, didn't it?" he shouted. "Now shut up before I blast you away right here and drag you the rest of the goddamn way."

Presently, we reached a point where I got a glimpse through the rain at the surface of the Long Island Sound. I knew we could not be too far from the hole he'd started digging in which to bury me.

"Off to the left, here," Brisco said. "And no quick moves."

Doing as I was told, I covered about ten feet before my foot again sank below the surface of the ground. I maintained my balance and kicked my other foot around in the nest before I resumed walking.

A fierce buzzing gained a menacing urgency. When I heard Brisco grunt loudly, and slap at his face, I dove to my left as a single gunshot shattered the silence of the night.

On all fours, I scuttled along the wet leafed floor of the forest and concealed myself behind a pine tree. When I peeked through the brush, Brisco was screaming and waving his arms madly. Helpless in his efforts to beat the insects off, and locate me at the same time, he turned and fled toward the rear of Vera's property.

As he stumbled and crashed through the woods, all the while cursing, I braved a cloud of yellow jackets to get my hands on the shovel he'd dropped. Then I cut a course to intercept him, while ignoring the stings on my face and hands.

Creating a ruckus of sound, he was an easy target to follow thrashing through the forest like a wounded bear. So intent on running and fighting the yellow jackets off him, he didn't hear me making up ground behind him.

The old shovel rang hollowly when I slammed it across the side of his shaved head. The force broke the handle. He wailed from the shock of the blow and stumbled several feet before going down in a heap of flying arms and legs. I tripped over a rock and fell trying to get to him.

When I got to my feet he was already up again and running toward the nightlights surrounding the greenhouse. Over his shoulder, he fired another errant shot. As we broke from the shadows of the forest I closed the distance between us. When he turned to fire another round, I left the ground and buried a shoulder squarely into his chest. Locked in a furious ball, we crashed through the greenhouse's rear window and part of the fragile wall.

Amid the inner darkness, scrabbling on shards of slippery glass and slick tile, we fought to our feet. Uttering a steady stream of curses, Brisco still clutched the gun. But I forced that arm up and away from me as we struggled for supremacy.

Suddenly, the lights in the greenhouse came on. Then Brisco kneed me in the groin and hit me in the jaw with a left cross. As I reeled backwards, I saw Chester leap through the crashed window.

Brisco, alerted by Chester's menacing growls, whipped around as the big golden dog landed on the glass-dusted floor. Brisco fired once and missed. Chester slid off balance. Two more shots found their mark and Chester slid to a dead halt at Sam's feet.

Before he could turn his attention back to me, I slammed into him from behind. Again we crashed to the floor. I saw the gun slide away from us.

Desperately clambering across the tiled floor, I crawled toward the gun. Inches from my grasp, Sam came down on my back with the full force of his heavyweight body.

With a thick arm locked around my neck in a deadly grip, I squirmed and wiggled to get free. But his powerful legs wrapped around my waist and squeezed. Then he rolled on his back, his grip tightening on my neck and around my waist.

I tried gouging at his eyes, but he clamped onto my fingers with his teeth and rolled on his side to pin my other arm down. Locked together, wrestling and squirming like an ugly two-headed bug, the world around me became fuzzy and I began losing consciousness.

Now whenever I recall the series of actions that followed, I see it all as a rapid flash of color followed by a dense cloud of smoke, which I never actually got to see.

With Lillian standing above us, I fought for one more precious breath of air. But I did clearly see Brisco's gun clutched in both of her hands. With her wet eyes wide, she yelled for Brisco to let go of me. Her voice rang dully as though it were a dying echo twisting through a windswept tunnel. Then my eyes went back to her face. Her head was shrouded in white gauze like some saint, still gripping the gun in her trembling hands. The working end of the revolver, the big black muzzle, grew larger and larger.

"The gun's empty, Lillian," Brisco's voice rumbled densely. "Go…ahead…and…pull the…"

Then everything, all sight, all sound, all feelings faded, as an overpowering insipid blackness swallowed me whole.

CHAPTER 27

Lillian and I vacationed the last two weeks of August in Bermuda. We spent lazy days rewarding our palates with new delicacies in the many fine restaurants, as well as in the more remote haunts where most sightseers seldom wander. Together, hand in hand, we strolled the pink-hued beaches, collected colorful seashells and waded in the cool currents of the emerald sea.

Often we took Polaroid snapshots of each other. The vibrant sunlight became Lillian and the deep cobalt sky framed and added a pleasant background to her winning smile. Her hair had grown out to be about three inches long, and the thin scar on the side of her forehead was hardly noticeable. In the evenings we wined, dined, danced to calypso bands and on a couple of occasions stayed up all night to witness spectacular sunrises.

On our last day there we packed a picnic lunch into a straw-weave basket we bought at the hotel. Then we hiked to a cove that was as picturesque as any glossy postcard I'd ever seen. We ate sumptuously and sipped wine straight from the bottle because we'd forgotten to bring cups. Then we dozed on a blanket with a beach umbrella shading us. When I awoke she was walking toward the shoreline into the lowering sun. I watched her skirt the edge of the white foam that licked at her calves and sent her scurrying away from a larger wave that followed.

While she played at the edge of the ocean, I sipped dark burgundy wine, pulled my straw hat down to shade my eyes and reflected on the dramatic changes in our relationship. The day after Lillian pulled the trigger that blasted Brisco to hell, she made me promise to never bring up the subject in any way, shape or form. At the time it had seemed like a reasonable request, and I complied. But now the unspoken had become a barrier which seemed to be slowly wedging itself between us more day by day.

Vividly, when I least expected it, I could still hear Brisco's thick voice telling Lillian his gun was empty. A span of eternity seemed to exist in those few seconds while my mind tried to recount the shots he'd fired off at Chester and me. As I'd desperately struggled and prayed for one last breath of air, the waiting seemed to go on forever.

If Lillian had hesitated to pull the trigger even a second longer I might not have been around to learn that one shell was still in the chamber of the gun. Even so, my heart, choked of oxygen, had stopped ticking. Vera, calling on her nursing experience, was able to coax it into beating again by pounding on my chest and giving me mouth-to-mouth resuscitation.

Twenty minutes later the local hick cops showed up, responding to a neighbor reporting the sound of gunshots. I told them that I had shot Brisco in the head. I had already coached Lillian and Vera to say that when they heard the commotion and ran into the greenhouse, Chester and the shaved-head man were already dead and I was holding the smoking gun. Vera also explained that she'd tried calling them to discover that her phone was inoperable.

As I'd expected, the hicks took me in for questioning. Predictably, they weren't too anxious to accept my story since Sam was the one with a NYCP gold shield. We kept going round and round. But I was eventually released from custody when a concurrent investigation, back in the city, turned up Brisco's dirty gun. A ballistic test on the .32 soon traced it back to all the phantom junkie killings. It was found tucked under a loose floorboard near the sink in the kitchen of Sam's Lexington Avenue flat. Hidden away in the same cache, they also discovered nine thousand dollars and a plastic, pink-colored Halloween mask.

However, despite the situation, or how evil and despicable Brisco had proven to be, I knew Lillian was struggling with guilt associated with willfully taking a human life even though she'd saved me from dying.

At odd times a pensive silence would come over her, darken her spirit and cloud her whole aura. Often during those times I was tempted to break my promise about avoiding the subject and persuade her to talk things out.

Instead, tough as it was for me to abide by the silence I'd pledged, I'd pretend to not notice her severe mood swings. At the same time I vowed even more deeply to never bring the slightest threat or hint of harm her way ever again.

After all, it was my reckless ways that had caused all our problems. Knowing how true that was, I wondered how much Lillian suspected me of doing that I had not already confessed to and whether she was not revealing everything she knew or suspected. All of that was part of the guilt and a host of secrets I harbored and did my best to deal with each day. I could only hope and pray that in time both of us would pull through the psychologically confusing maze we were stuck inside to eventually go back to living normal lives.

On another front, I'd kept up-to-date on the local news. Captain Owen Frye and Lieutenant Lyle McKellerhan had Tommy O'Brien's ghost to thank for getting them out of the slammers in time to ever see the light of day. Without O'Brien alive to testify against them, the DA's office and the Feds, in all their closed-door wisdom, had decided their case was too flimsy to indict the men. It also didn't help that the bug I was wearing to tape the showdown had malfunctioned and not a single word spoken in the warehouse had been recorded.

I also suspected that the governor and the mayor had both decided it would be wiser to drop the case than deal with all the bad publicity it would certainly create, not only for the Dirty Thirty Precinct but for the entire NYPD's reputation.

Summarily, the captain and lieutenant were both suspended from the force pending further investigation. As best as I could figure, even if neither one of them spent another minute in jail, their lives were irrevocably ruined. With the highly publicized blemishes and questions of honor staining their reputations they would be lucky to get jobs as floorwalkers at a Macy's store.

A single sense of satisfaction gave me reason to rejoice, however. That satisfaction came in knowing that Michael Tanner, the man who had sicced his goons on Lillian and me, was now buried six feet under. Although he was dead and I had a hand in bringing him down, never once did I delude myself into thinking I'd made a significant dent in stemming the flow of heroin into Harlem.

I knew better than that. Waiting in the wings were dozens of Tanners, Fryes and McKellerhans, all eager and willing to fill the void to keep the game alive. For on the gritty edge where reality meets the surface of the bottom muck, the Freddie Tuckers, the Johnny Gs, the Rudy Yancys and the Puddings were also ready to assume their pathetic and sorrowful roles in the game; a real life rendition of life going to hell in a hand basket.

Anger and contempt for the game still simmered inside of me. But there was something else alive in me that previously hadn't counted for much. I had a devoted love for Lillian, which galvanized for me a brand-new set of priorities. For regardless of the costs or sacrifices, I was determined to focus all of my God-given strength, patience and perseverance on healing and bridging the gulf between us.

Often, during times of reflection I recalled Horace saying that the drug dealers who killed Rudy would have to realize that there were consequences for the action. At the time I had no idea how far those consequences would stretch or how my actions would create such long lasting negative consequences, too.

Lying there on the warm beach, watching Lillian playfully cavorting with the undulating waves, knowing that Harlem was more than a thousand miles away didn't stop me from feeling as though it, and our future there, was right around the corner.

I was also looking forward to seeing young Joe Weathersby again. As he'd predicted the last time I saw him, he'd managed to convince his parents to let him continue his dream of becoming a musician and attend classes at Boston's Berklee School of Music.

Sipping on the last dregs of wine floating in a corner of the bottle, I kept remembering that cold and windy day in April when Blinky Carlson walked through the front door of Wally's dive. And often, from beginning to end, I ran through the subsequent events over and over again from top to bottom and side to side. I knew it would be years, maybe another lifetime, before I could put those thoughts behind me.

Sometimes I even imagined telling the whole story to someone as a catharsis. For a heartbeat or two I even flirted with writing it all down. However, before that wild notion was allowed to take any shape or semblance, I'd laughed to myself long and hard. I realized if I committed the story to writing I'd risk arrest, being tried, convicted and executed. Even if I arranged it so the story did not see the light of day until I was dead and gone, I knew it was unlikely anyone in their right mind would believe the veracity of such a tale.

I lay there on the pink-colored sand for a long time without one voluntary muscle acknowledging that I was alive. Distant clouds painted a hazy face on a serene sunset. Then, reacting to a sudden inspiration, I sprang to my feet. Tossing my straw hat aside, I trotted down to the shoreline, wanting nothing more than to be nearer my one love, Lillian Warren.

781 407-1657
DeDe

Made in the USA
Lexington, KY
15 September 2012